AF609007

THE SECRETS FROM THE DEEP

Satu Rämö is a bestselling Finnish-born crime author who has lived in Iceland for the past twenty years. Her Nordic crime *Hildur* series has sold over one million copies worldwide and has been a bestseller in Finland, Iceland, Sweden and Germany. A TV adaptation will premiere in 2026 and the series has also been adapted for the stage. Satu has also published numerous best-selling, prizewinning non-fiction titles in her native Finland.

She lives with her Icelandic husband and two children in the small town of Ísafjörður in northwest Iceland.

Also by Satu Rämö

The Clues in the Fjord
The Grave in the Ice
The Shadow of the Northern Lights

THE SECRETS FROM THE DEEP

Satu Rämö

ZAFFRE

First published as Rakel by Werner Söderström Ltd in 2024
Published in the English language by arrangement with
Bonnier Rights Finland, Helsinki, Finland

First published in the UK in 2026 by Zaffre
An imprint of Bonnier Books UK
5th Floor, HYLO, 105 Bunhill Row,
London, EC1Y 8LZ

Copyright © Satu Rämö, 2024
English language translation © by Kristian London, 2026

All rights reserved.
No part of this publication may be reproduced, stored or transmitted in any form or by any means, electronic, mechanical, photocopying or otherwise, without the prior written permission of the publisher.

The right of Satu Rämö to be identified as Author of this work has been asserted by her in accordance with the Copyright, Designs and Patents Act, 1988.

This is a work of fiction. Names, places, events and incidents are either the products of the author's imagination or used fictitiously. Any resemblance to actual persons, living or dead, or actual events is purely coincidental.

A CIP catalogue record for this book is available from the British Library.

ISBN: 978-1-80617-274-0

Also available as an ebook and an audiobook

3 5 7 9 10 8 6 4 2

Typeset by IDSUK (Data Connection) Ltd
Printed and bound by CPI Group (UK) Ltd, Croydon CR0 4YY

The authorised representative in the EEA is
Bonnier Books UK (Ireland) Limited.
Registered office address:
Block B, The Crescent Building
Northwood, Santry
Dublin 9, D09 C6X8
Ireland
compliance@bonnierbooks.ie
www.bonnierbooks.co.uk

The verses on p. 4 and p. 332 are from the song 'Stál og hnífur' (1980) by Bubbi Morthens.

The verse on p. 272 is from the poem 'Hávamál' from the *Poetic Edda*, or *Codex Regius*.

For my grandmother Sirkka (1933–2024)

If I drown, I drown tonight
If they find me
Come seek me out
Let this be my reminder

Prologue

Kotsdalur, Westfjords, March 1995

The change didn't originate in Rúnar's deepest self. Whether or not it would have eventually made its way there remains a mystery, for this was his last day.

Rúnar struck the frozen earth with the spade and muttered to himself. When work appeared, it had to be done. The bleak backyard was dotted with piles of rocks and served no purpose other than accepting the changes in season. The snow fell, the snow melted. The wind lashed the homestead every day, as it was lashing now. Winter was far enough along for the sun's rays to reach Kotsdalur valley, but Rúnar was blind to them.

Rúnar was a hard worker, not one to give up easily. When he wasn't out on the fishing boat, he did odd jobs. Tilled, wheelbarrowed, hauled, heaped, dug. His shoulders ached. Time for a break. He'd excavated this same spot several times, even in winter, but today he was taxed by the effort. Although temperatures in the valley had held above freezing for the past couple of weeks, just inches beneath the surface the soil was frozen solid.

Rúnar paused and looked around. The fence needed repainting this summer. The wet winds from the sea had softened the wood, sloughing off its surface in big strips. And bubbles had formed in the living room ceiling since the autumn rains. The rust-eaten roof would have to be replaced soon too. Damn it. There was always something that sucked up his cash.

Rúnar had returned from sea earlier that day, and here he was now at his farm, surveying all the work that needed doing. He glanced at the corpse lying on the wet grass and reached into his pocket for his bottle of liquor. The cork was off in a flash. As the liquid seared his throat, a comforting warmth spread throughout his body.

If anything in this world needed doing, it was best to do it yourself. There was no point expecting help from others. Rúnar had always wanted to do things his own way. Who else would understand a man's troubles better than himself? No woman, that's for sure. They'd never been anything but trouble.

Except Mum. But she'd been gone for years. She'd died of old age, her dignity intact.

In contrast, the individual who sprawled spread-eagled on the ground had died of foolishness. If she'd just kept her mouth shut and done her part without complaining, Rúnar wouldn't have to be standing here, hacking away at the icy soil.

After an hour of toil, Rúnar was forced to take a longer break. He pulled the long grass over the pathetic start to a hole. He left nothing to chance, no tools scattered around. Nor did he leave any task unfinished.

Rúnar entered the house, wiped his feet on the mat, and stomped into the kitchen. A moment later the coffee was percolating.

Rúnar took a fatty hunk of lamb from the fridge, buttered a disc of flatbread, and cut a thick slice of the meat. The kitchen was filthy: the table strewn with breadcrumbs, the sink heaped with dirty dishes. The only thing in the fridge aside from the lamb and bread he'd bought was a block of butter.

Rúnar wondered where his wife was. Rakel had grown increasingly distant since Rósa and Björk's disappearance the previous autumn. Where was she gallivanting now? The house looked like it had been empty for days. It was a weekday. Hildur ought to have been at school. Rúnar considered whether to call his sister-in-law Tinna and ask where his wife and daughter were. He turned off the coffeemaker and finished his coffee.

And then he heard sounds. Rúnar stepped outside and grabbed his spade.

Rakel climbed slowly from the car. Her voice was subdued: 'Hey. You're back already.'

Rúnar's fingertips were tingling. The red, pulsing itch rose from his feet to the nape of his neck. He flung his shovel to the ground. 'Where the hell have you been?'

Rakel said she'd been at therapy. They'd discussed her need to see a therapist in Reykjavík to process the trauma of their daughters' disappearance, surely Rúnar remembered.

'Hildur has been staying with Tinna,' Rakel explained, adding the neighbours had fed the horses during her absence. Her voice was supremely calm, but her clipped intonation gave away her welling panic.

'Don't lie to me,' Rúnar spat. He pushed Rakel. 'You've been up the road with Hallgrímur.'

Rakel denied it, despite knowing from experience her words would have no impact. Her husband was in a perilous mood. He'd shut himself off in his own reality, and words couldn't penetrate his cloak of fury. But Rakel had no idea how bad things would get this time.

Rúnar yanked open the car door. He reached for the overnight bag in the back seat and started tossing the contents around. Underclothes, slippers, a jar of Rakel's homemade ointment. A plastic bag he tore into like a raven, strewing Rakel's dirty laundry around. He reached into the side pocket and fished out a folded piece of paper. One glance at it, and a look of victory washed over his face. Rúnar had found proof Rakel was lying. The slip of paper was a boarding pass for a Smyril Line ferry. Rakel had been on a pleasure cruise!

Rúnar built up force and kicked his wife in the ribs. 'You've been to the Faroe Islands!'

He paused. His stomach rose and fell in time to his heavy breaths. Rúnar picked up the spade he'd just flung to the ground, took it in both hands, and raised it into the air. There was a dull thump as the edge of the pointed shovel struck his wife in the shoulder.

Rakel curled up like a snail retreating into her shell and tried to shield her head from the blows. She coughed up blood and mumbled something Rúnar couldn't make out.

He kicked his wife again. That helped.

Rakel apologised for having been such a bad wife. Rúnar grabbed her by the shoulders and forced her to look him in the eye.

Rakel groaned and said: 'Now I see you've had to teach me. I deserve it. I shouldn't have pressured you. I know you did your best.'

She was gasping in pain. Blood trickled from her forehead to her chin and slid under the silk scarf at her throat. Rakel said she'd taken Rósa and Björk to safety in the Faroe Islands, but she realised she'd made a mistake and wanted to fix things.

'I want you to come with me. If we start driving right now, we can make the ferry tomorrow.'

There was no ferry tomorrow, and Rakel knew it. But Rúnar had no idea what the ferry schedules were. The lie was Rakel's only way out of the situation. She couldn't allow Rúnar to find the girls.

Rúnar stood there, staring in confusion at his wife as she whimpered on the ground. The story she'd just told him sounded so outrageous that he had to find out whether it was true.

But Rúnar always finished what he started. He couldn't leave evidence in his yard. He had to get rid of the corpse.

He ordered his wife into the car. The rolled-up tarp and spade fit in the back seat, no problem. He could finish the job on the way.

Rúnar opened the passenger door and collapsed onto the seat. Rakel stared straight ahead, eyes blank. She didn't snap out of it and start driving until Rúnar smacked the dash. The car shuddered down the bumpy drive.

Rakel was revolted. She hated her husband. She hated herself for having chosen such a vile spouse. A husband who marinated in disappointed rage and suspected his neighbour of being the father of his two younger children. Rakel's face was bloodied and one of her teeth had cracked, but she had the air of someone who knew what she was doing. She had a plan.

She drove faster. The road entered into a climb, and Rakel gave the car more acceleration. At the top of the hill, the road would veer to the right. Her self-confidence and defiance swelled as the car picked up speed. Her voice turned honey-soft, confusing Rúnar.

'You know, all three girls are yours, but I never was. I love someone else. Someone who always fixed what you kept breaking. But we didn't want to hurt Hallgrímur, so we kept it a secret.'

She turned to her husband. His dumbfounded expression made it plain the words hadn't sunk in yet. Rakel relished the look on his face.

'For me, Helga was everything you never were. I truly loved her.'

A tender male voice came from the radio, singing one of Rakel's favourite songs. It was as if fate had wanted her to hear it before the end.

The bend in the road was approaching. Rakel gave no indication of turning the wheel. She raced faster. The sea shimmered at the horizon. Rakel laid into the accelerator, gripped the steering wheel with both hands, and then let go for the last time.

The weather in Iceland could be anything at all on the cusp of spring. That night, temperatures dropped below freezing and a dusting of snow fell. A farmer driving past the bend early the next morning saw tyre tracks in the snow, heading toward the cliff. He called emergency services from the nearest house.

Fire and rescue were on the scene within a little over an hour. They saw a car submerged at a depth of three metres. Two police officers stood at the brink above, shivering in the damp, frigid air as they monitored the retrieval operation. The sound of the crane's motor mingled with the crash of the waves.

When the car's roof finally broke the surface, the roiling, dark-blue sea turned to white foam. The nose of the vehicle was flattened. The left side was punched in, and the driver's door hung on a single hinge. The impression was one of an injured bird.

The police officers moved from the edge of the cliff to the patrol car, and the mangled vehicle was lowered next to it. Tyres hit snowy ground. The crane's cables were detached.

The police officers approached the vehicle and peered in. They could see two badly battered bodies. A male had been caught under the nose of the crushed vehicle. The second victim was so horrifically disfigured that it turned the stomach. The face was a gory pulp; ribbons of chestnut hair clung to it like seaweed.

Chapter 1

15 April
Hey!
I finally arrived yesterday. The trip went well.

I'm so happy no one knows me here. I feel like a blank canvas no one has painted on yet. Like I'm starting something new.

My address is on the other side. Write if your plans change and you want to meet.

Greetings from the coast,

R.

PS. I'm really sorry I didn't have time to say goodbye.

Chapter 2

Ísafjörður, June 2022

The call had come at 5.35 a.m. Detective Hildur Rúnarsdóttir knew the exact time, because she'd been lying awake, staring at the red numbers on her clock radio. The summer sun had found its way into her bedroom around five, and she'd slept poorly as it was. The night before, she'd tossed and turned for hours before sleep came.

Hildur's partner, junior constable Jakob Johanson, lived next door, in the other half of the duplex Hildur owned. After the call came, Hildur had phoned him, quickly pulled on some clothes, and splashed her face with cold water. A piece of mint gum had dispelled the nighttime funk from her mouth. It had been a speedy departure: they'd arrived at the address within thirty minutes of receiving the call.

A two-day old stubble sprouted from Jakob's face, and his eyes were still puffy from sleep. He and Hildur were standing in front of a one-storey rowhouse at the edge of Ísafjörður.

'Have you ever been on an assignment like this before?' Hildur asked, reaching for the gate. It creaked as it opened, and on the other side the flagstones forked into three paths.

Jakob replied this was his first time.

'It's my third. Luckily, they don't come often,' Hildur said. She and Jakob had agreed she would handle the talking.

Hildur knew there were four adults inside the residence: the couple that owned the place and some friends visiting from Reykjavík.

The female visitor had woken at quarter past five and peered into the travel cot to see if her three-month-old baby was hungry. According to the mother, the baby had last eaten at ten, before everyone went to bed. She'd stroked her sleeping child's back and panicked. The baby's body had felt cold. That was all the information Hildur had received from dispatch. By the end of the call, the father, who was the one who'd placed it, hadn't been able to say anything except three words repeated over and over: *cold* and *not moving*.

The spacious entryway was unlit. A woman in a long white T-shirt and knee-length shorts stood in the middle of the room, hugging herself at the elbows. Dark, tangled hair hung at either side of her face, hiding it, but Hildur could hear her crying. A slim, tall man had wrapped his arms around her and was looking directly at Hildur. He'd pulled a loose sweater over his pyjamas before Hildur and Jakob arrived. One could have mistaken the flash in his eyes for anger, but Hildur knew better. The piercing look was one of grief.

'Kristína and Óskar?'

'Yes.'

'My condolences,' Hildur said softly.

A faint grunt of acknowledgement escaped the man's lips. The woman's wails grew louder. Her jiggling shoulders rose and fell. Rose and fell, like a pulsing wave.

The door at the far end of the hall was ajar. Hildur nodded toward it, and the man nodded back. Hildur and Jakob didn't take off their shoes. It would be best for everyone for the police to enter and depart without delay.

The walk down the hall felt endless, Hildur's body like lead. For the first time in months, she felt the pressure accumulating under her breastbone. The spring had gone well. She'd taken a long vacation to Hawaii with her Finnish friend Anton. The two of them had surfed, laid on the beach, and ordered drinks decorated with colourful paper umbrellas. Neither was a huge fan of hot weather or sunshine, but they'd enjoyed each other's company and continued to stay in touch after their return. Work had been manageable too; discounting the arrests of a few drunk drivers, the Westfjords had seen little drama for months.

The days had come and gone, and Hildur had sailed through them without any major crises. She'd felt buoyant. She didn't usually care for summer; the bright light assaulted her from every direction and at all hours of day and night. Even so, she'd been sleeping like a log – until last night, when weighed down by a heaviness, she'd drifted off too late and woken too early.

There was a strong smell in the guest room. It wasn't the usual funk of death, which Hildur had become familiar with as a detective. A corpse gave off a pungent odour if a long time had passed between death and discovery. This baby had died very recently. What hung in the air now was the stink of horror and sweat. Hildur had the urge to vomit.

The sofa bed was unmade, and a suitcase lay open on the floor with a stroller next to it. The travel cot stood to the right of the sofa bed.

'The stroller's seat is removable. Should we use it?' Jakob asked.

Hildur nodded.

Jakob freed the bassinet from the stroller and flattened it on the bed.

Hildur shifted the small, polka-dotted blanket, revealing the baby's feet. She picked up the body and placed it in the bassinet. The sensation of the tiny corpse in her arms made her realise she couldn't remember the last time she'd held a living infant. It must have been years.

Jakob turned away, and Hildur understood why: blue splotches the size of fingertips had formed on the baby's face. She had died in her sleep on her belly. The parents wouldn't have been able to do anything even if they'd woken a few hours earlier. SIDS arrived without warning, slinking in when least expected.

Hildur saw no signs of violence on the body, but the forensic pathologist would perform a more detailed examination. Hildur covered the corpse with the polka-dotted blanket and did a quick check of the bedroom. The police were charged with ensuring no crime was involved in the death.

Cases of SIDS were so rare these days. *And today a rare event became this family's reality*, Hildur reflected as she reached for the baby seat.

The parents were still leaning against each other in the entryway. They'd been joined by another couple around the age of thirty. The second woman, who had short hair and a red robe, introduced herself as Elín and added that this was her and her husband Páll's home. She worked at the local pharmacy, and Páll worked for municipal social services. They explained Kristína and Óskar were visiting them.

'We were woken up after five by a shout . . .' Elín said. 'I don't understand . . . I can't believe this has happened.'

Hildur noticed wet spots had appeared at the breasts of Kristína's T-shirt.

'The social workers are on their way. They're coming to help you through this difficult time,' Hildur said. 'We can also arrange for you to see a doctor if you'd like.' She knew Kristína would at least want a lactation suppressor to stop her breasts from producing milk.

'Where are you taking her?' Óskar asked, squeezing his wife's slack body more tightly.

Hildur knew that in moments like this, it was important to answer questions clearly and directly. Beating around the bush was of no use to anyone.

'To the local hospital. Later today the body will be transported by aeroplane to Reykjavík. After the forensic examination, permission for burial will be granted.'

Kristína was still hanging her head, unable to look anyone in the eye, but there was a pause in her weeping. Her voice was calm and determined: 'My child is not going in the hold with the baggage.'

Corpses generally travelled in special caskets transported in aeroplane holds. Hildur had no trouble grasping how horrific the thought of the tiny coffin packed in with a bunch of suitcases must seem. But the body wouldn't be released for burial until the forensic pathologist had performed an autopsy. Besides, the funeral would presumably be held in Reykjavík, where Kristína and Óskar lived. Hildur shot a questioning look at Jakob, who nodded lightly.

'I don't think either one of you is in any condition to drive. My colleague can drive your car, and I can drive your child. You can ride in either vehicle.'

Chapter 3

The temperature was 15 degrees Celsius, but in Iceland even that was high. Summers on the island were cool and bright. The little harbour at Ísafjörður dozed in the sunshine and still air. The sea's surface was like a thick, congealed liquid. The wind was such a persistent presence in the Westfjords that completely calm and sunny summer days were a rarity. The south wind brought rain, and the north wind brought cooler temperatures, even in June.

Some shops had closed early so employees could enjoy the day. Children scampered along the sandy beach and in the shallows, and adults paused to praise the weather to passers-by. Everyone reminded themselves and each other to take full advantage of it until nightfall.

The cries of hungry gulls carried from the sea. They were wheeling around a small fishing boat returning to port. Fishing boats often tossed damaged fish or catches of the wrong species overboard, and the gulls feasted on the bounty.

Also gliding into this seaside town on this fine summer morning was *Diamond Adventure of the Seas*, a white cruise ship carrying two thousand passengers. The vessel was twelve storeys tall and over two hundred metres long. The distance between the northern and southern edges of Ísafjörður was no more than a kilometre, so the huge ship looked preposterous in comparison to its surroundings. The passenger bridge was locked in place and the doors opened. For the next hour or so, Americans, Canadians, and Central European tourists disembarked. They looked around, enchanted, and scanned the cluster of tour guides for the one carrying the right coloured sign.

The guides in ball caps steered groups onto the buses. The green buses would be taking passengers on a day trip to the handsome Dynjand waterfalls, including a lunch of fish soup at a rural restaurant, while the yellow buses would convey visitors to a fishing museum on the shores of another fjord not far to the west.

After the back of the last bus turned right down the road and vanished, the stillness resumed. The only sound now was the faint screech of gulls.

Ísafjörður was committed to investing in growing cruise-ship tourism. The harbour was being dredged to accommodate even bigger ships and altered to meet the needs of more demanding tourists. The expansion wouldn't be finished for another couple of years, but the small improvements that had been completed already had made the place prettier. Buildings showing the patina of the ever-changing weather had received a fresh coat of paint, and public toilets had been installed at the port. Stout concrete planters overflowing with masses of white petunias lined the harbour basin. Petunias bloomed and thrived even in these northern climes. A few bees buzzed among the flowers.

An unexpected clattering suddenly echoed from the passenger bridge. A couple of faint thuds, then a sharp sound that reverberated across the deserted harbour yard. A slim, dark-skinned young man stumbled violently down the bridge, crashing into the walls. He groaned, doubled over and covered his face with his hands.

A closer look at his uncontrolled shambling revealed that he wasn't shielding his face; he was suppressing his injuries. Red liquid sprayed between his fingers and onto his white dress shirt and light-blue trousers. His entire torso was drenched in blood.

The man staggered from the bridge to the harbour yard and collided with a ponytailed young woman deadheading the petunias, a summer worker hired by the local youth employment initiative. She took one look at him and screamed. Her sharp shriek welled up from deep within and lingered, reverberating in the air.

The man fell at her feet and wailed something unintelligible. His words were swallowed by the garble of gushing blood and the saliva spilling from his mouth.

The young woman steadied herself against the planter and breathed deeply to regain her composure. She knew she ought to call emergency services, but there was only one thought running through her mind:

How could such a skinny young man have so much blood in him?

Chapter 4

Hólmavík, June 2022

The shoreline road began to climb. There was a blind spot at the peak, followed by a sharp curve to the right. It was impossible to see oncoming traffic until you reached the top, so Hildur chose to drive carefully. Brenda – as Hildur's Toyota Land Cruiser had been christened – chugged up the hill at thirty kilometres an hour. The tarmac was pitted with small potholes. The Icelandic Road Administration prioritised repairs in the greater Reykjavík area and on Route 1 circling the island. Lesser-used roads were repaired later in the summer. Hildur felt Brenda shuddering too keenly over the bumps. She'd have to ask someone to take a look at the right-side suspension.

Hildur saw a blur of white in the right periphery of her vision and slammed the brakes. Brenda came to a stop just before hitting a sheep that had bounded into the road. Two tiny lambs capered behind a moment later. The ewe and her offspring crossed in front of Hildur and continued down the hill toward the meadow that reached the shore.

Free-ranging sheep made summer a dangerous time to travel Iceland's highways. Over a million sheep were set loose at the beginning of summer and grazed until the end of September. They always caused traffic accidents, especially on narrow, winding rural roads.

Hildur glanced in the rear-view mirror. Luckily, the transit coffin they'd been lent by the hospital hadn't been dislodged by the sudden stop. She pressed her hands against the wheel, straightened her arms, and let her breathing steady. Then she started driving again. This was the curve that had made her an orphan, the spot where her parents' car had driven off the cliff and into the sea. Thinking about the accident no longer made Hildur sad. Life went on. It was true the sense of aloneness had never dissipated, but then it might have been an inherent part of Hildur anyway. Sometimes things just were the way they were, and that was that.

Jakob hadn't gained too much of a lead. Kristína and Óskar had wanted to sit side by side in the back seat so they could maintain eye contact with the vehicle transporting the coffin through the rear window.

Hildur felt it was important to help the parents during their time of devastation. For some inexplicable – and, considering the sad circumstances, perhaps slightly inappropriate – reason, she felt energetic and eager to take action. There was something she could do, and that felt meaningful.

The winds of life had been favourable for Hildur lately. She'd kept her spirits up. Months had passed since she'd been plagued by anxiety, intrusive images, or intensified sensory reactions. She hadn't had any dreams or experienced any anguish over impending misfortune.

Hildur had inherited the gift of foresight through her maternal line. One of her ancestors had been a renowned seer in the area, capable of telling the future and advising people on major decisions. Consulting a seer had once been commonplace among Icelanders. Farmers would ask about weather forecasts for the coming summer, fishermen about the movements of fish stocks. Naturally, seers had been sought out for counsel on matters of the heart as well. Hildur had never seen future events very clearly, but since adolescence she'd had premonitions about major accidents and serious crimes. The hardest thing about this ability was knowing something bad was about to occur, but never when or to whom. It was a curse, knowing too much, yet at the same time too little.

Although last year had been more eventful for Hildur than an entire lifetime was for many, her angst had diminished. Maybe she was gradually coming to terms with her past.

Her mother and father were dead. Her sisters, who had been missing for decades, had been found. Her reclusive sister Rósa, who had supported herself for years collecting mares' blood, had made a life change and found a comfortable indoor job working for a big mobile phone company. Allowed to work remotely, Rósa had moved to the Westfjords. She didn't need much to get by on. Rósa said anything she had left after mandatory expenses went to paying off her debts. Hildur didn't know who Rósa owed money to – she'd asked, and Rósa had refused to answer. Hildur hadn't asked again. There was no point trying to change her sister.

Rósa had returned to Kotsdalur. The childhood homestead had fallen into disrepair over the decades, but Rósa was handy and happy to re-establish herself in a familiar environment near Hildur. She was naturally less inclined to crave change than Hildur, but maybe that was the reason the two of them got along so well.

The youngest, quietest, and most sensitive of the three sisters, Björk, had been sentenced to prison without parole for a string of assaults carried out the previous spring. Björk had claimed she'd been protecting Rósa while Rósa collected blood from Icelandic mares. According to the prosecutor, Björk had wanted to intimidate a group of animal rights activists who threatened Rósa's livelihood, with profound consequences. Björk had been found guilty of several aggravated assaults. Two activists had died, but the courts had found that in one instance the crime was desecration of the dead, not assault, and in another manslaughter, not murder, leading to a lighter sentence.

Hildur didn't believe for a second that Björk was guilty, but what Hildur believed made little difference. Her youngest sister had stuck to her story and taken the rap. Björk was serving time at the women's prison outside Reykjavík. Hildur would be seeing her later that day, even though her sister didn't talk much during their visits. *If you live too close to a mountain, you turn into one yourself one day.* Presumably that was what had happened to Björk, who'd grown up in the mountains of the Faroe Islands.

For the first three hours on the road, the landscape had varied from seaside to mountain roads to lush valleys. Since pulling out of Ísafjörður, the tiny body's escort had driven past one small town and a dozen farms. The Westfjords were sparsely inhabited. The first service station they came across was in the village of Hólmavík, population a few hundred, where the main road was swarmed in the summer by tourists. Hólmavík was home not only to a small public pool and a restaurant, but also a museum of Iceland's history of witchcraft. The country's eighteenth-century witch hunts had largely been focused on the Westfjords. The motive for the persecution had been simple: the rich, prominent families who resided in the area at the time protected their wealth and power by accusing problematic personalities of witchcraft. Hildur had been to the museum some years before and enjoyed the way it told offbeat stories about the country's history. But today they'd only be stopping in Hólmavík long enough to refuel.

Hildur pulled in next to Jakob and killed the engine. Jakob emerged from Kristína and Óskar's car and walked into the service station to get himself a coffee.

The parents took their time climbing out. The husband wrapped his arm around his wife as they leaned against the back bumper, clinging to each other with their eyes closed. With their faces bathed in sunlight, they looked like an ordinary couple on the road, hunting for pleasant vacation weather.

Hildur leaned against Brenda's rear bumper and glanced at the parents. 'Is there anything I can bring you? I'll be going into the shop soon.'

Kristína blinked a couple of times and turned to Hildur. 'That's thoughtful of you, but no thanks.'

Hildur nodded in reply. She drew little patterns in the dirt with the tip of her toe and pondered the parents' composure. Neither had shouted, raged, or cried out loud. The eye of the storm was disturbingly calm.

Kristína tucked her hair behind her ear and gazed into the distance. 'This might seem strange to you, but . . .'

Hildur stopped moving her foot, leaving the design in the dirt unfinished. 'I can guarantee you, nothing seems strange to me. Feel free to say whatever you want.'

A faint, internalised smile formed on Kristína's face, completely devoid of joy. 'When the worst happens, you stop being afraid.'

Hildur nodded. She knew exactly what Kristína was talking about.

Husband and wife were still leaning against each other. Hildur kept watching them out of the corner of her eye.

And suddenly she was sure she'd seen the husband before somewhere.

Chapter 5

Reykjavík, summer 2022

It was coming up to 4 p.m., and the sun was still high in the sky. Hildur lowered her sunglasses and turned on the car radio. She had no interest in the national track and field results, but the monotonous male voice momentarily transported her to another reality. She needed something else to think about.

It had been an incredibly long day. After reaching Reykjavík, she and Jakob had dropped Kristína and Óskar off at their home. Hildur and Jakob hadn't wanted to leave the parents alone in their present state, so they'd waited until Kristína's sister arrived. Hildur had given the sister contact information for the crisis centre; the grieving parents could find someone there to talk to if necessary.

Kristína and Óskar's house was in a suburb near lake Elliðavatn. Hildur was familiar with the area. Years ago, when she'd worked as a police officer in the capital, she'd been in the habit of coming out here to exercise. There had been good running paths around the lake back then, before the area was developed. Now spacious single-family homes sprouted near the water. A little higher up, there were rowhouses, and behind them, a few low-slung apartment buildings. The lake lent the area a special beauty; it was no wonder the ever-growing capital had unfurled its streets, streetlamps, and bus network here.

After bidding Kristína and Óskar farewell, Jakob and Hildur had delivered the infant's body to the forensic pathologist's office downtown, where it would be examined. Then Hildur had dropped Jakob off at the airport. He flew back to the Westfjords that same afternoon to make it home to his son before evening. Although Matias's iPad would help him pass the time after school and his after-school activities, Jakob didn't want to leave his son alone too long. Hildur understood. Matias was having trouble adjusting as it was – which Hildur thought was perfectly natural. Matias had lost his mother the winter before and been forced to change countries, languages, and schools yet again, moving with his father to Iceland. She agreed it would be wisest for Jakob to fly home without delay.

Hildur wouldn't be driving home until tomorrow. She meant to take time to visit her sister at Hólmsheiði prison outside Reykjavík. Some men were held there on remand but by and large the facility was reserved for women. The opening of Hólmsheiði had meant a huge improvement in conditions for Iceland's female prisoners, as in mixed prisons many had been sexually harassed or mistreated.

Currently, about forty women were serving longer sentences in the prison's two units. The units were divided by nationality: Icelanders did time in one, foreigners in another. There were three fenced yards, the indoor gyms were top of the range, and prisoners had the opportunity to study and work while incarcerated. Like her fellow inmates, Björk made objects out of wood and other handcrafts to sell on the prison website.

Hildur glanced at her mobile phone as she walked toward the main door of the rust-brown building. She'd received a message from Anton:

> Hey, gorgeous lady! How are you? Calf-marking is just around the corner. Busiest time of year.

Hildur found it amusing that Anton always called her *lady* in his brief English-language texts. And that his topics of conversation rarely ventured beyond his reindeer. Hildur slipped the phone in her pocket. She'd reply later.

Each inmate had to provide prison staff with a list of people allowed to visit them. Björk had given two names: Rósa's and Hildur's. Hildur recognised the guard working the desk. An amateur weightlifter, Kári often had a protein bar or shake at hand. Today Hildur noticed he had both. His neckless head twitched a couple of centimetres to signify he'd recognised Hildur. She still flashed her ID as a formality.

After the reception desk came the security check, where the next guard inspected Hildur's bag. Hildur had brought Björk some reading material. The guard flipped through the four books to make sure they contained no contraband. Visitors didn't receive special treatment just because they happened to be police officers.

Hildur sat down to wait, and a moment later Björk walked in. Her escort nodded at Hildur and exited. Prison rules required the first three visits to take place in the visitors' room, where the inmate and her guests were separated by a sheet of bulletproof glass. Since those encounters had gone smoothly, the sisters were now able to meet in a private room.

'Hey, sis,' Hildur said, reaching across the table to pat Björk on the shoulder. 'How are you?'

Björk shook off Hildur's hand and pushed her chair back a few centimetres. 'I don't feel like hugging.'

Hildur asked how things were going with the other prisoners. During the previous visit, Björk had reported she was most comfortable alone.

'There's only one thing we have in common,' Björk said.

The wall clock ticked as the minute hand advanced. Hildur looked quizzically at her sister.

'Everyone is here because of some man. That's it. We don't have anything else in common, anything to talk about.'

Hildur let the matter drop. She pulled the books out of her bag and stacked them on the table. Björk looked delighted.

'There's the latest from Arnaldur, Yrsa, and Ragnar,' Hildur said. She'd popped into a bookshop in central Reykjavík. Björk loved crime novels and television police procedurals. She didn't have her own television in prison, but she could read to her heart's content.

'Thanks,' Björk said. She pulled the books toward her and went through the stack, nodding in approval.

Hildur's relationship with Björk and Rósa wasn't wholly uncomplicated. Her sisters still occasionally expressed bitterness at how they'd been sent to a foreign country to live with a stranger while Hildur had been allowed to stay close to home with Aunt Tinna. None of them fully understood the reason the younger girls had been ferried to the Faroe Islands. What had their mother been thinking? Why had things gone the way they had?

Now, finally, all three of them were on the same island. But rebuilding a connection wasn't simple. All three sisters were lost, in one way or another.

'I like the hair,' Hildur said, trying to drum up conversation.

'Bah,' Björk said, rubbing her nearly shaved head. She was being reticent. Or maybe recalcitrant.

'How are the classes going? Have you started yet?'

Björk had earned a nursing degree in the Faroes. After being sent to prison, she'd applied for specialist training in mental health and substance abuse.

Björk cleared her throat and fiddled with the books she'd been given. 'Fine. I'll be done in a year.'

She turned her attention to the topmost book and started reading the back cover. It was Yrsa Sigurðardóttir's *I See You.*

'*A family's dark secrets come to light in remote Hvalfjörður,*' Björk read. She gave a dry chuckle and dropped the book on the table. 'Sounds just like us.'

Damn it, Hildur swore to herself. She hadn't checked the books' themes; she'd just bought all the latest releases she knew Björk would want to read. Björk squeezed out a tiny smile. Hildur knew it meant she wanted to get along.

'Yrsa's good. I went on her walking tour in Reykjavík last winter. She took us around to all the places that appear in her books,' Björk said, thanking Hildur again.

Hildur was delighted by her sister's sincere enthusiasm.

She also wanted to share the latest about Rósa. 'Rósa likes her new job working for the phone company. She can do it from home.'

Björk raised her left eyebrow.

'She'll come next time,' Hildur chattered. 'She had to hang around Kotsdalur today to keep an eye on some excavating work she's having done. They're supposed to install a septic tank this week.'

Björk nodded.

Hildur kept trying: 'She asked me to say hello.'

Björk turned away and studied her cuticles, then drily said: 'Don't lie. Rósa isn't the type to ask anyone to say hello to anyone else.'

Hildur glanced at a white needlepoint that hung over the door: *God bless this home.* Some version of it appeared in nearly every Icelandic residence.

'I want to go back to my cell now,' Björk announced. She stood and knocked on the door.

Hildur felt bad. They still had time left. 'But I just got here.'

Björk lightly tapped her foot against the floor, the signal that she'd made up her mind. As the time for saying their goodbyes was approaching anyway, Hildur decided to ask the same question she did every time.

'I don't believe you committed those crimes. Why won't you say what really happened?'

Björk clutched the books to her chest and looked at the door. 'Just let me handle my own affairs.' Relief washed over her face when the guard opened it. 'I study. I kill time. I read. Just now things couldn't be going any better for me. You go worry about other people's problems. It's enough for me to be on time for a meal that's been prepared for me.'

Six whole sentences, Hildur silently counted. Björk was most talkative when standing up for her views. Hildur exited through the visitors' door. She didn't get her little sister's behaviour, but in the end, who did understand every one of another individual's motives?

Once she was outside, Hildur marched straight to Brenda. She'd pick up something from the grill at the nearby service station, drive to the roadside hotel in Borgarnes, and go for a run to ease some of the stresses of the day.

Before starting the car, she replied to Anton:

Hey, handsome man. Things are fine here. When are we going to see each other?

The mountains at the horizon, the Bláfjöll, didn't live up to their name just now. Their slopes weren't blue, but orange in the westering sun. Hildur turned up her nose. She couldn't stand dull, warm summer tones. The only reason she could tolerate the entire season was because it was short and was followed by autumn and the even-longer winter.

She buckled her seatbelt and backed out of the parking spot. Something her sister had said nagged at her: *Everyone is here because of some man.*

Who was the man Björk was in prison for?

Chapter 6

Ísafjörður, June 2022

Jakob sniffed the brown swill in the coffee pot. His nose told him it was no longer drinkable.

'Should I make a fresh pot?' he asked loudly. The question was aimed at his boss, Elísabet 'Beta' Baldursdóttir.

'No thanks. I have dance class soon.'

Beta had picked up dancing since her divorce and was committed to her new hobby. Her dance class was at the same time every week.

Beta had worked as police chief in Ísafjörður for ages, but the year before she'd moved to Reykjavík for personal reasons and taken a short-term position in the narcotics unit. When the position of Westfjords police chief had opened up again this past winter, no one had applied. Finding competent professionals willing to work in the remote, sparsely inhabited region was a challenge: the few villages and towns spread across over twenty-two thousand square kilometres were home to a total of about seven thousand people.

And so Jakob and Hildur had come up with a plan. They'd suggested to Beta that she return to the Westfjords for one more year. Jakob knew he wanted to build his law enforcement career in Iceland, and he enjoyed living amid the stark, mountainous terrain of the Westfjords. He also had a family in Ísafjörður now, consisting of his son Matias and partner Guðrún. Jakob had been keen on the supervisory position but couldn't apply yet because he didn't meet the criteria. He was currently studying law at the University of Iceland in his spare time. The university offered the flexibility of remote study, and Jakob had taken up his studies a couple of years earlier without telling anyone. Once he'd committed to his dream of becoming police chief, he'd shared his plans with Hildur. In Iceland, one had to have a Master of Law degree to serve in the role, and Jakob meant to earn one. Although he understood Icelandic almost perfectly, writing was harder. Luckily, Hildur had helped him with his coursework; he was eternally grateful for her assistance.

Jakob would continue working away at his degree over the next year. He'd be receiving Icelandic citizenship soon, as he'd passed the language test and nearly met the requirement of four years' residency in Iceland. He had his police degree from Finland and experience working as a police officer in the Westfjords. Jakob believed he'd get the position of chief the next time it was opened up, even if he were missing a few credits from his law degree. Over his years of living in Iceland, he'd learned that rules bend when necessary.

Despite having just moved to Reykjavík, Beta had found the proposition tempting and agreed to return for a brief stint. *But just for one year*, she'd said.

Beta had twin boys who split their time between the Westfjords and their father's home in Reykjavík. She didn't want the boys to have to travel between two homes for any longer than a year, especially since the distance between those homes was well over four hundred kilometres. The boys attended school in both places, alternating weeks. The arrangement required a little effort but was in no way out of the ordinary. Many Icelandic children spent their time between two homes, and some switched back and forth between schools that were nowhere near each other. Nothing was impossible to arrange if you wanted it badly enough. Beta's decision had been made easier by the fact that her temporary position with the Reykjavík police was nearing its end. She'd have had to look for a new job anyway.

Jakob was fond of Beta. She was the one who'd originally brought him to Ísafjörður as an intern. She was a fair boss who gave little heed to hierarchies and didn't breathe down her subordinates' necks. She trusted her staff and let them do their work without micromanaging them.

Jakob shook the mouse on the desk to banish his computer's screensaver. His next task was finalising the report on the baby that had died of SIDS. After that, he had to delve into a series of break-ins that had been taking place at local cabins since early May. The investigation was still in its preliminary phase, and there weren't many clues, let alone any suspects. He'd have to talk to the owners of the cabins that had been targeted most recently.

Before he could get down to work, the phone rang. Jakob answered using his full name, although most Icelanders answered with their first name only, even at work.

'Hi, this is Hilmir from the emergency room at the hospital.'

The deep-voiced Hilmir cleared his throat into the phone. He had the uber-Icelandic habit of inhaling at times when speaking. It made it sound like he was perpetually worried.

'Damn it. Our shift lead forgot to call you yesterday. It was his last day of work before vacation, so the only things on his mind were beer and football.'

Jakob waited for Hilmir to get to the point. 'OK. What is this about?'

Hilmir's voice grew serious as he explained a patient from a cruise ship had come in yesterday.

Jakob grunted to indicate he was listening. He'd picked up the fundamentals of cruise tourism during his time in the Westfjords. The massive vessels circled Iceland. Their passengers slept and ate on board. During the day, the ships made stops at coastal towns – for instance, Ísafjörður, where disembarking tourists overran the centre every morning from May to September. On the busiest days, there could be as many as three ships in town.

'*Diamond Adventure of the Seas* is a mid-sized vessel,' Hilmir explained. 'It docks instead of dropping anchor out in the fjord.'

The biggest cruise ships were so gargantuan they didn't fit in Ísafjörður's small harbour, so tender boats were used to transport passengers between ship and shore.

Jakob was afraid Hilmir would forget the reason for his call. 'What was it you wanted to tell us about the patient who came in?'

'His face was gone. Shredded.'

Jakob asked Hilmir to be more specific: was the patient a tourist or a local resident? Maybe there'd been an accident on one of the fishing boats.

'He'd just stumbled off the cruise ship. He had the ship's logo on the front of his shirt, so we figured he worked on board.'

Hilmir went on to explain that when the bleeding man reached the emergency room, they thought he was drunk, because he just wheezed and shook and was unable to get a word out.

'But we were wrong. He was just in really bad shape. Potentially fatal cuts all over his face and multiple broken ribs. He didn't understand English, at least not in his state of shock,' Hilmir said. He'd eventually deduced that the man spoke Spanish.

'Fist fight?' was the first idea to pop into Jakob's mind.

'The cuts are so uniform that I suspect a steel blade. It took us hours to stitch his face back together. We had to put him under for the duration of the operation.'

Odd that no one at the station had been informed right away. Most of the time emergency rooms automatically reported life-threatening cases to the police. A frustrating oversight. Jakob rubbed his man bun with his free hand. He found it irritating when even seemingly simple procedures suffered from lack of follow-through. He and his colleagues would have to speak to the victim as soon as possible.

'Is he conscious?'

Hilmir said the patient was sleeping now and guessed he wouldn't wake till afternoon at the earliest. 'It's a doozy of a case. I've never seen a face cut up like that.'

Jakob ended the call. He was just stepping out of the office when the phone rang again.

'Hi, it's Birkir, Matias's teacher's assistant,' said a hurried-sounding male voice.

Jakob felt a cold sweat travel up his neck to his forehead. *What now?* 'Is Matias . . .?'

He left the question hanging and pressed the phone more tightly to his ear.

The way Birkir sighed didn't bode well. 'We've had a bit of a tough morning again.'

We? You mean Matias. Jakob could hear it in the teacher's voice. It wasn't the first time he'd received a call of this nature.

'Matias pushed a classmate into the bathroom and threatened to set the cubicle on fire. When I took his lighter away and told him that was unacceptable, he told me . . .' Birkir paused, as if searching for the words, '. . . he told me to "chill out and go click on OnlyFans".'

Jakob almost dropped the phone. *OnlyFans?* How could a seven-year-old know anything about OnlyFans? He drew a breath and exhaled, emptying his lungs. It had been a difficult spring for Matias. Jakob wasn't surprised: Matias had undergone some major unanticipated changes in his life. Jakob might have been naïve, assuming Matias would adjust to life in Iceland with little trouble. A small town, a small school, a safe place to grow up, a stable father, and patient, kind-hearted Guðrún living in the same household. But Matias had begun acting up as soon as he started school. He couldn't sit still, constantly pestered the other students, and instigated bullying incidents during recess. *Where on earth did Matias get a lighter?* Luckily, the school year would be ending soon.

Things might settle down over the summer, Jakob thought to himself.

At least he hoped so.

Chapter 7

Hildur rolled her neck, resulting in a faint rasp reminiscent of grains of sand sliding across a tilted sheet of paper. Ten times clockwise, ten times counterclockwise. The small, targeted movement relieved the shoulder aches that frequently troubled her after long drives.

'So he didn't say anything?' Jakob confirmed from his seat at the table. He looked at Beta and Hildur without his hands slowing. Watching his knitting needles move was hypnotic. Hildur had lost count of how many sweaters Jakob had knitted over the past spring and early summer alone.

It was approaching 4 p.m., and the three of them had gathered in the station break room for a quick status update.

Beta had just dropped by the hospital with a Spanish-language interpreter, but the man with the sliced face had been too out of it to talk. Even if he hadn't been, talking would have been hard, as his head was completely swathed in bandages. The doctor who treated him had told Beta to come back later.

The twenty-two-year-old patient's name was Manuel Pérez, and he was from Venezuela. His name, age and citizenship had been determined from the passport he carried in his back pocket. They'd established his employer from his clothing: his trousers and his shirt bore the ship's logo. Beta said Pérez's clothes had smelled so strongly of grease that she'd deduced he'd worked in the ship's kitchens.

'The doctor wants to keep him for observation for at least a few days,' she added.

Hildur buttered herself a piece of bread. The drive from earlier that day had made her hungry. As she fixed her snack, she pondered questions that needed answering. The ship would be returning to Ísafjörður in a week, which gave her and her colleagues plenty of time to talk to Pérez. Who had done this to him? And with what weapon? A kitchen knife? Why had he been attacked?

Assaults were reported to the police every week. The incidents often involved drunken scuffles after the bars closed. But most took place in the home and were not necessarily reported. Hildur had encountered all sorts of things on the job but never knife-work like this.

There was one thing in particular that bothered her about the Pérez case: 'Don't you guys think it's a little weird that no one's called looking for him? His employer, for instance?'

Jakob's knitting needles stopped for the first time during the meeting.

'Now that you mention it . . . You'd think they'd care if an employee didn't show up for their shift.'

The cruise ship had continued to the town of Akureyri on the northern coast. Hildur wondered, mostly to herself, how it was possible no one on board had noticed anything. Maybe Pérez had had the day off.

Beta pulled her T-shirt away from her torso and fanned it to cool herself. It was wet at the armpits. The windowless break room was stiflingly hot.

'We need to inform them,' Beta said. 'I'll contact the ship.'

She looked down at the notepad where she'd recorded some notes on the doctor's observations. Pérez had four broken ribs. Most of the roughly dozen cuts on and around his face ran from the hairline to the tip of the chin. Apparently, he'd been fortunate they'd skirted the eye and hadn't reached his throat.

'Did someone put him through a paper shredder or what?' Hildur said with a snort. The injuries suggested such intense violence that there was no way anyone in the vicinity could have been unaware of it. Not to mention Pérez had lost so much blood he must have left a visible trail, and the assailant must have received their share of the spatter too. Someone had to have seen or heard something.

'Whoever it was really wanted to hurt him. A spontaneous, angry slash wouldn't result in wounds like that,' Jakob said, pulling more yarn from the skein. He suggested maybe Pérez had been spending a day off with friends, someone had over-indulged, and a fight over something trivial had broken out.

Beta sighed. 'Party or not, he didn't have any alcohol in his blood. We're still waiting on the narcotics panel.'

The interpreter had promised to return the next day, when they'd try to talk to Manuel again.

'Should someone board the ship and do some asking around?' Jakob said. 'I bet our colleagues at the boat's next stop would help. It would be good to ask questions as soon as possible, the next time the boat docks.'

The vessel would be berthing in Iceland's northern and eastern harbour towns over the next few days.

Beta rejected the idea. She stood, signalling that the day's fights had been fought, and said she'd contact the ship soon. But boarding wasn't necessarily very likely. 'We'd need the captain's permission, and I can tell you from experience that getting it is by no means a given. We don't have the authority to board at will.'

With that, Beta said her goodbyes and headed home.

Jakob was still knitting. It was mind-blowing to Hildur that someone could move their hands so fast without constantly making mistakes.

'Hildur, can I ask you something?'

Hildur grunted to indicate she was listening.

'We moved a lot when I was a kid. I've never even gone to see my first home, in Helsinki. What's it like going back to Kotsdalur after such a long time? I'm thinking about Matias . . . He's probably never going to see his first childhood home in Oslo. Is he going to miss out on something?'

'I'm pretty sure he won't miss out on anything. There's no point getting attached to things that will eventually rot and fall apart.'

Jakob laughed for the first time that day. 'At least no one can accuse you of having a toxically positive life philosophy.'

Hildur wiped the counter.

'If you're always longing to be where you used to be, you'll get stuck in place. And then a landslide will come along and sweep you away.'

Chapter 8

Hildur attached her surfboard to Brenda's roof and opened the cargo space. She groped at the back of her wetsuit to unzip it.

She used this one wetsuit year-round. This far north, the sea stayed cold even in high summer. The only real difference between summer surfing and winter surfing was the sea was a lot less interesting in the summer. In the winter, big storms in the Bay of Greenland sent long waves to the shores of the Westfjords. In June, the sea rarely offered any challenges.

Hildur grabbed the towel next to the garbage bag and dried her hair. As she rubbed her scalp, she decided she'd drop by the nursing home. She'd cut her surfing short due to the boring waves, so she had time to visit Helga before evening. Helga and her husband had once owned a sheep farm up the road from Hildur's family when Hildur was a child.

As an adult, Hildur had learned that Helga had been Hildur's mother's Rakel's lover. Helga had said that Rakel had been willing to divorce Hildur's father and make a fresh start with the children and Helga, but Helga hadn't had the courage. On multiple occasions, Helga had repeated to Hildur how profoundly she regretted her decision.

The previous winter, Helga had moved from the assisted living home to the nursing home attached to the hospital. Her legs had deteriorated to the point that she couldn't wash herself or manage her affairs alone. The move had only taken her across the street, but it had been a big step.

My last home before they put me in a coffin, she'd said upon seeing her new room for the first time.

Hildur had made a habit of visiting Helga at least once a week, sometimes more. She'd told Helga about her sisters and what had befallen them. Helga hadn't interrupted a single time, even when Hildur told her about Björk's confession and subsequent incarceration. Helga had just sat calmly at the kitchen table, slender fingers fiddling with the fringe of the tablecloth. *Jæjja. That's life for you.* That sentence had been the start of their deeper friendship. Helga was right. The most suspenseful movies plot twists were nothing compared to everyday existence. There had been plenty of times on the job when Hildur had seen things happen in real life that were beyond imagining.

Maps of the Westfjords and old photos of the town and its inhabitants were displayed in the nursing home corridor. The hallway opened up on a bright, spacious common area with an eastern exposure that was all glass: the floor-to-ceiling windows had a stunning view of the mountains. The residents spent a lot of time in this shared living room.

'Here comes our little policewoman again. Have any news for us?' The greeting was from a talkative old woman Hildur often saw sitting in the same chair, knitting mittens. She peered at Hildur from behind her glasses and smiled inquisitively. 'Helga's a lucky girl, having a visitor as often as she does.'

Hildur stopped and asked the old woman who she was knitting mittens for. The old woman looked at her coyly and lowered her voice: 'For those handsome devils. For next winter. I've already finished four pairs.'

Hildur glanced at the group gathered at the window table. Two wiry men in glasses were playing chess. The taller one was stretching his neck like an athlete preparing for a race. Four other men watched the game in silence. Hildur bid the old woman goodbye and moved on.

The neck-stretcher with thick-framed glasses whistled at Hildur as she passed, sparking murmurs of approval among his comrades.

'You've got great legs,' another added.

The old men's catcalls continued to amuse Hildur as she knocked on the door of Room 12. A moment later, she heard a lively, 'Come in, whoever you are.'

Despite her strong voice, Helga's appearance was frail. She sat in an armchair with a blanket across her lap, reading the paper. She and Hildur hugged and exchanged cheek kisses.

'Push that rollator out of the way and get yourself a stool,' Helga said. 'There's toffee in the drawer.'

Hildur knew it was important to Helga that she accept when Helga offered. She took two toffees from the nightstand drawer and popped them in her mouth.

'How's Tinna? Did they leave on their trip yet?'

Hildur nodded and shifted the sweet over to her other cheek so she could talk. 'As soon as Ívar's summer vacation began. They won't be back until autumn.'

Hildur's aunt Tinna lived in Ísafjörður. Tinna had recently begun dating Ívar, who maintained aluminium plant machines. This summer the pair of them had set out in his recreational vehicle to tour Iceland together. Tinna's absence felt odd. It had been years since Hildur had spent any appreciable amount of time away from her aunt. Now it looked like they wouldn't be seeing each other until late August.

Helga folded up the newspaper in her lap and interlaced her fingers. Hildur saw sadness in her eyes.

'It's almost June seventeenth,' Helga sighed. It was both Icelandic independence day and Rakel's birthday. 'Your mother couldn't have been born on a more fitting date.'

Hildur nodded. She already knew what Helga would say next: 'She was more independent than Bjartur of Summerhouses.'

Bjartur of Summerhouses was the protagonist of Nobel Prize-winning author Halldór Laxness' work *Independent People*. Bjartur toiled doggedly to build himself a better life and rejected offers of help.

'But your mother had better intentions. She didn't crave total separation from others, just a sensible independence. There's a pretty big difference, you know?'

Hildur nodded. The chewy toffee was stuck in her molars. She moved her jaw back and forth to loosen the sweet. Hildur knew Helga liked reminiscing about Rakel, so she always asked about her mother during these visits.

'Tell me something about my mother that I don't know yet.'

Helga stroked her thin hair and sank into long-ago memories. 'Rakel always put on lipstick before we saw each other.'

This was a detail Hildur recalled. 'Those were the only times she ever wore lipstick. When we came to visit you.'

Helga winked at Hildur and lowered the newspaper to the floor. 'She was such a beautiful person. When she stepped into a room, she always brought generosity of spirit with her.' Helga shifted in her armchair. Her bony fingers fiddled with the blanket's fringe. 'She was a real nail.' This Icelandic compliment was used to describe hardworking horses and people. 'She never complained and didn't believe in lightly made promises. She sold those ointments of hers tirelessly.'

Hildur didn't remember many details from her childhood, but the coarse, scratchy gunnysacks and the smell of ointment were an exception. Her mother had kept the bearberries, tea-leaved willow, yarrow, and mother-of-thyme she harvested in the highlands in the sacks. She'd occasionally taken Hildur to go picking with her. Hildur could still identify a lot of the plants. Seeing tiny white chickweed flowers in the bowl of a valley warmed her heart, even now.

'The recipe for the ointment had been passed down in your family since Hrafntinna's days,' Helga said, grazing her wrinkled cheek with the tip of her forefinger.

Hildur knew this. Tinna had told her about Hrafntinna, their ancestor and seer who had extensive knowledge of herbs. Hildur remembered the sharp smell of the greenish salve. Mum would pick the plants, clean them in the yard, store them in sacks, and blend them with beeswax.

'Do you think she was happy with my father?'

Helga shook her head. 'Rakel never said a bad word about your father. But she didn't say a good one either.'

They chatted about Rakel, then the weather over the past week, the food at the nursing home, and of course the tourists. Helga's delicate frame jiggled with laughter when she reported an encounter she'd had with cruise ship tourists the day before, as a group of the curious tourists had ended up in the grounds of the nursing home.

'They looked in the windows. I made the mistake of waving at them, and that really got them going. Pressed their mobile phones up to the glass and took pictures.'

Hildur glanced at the sports watch on her wrist. She had to get home. Matias was scheduled to come over that evening.

'Your mother is also really good at fooling people,' Helga whispered.

Hildur felt a twinge inside. She'd learned to recognise this tone in Helga's voice.

'She sneaks past the night nurse and visits me. And no one notices anything; the two of us just lie here together!'

Helga's eyes were those of an old woman and a young girl at the same time. Her mind was usually sharp, but there were times she flitted elsewhere without warning.

'I hear her coming. I can hear her shuffling down the hallway,' Helga added, with another wink for Hildur.

Hildur responded with an encouraging smile and acted as if Helga were talking about something totally ordinary.

Chapter 9

Hildur had just stepped out of the shower when she heard a knock. She wrapped herself in her bathrobe and walked to the front door, leaving wet footprints on the hall floor.

'Come in,' Hildur said. Matias didn't speak Icelandic fluently yet, so she spoke to him in English. 'Have you had dinner?'

Matias shook his head and smiled. He made a beeline for the basket in the living room, grabbed his favourite Icelandic-language comic book – *Leðurblökumaðurinn*, or *Batman* – and sat down at the kitchen table to read. The short sentences facilitated his learning of the new language.

Meanwhile, Hildur put a pizza in the oven and set out two plates. She thought about the message Anton had sent her, asking her to visit. Why couldn't he come here to Iceland? The distance made scheduling a time to meet an endless back-and-forth. Hildur liked getting texts from Anton, but they weren't going to lead to anything.

What did she know about Anton in the end, anyway? He was Jakob's childhood friend from Finland. A childless reindeer herder whose wife had died of cancer years ago.

The previous spring, Hildur and Anton had taken a long overseas trip to a tropical island. It hadn't taken Hildur long to realise how raw Anton was inside. Both parties' quivering ghosts had crept out of the chambers where they'd been lurking for years, Hildur presumed. Two broken humans had recognised each other. That was no doubt one reason such a deep connection had formed between them over the few weeks they spent in each other's company. Now that connection hung on the delicate rhizomes of text message exchanges.

Hildur realised she'd ended up in a situation she had no interest in being in. She hadn't wanted to share her life with anyone. Living alone as she did, she was responsible for no one but herself. She had her daily routines and was satisfied. She'd trained herself to constantly prepare for the worst, and she preferred to do so on her own. And yet she enjoyed getting Anton's messages.

It made no sense.

Hildur thrust the pointless thoughts from her mind. She turned off the oven, pulled out the pizza, and set the baking sheet down on potholders on the counter. Hildur cut equal slices for herself and Matias and set out the garlic-infused oil. The beverages on offer were orange soda and water. Matias chose soda.

After a few mouthfuls of salami pizza, Hildur broke the silence: 'Are you enjoying school?'

'Not really.'

Hildur considered a response of more than a single word a victory. Matias didn't much care for talking about school.

'What's the most annoying thing about it?'

'They're all losers and no one understands anything.'

Hildur laughed. 'Sometimes I feel exactly the same way.'

Matias laughed too. The connection between Hildur and the boy was slender but woven of goodwill.

'Even so, I don't try to set my colleagues on fire,' Hildur noted, adding that Jakob had told her about what had happened at school. 'Do you even know what OnlyFans is?'

Matias squirmed uncomfortably in his chair and shifted his slice from one side of his plate to the other.

'It's a website where grown-ups post videos for other grown-ups,' Hildur explained. 'Videos about sex.'

Matias stared at Hildur, eyes wide. He was spellbound by what he was hearing, so Hildur continued.

'If you have any questions, ask me or your dad. Or Guðrún. But don't talk about this sex stuff at school, OK?'

Matias thought for a moment, then shrugged and kept eating.

'And don't bring lighters to school.'

After dinner, Matias delved back into his *Batman* comic book. Hildur leaned against the counter and stared out the window into the summer evening. A pair of songbirds were hopping about at the base of a bush. She thrust Anton from her mind and turned her thoughts to the Venezuelan from the cruise ship. Hildur had dropped by on her way to Helga's to inquire about his condition. A passageway connected the hospital and nursing home, facilitating swift movement between the two.

Pérez had still been asleep. He'd looked so small and delicate. Whose hatred of him had been so intense they'd almost sliced his face off? How come no one was asking about him? What was his secret?

Chapter 10

The thin clouds cut the keenest edge of the morning sun. The time was nearly eight, and Ísafjörður was awake. It was the last day of the school year. Summer vacation was about to begin.

Hildur and Jakob were walking over to the hospital to talk to Manuel.

'The ship claimed no one by that name was missing,' Hildur said, kicking a rock. It struck a stone wall and bounced off. Hildur recounted everything Beta had told her on the phone the night before. There weren't any Manuel Pérezes among the personnel, and the name didn't appear on any passenger manifests. Or so the ship's director of communications and community relations, or whatever her title was, had indicated.

Jakob considered the possibility that perhaps Manuel had been a stowaway and stolen the employee uniform he was wearing. 'There are hundreds of crew members and thousands of tourists on a vessel like that; it would be easy to blend in if you wanted.'

Jakob's theory could well be possible. Hildur glanced at the sea. A huge cruise ship had just anchored in the fjord, and the tender boats were chugging toward it. The water's calm surface reflected the surrounding mountains.

Luckily, a Spanish-language interpreter had been able to accompany Hildur and Jakob today. Booking an interpreter was never a given. There were a few Spanish speakers living in or near Ísafjörður, and the police would call them in as needed. But most of them worked in tourism during the summer and were no doubt leading tour groups today.

'I checked the cruise ships' schedules. The vessel Manuel disembarked from is circling Iceland until the end of July. In other words, it'll be stopping here a few more times.'

In August, the ship would set out on a longer voyage from Greenland to Iceland, the Faroe Islands, and finally Denmark. There were plenty of cruise options, even in northern seas.

The sun was behind Hildur and Jakob now. When they reached the seafood warehouse, they turned left and cut along the edge of the old cemetery toward the hospital.

Up until recent decades, remote small towns like Ísafjörður had lived off fishing. When the industry had concentrated in a few major harbours and employers had abandoned small towns and villages, rural Iceland had emptied. Cruise ship tourism had changed things. The harbours had come back to life.

'I'm not sure the local infrastructure can handle this many people,' Hildur remarked.

'The cruise ships create jobs and generate income. That's what's going to pay for that infrastructure,' Jakob said, glancing to the side before stepping into the crosswalk.

Hildur saw the interpreter waiting for them at the hospital entrance. Finnur Bogason had thick reddish hair, a lot of freckles, and a strikingly sharp Adam's apple. Finnur was a part-time Spanish teacher at the local high school. He also translated Spanish literature into Icelandic and worked as an interpreter. Beta had relied on a different interpreter during yesterday's attempt, so Hildur briefed Finnur on the situation.

'Venezuelan pronunciation is a little different than European pronunciation. But I'm sure I'll manage,' Finnur said. His Adam's apple bobbed up and down as he spoke.

The hospital smelled of disinfectant and stale coffee. Hildur greeted the receptionist and said they were here to see Manuel Pérez.

Manuel's bed had been propped up so he could sit. His face was completely swathed in bandages: only the eyes, mouth, and badly bruised nose were visible. A rerun of the Icelandic comedy *The Night Shift* was playing on the television. Manuel glanced at the newcomers but quickly turned back to the TV. Hildur introduced herself and Jakob and the interpreter and explained they were there to find out how Manuel had been injured.

'Are you feeling well enough to talk?' Hildur asked.

Finnur translated. Manuel kept staring at the television. There was no response to translate, because Manuel didn't speak.

Hildur decided to press on nonetheless. 'What were you doing on the cruise ship? Did you work on it?'

Manuel kept his eyes glued to the television.

Jakob decided to give it a try: 'Were you on the vessel without permission?'

Equally slim results.

'We don't care if you were a stowaway. We're just trying to find out what happened to you and if we can help,' he continued.

Hildur scanned the room and pondered. Manuel had a private room. He was in his early twenties but seemed younger. His threadbare hospital pyjamas emphasised his scrawny physique.

'Is that show funny if you don't understand the language?' Hildur asked.

Finnur took the only chair in the room and sat down at Manuel's side.

'Is this a comedy? I can't believe how sad it is,' Manuel replied.

Hildur was delighted. Manuel had answered, and with more than one word. Maybe they'd still find a shared language.

The show was about three service station employees who worked the night shift. 'That one who plays the pompous boss was the mayor of Reykjavík for years,' Hildur said, then fell silent. She waited for Manuel to keep talking.

'Do so few people live in Iceland that politicians have to act on TV? Or maybe that's a good skill for a politician, being able to act. It's the same in my homeland . . .'

Hildur grunted. She didn't know much about Venezuelan politics. She knew the name Hugo Chávez, the former president who had died a few years ago, but that was it.

'We want to know how you got those injuries on your face,' Hildur said, gesturing at her own cheek. 'You were in pretty bad shape when you were brought in. What happened?'

Manuel withdrew into his shell. He adjusted himself into a more comfortable sitting position and tried to fold his arms across his torso.

'You were brought here from the harbour. According to an eyewitness, you ran off the ship trailing blood. You've been cared for here since. The ship left and will be back in a week's time. By then you'll probably be well enough to return to the boat. You'll have to continue your recuperation there.'

As Finnur translated Hildur's words, Manuel's thick but barely visible eyebrows rose, his lower eyelids tightened, and his mouth opened halfway. As if someone were tugging on his face and he was trying to resist the pull. Judging by his micro-expressions, Hildur decided he was afraid. She could hear his breathing accelerate.

'No,' Manuel said.

Hildur glanced at Jakob. Maybe he could get the young man to open up.

'Listen, if we don't know why you don't want to go back, there's no way we can help. All you have on you is a passport. We assume all your other belongings are on the ship. No one from the boat seems to be missing you, but you're wearing an employee uniform. There's something fishy about this whole scenario.'

There was a knock at the door, and a nurse stepped in to check on Manuel. She carefully adjusted the bandages on his face, and Hildur noticed she addressed him in Spanish. Only one of the nurse's hands was fully functional. She held the other one close to her body.

'It's almost time for his medication,' the nurse said with a pointed look at Hildur.

Hildur nodded. She presumed she and Jakob would be finished by the time the nurse returned.

Manuel still wouldn't speak. Jakob walked over to the window and closed the blinds. He tightened the man bun at his nape and let out a weary sigh. 'So should we arrest you for entering the country illegally?'

Hildur was caught off guard by her colleague's bold attack.

'No jail!' Manuel cried out.

'My colleague here is exaggerating a little,' Hildur said in a reassuring tone. 'We just want to know what happened.'

Manuel shifted in his bed. He fiddled with a wrinkle in the sheet as he appeared to weigh his options. He sighed lightly, then said in a quiet voice: 'I work in the ship's kitchens.'

'So was it a workplace accident?' Jakob asked, stroking his own face.

Manuel nodded shyly. His chin trembled. 'I'd cut up over a hundred chickens. I was very tired. My grip slipped, and I tripped and fell on my knife.'

Hildur was sceptical. If the injury had been an accident, it would have resulted in at most one cut, not full-face lacerations. But she didn't want to challenge Manuel's account right off the bat. 'You said you were tired. Had you worked a long shift?'

'A normal one,' Manuel replied. He leaned his head back against the pillow and closed his eyes.

'We'll leave you alone in a moment so you can rest,' Hildur said in a conciliatory tone. That seemed to do the trick.

'Thirty hours on a three-hour nap.'

Hildur glanced at Jakob. Manuel's claim stunned them both.

'Are shifts like that normal?' Jakob asked, immediately jumping to the next question. 'How did you stay awake?'

Manuel warily opened his eyes and lightly touched his bandages before answering: 'I sleep during my breaks.'

Jakob continued: 'How come no one on the ship knows your name?'

Manuel's shoulders shuddered, but there was no answer. Through Finnur, he said he was tired and wanted to sleep. He shut his eyes and turned away from his visitors.

Despite Hildur's efforts to continue the conversation, it didn't look like Manuel would be giving them any more today. She and Jakob had to leave, but they'd be back.

Out in the corridor, they came upon the nurse with the bad hand pushing the medication cart with the other one. Jakob and Finnur kept walking, but Hildur wanted to exchange a couple of words with the nurse.

The nurse introduced herself as Lára. She said she'd been an exchange student in Argentina for a year back in the day and done a lot of travelling around Latin America. That was why her Spanish was so good. Hildur asked whether Manuel had told her anything that could be of use to them. They were trying to figure out what had happened to him.

'He's a nice kid. Quiet, doesn't talk much. But I can still recognise the Venezuelan sense of humour,' Lára said. 'He gave me a nickname: No Hand.'

Lára laughed heartily. Hildur felt awkward.

Lára gave Hildur an amused slap on the back with her healthy hand and said it was totally normal. 'It takes a minute to get used to their sense of humour. It's a sign of affection to give someone an offensive nickname.'

Lára was just pushing the cart into motion when she suddenly stopped. 'Maybe it doesn't matter, but something happened early this morning.'

Hildur's interest was piqued. She asked Lára to elaborate.

'He had a visitor. Manuel did. Before visiting hours.'

'A nurse?'

Lára shook her head. She said she'd had her hands full with her morning rounds and hadn't had time to inquire any further.

'I'm sure she wasn't staff. She was wearing a red post office uniform and had a mailbag over her shoulder. Long, silver-blonde hair down to her bum.'

Chapter 11

Fifteen minutes later, Hildur and Jakob were standing outside the glass doors of the post office. Hildur had shared the nurse Lára's observations with Jakob during the walk. The post office opened at nine thirty, which was still a few minutes off.

'Thanks for yesterday, by the way,' Jakob said. 'Matias was in a much better mood when he came home.'

The compliment felt nice to Hildur.

Jakob's phone pinged. He took it from his pocket and glanced at it. Hildur saw his face freeze.

'Something important?'

'No,' Jakob quickly replied, shoving the phone back in his pocket.

Hildur eyed him, dissatisfied by his response. Lately, Jakob had been reacting strangely to the sound of incoming messages. 'I don't believe you. I've noticed you keep getting messages that make you twist your face up. What's going on?'

Jakob asked Hildur to drop it. He tried to look past her, but she didn't give in. Her eyes stuck to his like a burr. 'Who is it?'

'I didn't choose this shit!' Jakob shouted. He took his phone out again and waved it around. For a second it looked like he would hurl it into the street.

Then they both quickly pulled themselves together. An older woman with glasses opened the door to the post office and flipped the lock to the off position. Hildur introduced herself and Jakob and described the woman they were looking for.

The woman invited the police officers inside.

'We don't have any young women working here with long blonde hair like that. Are you sure you'd find her here?' The older woman took a cloth from her pocket. As she cleaned her glasses, something seemed to occur to her.

'There is a mail carrier who works here who has long blond hair. But it's a man. He dyed his hair silver at the beginning of the summer.'

This caught Hildur's attention. What was it the nurse had said . . .? She'd seen someone in a red uniform from behind and said their hair reached down to their lower back. Of course. There was no reason it couldn't be a man, was there?

The woman turned toward the open door behind the counter and shouted: 'Andri!'

Then she lowered her voice. She said Andri Ólafsson had worked there for about a year. She praised him, said he did as much work as two ordinary mail carriers. He was fast and didn't make mistakes.

A moment later, a long-haired man appeared in the doorway, carrying a stack of mail. 'I can't find recipients for these. The addresses are either wrong or incomplete,' he said, setting the mail down on the counter. His big blue eyes stared quizzically.

Hildur asked Andri if there was a place they could exchange a few words privately. They went through the back room to the storage area, where packages waiting to be picked up were arranged on shelves. The biggest deliveries stood on the floor. Hildur introduced herself and explained they'd been to the hospital.

The moment she mentioned Manuel's name, Andri's expression changed. 'I don't know anything about that,' he said initially.

Hildur saw through him. He wasn't a very good liar. His gaze roamed the walls and his chin quivered. One of his hands was resting on an empty shelf. His painted, dark-blue fingernails tapped the aluminium surface.

'You were seen there. We can check the security cameras to confirm,' Hildur said, although she was unsure whether there were any CCTV cameras in the hospital corridors. 'It would be better for you just to come clean. You're not suspected of anything. We're just trying to find out what happened to Manuel. He's in really bad shape.'

Andri leaned against a shelf and stared at the one opposite, as if searching it for something. 'The drugs weren't mine.'

His words caught Hildur off guard, but she didn't show it. 'We're not interested in whose they were. We just want to get to the bottom of what happened to Manuel.'

She asked Andri to continue. Andri lifted his long hair over his left shoulder and stroked the tips uncertainly. He backtracked and slowly told his story. Hildur and Jakob listened without interrupting. Andri explained that he'd worked on the cruise ship as an entertainer a couple of years ago.

'I play sax,' he said with a self-deprecating smile.

Andri had got to know Manuel, who worked in the kitchens. 'But I couldn't take the cruise ship life for more than a few months. I came back to land and found a job here.'

Once he was talking, Andri's sentences grew longer. Manuel had worked his butt off and still did. Without European citizenship, he couldn't just relocate to Europe. Now that the cruise ship had started touring Iceland again for the summer, Andri and Manuel had met up to party. Andri had requested time off on the days the boat stopped in Ísafjörður.

'We're good friends. We were supposed to hook up. I went down to the harbour to wait, but he never showed. He didn't answer his phone and wasn't even reading my texts. It was weird, because he always answered right away and was one of the first people to disembark.'

Andri paused. 'I was just leaving the harbour when I saw him stumble off the boat. A woman there called an ambulance. I didn't . . . There was nothing I could do. I freaked out and ran home like a huge coward.'

He sniffled once and held back his tears.

'Is that why you went to the hospital this morning?' Hildur asked.

Andri nodded. He pulled a rumpled paper towel from his pocket and dried his eyes. Mascara had smeared across his lower eyelid.

'You mentioned something about drugs,' Jakob said. 'What was that about?'

Andri blew his nose, then folded up the paper towel and slipped it back in his pocket. He looked disconsolately at Jakob and said Manuel hadn't been able to talk that morning. He'd been in too much pain.

'Before he crashed, Manuel asked me to take the baggie that was in the inside pocket of his trousers and get rid of it in case the police came to see him.'

Andri looked regretfully at Hildur and Jakob as he pulled a little freezer bag from the pocket of his red trousers. Hildur accepted it.

The baggie contained a small amount of a white powder. It would have to be sent to the lab in Reykjavík for analysis. Hildur asked Andri if he knew what the bag contained.

'It's probably speed. A lot of crew members take it to help them make it through long shifts. It keeps you going.'

Hildur took her card from her pocket and handed it to Andri. 'Give me a call if anything else comes to mind.'

Andri accepted the card and studied it, then asked in a panicked, confused voice: 'What exactly happened to Manuel?'

Hildur patted him on the shoulder. 'That's what we intend to get to the bottom of.'

Chapter 12

Westfjords, early 1990s

Rakel

An unexpected gust of wind snatched the door and yanked it open. Rúnar climbed out of the car and took hold of it with both hands to keep the hinges from snapping. He slipped out of the driver's seat, slammed the door, and, holding on to his ball cap, strode quickly across the yard to the front door of his home.

Rakel had witnessed her husband's arrival through the kitchen window. She'd hoped he'd be gone a little longer. Things were more peaceful around the house when Rúnar was absent.

A moment later, there was noise in the entryway: 'Put on some coffee. I have good news!'

Rúnar marched into the kitchen without stopping or taking off his shoes. Rakel had just swept the floor. She looked at her husband's muddy boots and then her husband. She was on the verge of saying something, but she shut her mouth and started measuring out coffee for the coffeemaker. She set the table, and Rúnar sat down.

The coffee percolated. The marine weather forecast was being broadcast on the radio. Rakel had packed a fresh batch of ointment into jars that morning. She'd deliver them to her customers the next day.

'I just made an excellent deal,' Rúnar announced smugly. He whistled, clearly in a good mood, and adjusted his cap.

Rakel's stomach lurched, but she maintained a casual tone: 'What deal was that?'

'*Herdís*,' Rúnar said with a smirk.

Rakel dried her hands on her apron and turned to Rúnar. 'You're kidding. You can't.'

Rúnar chuckled. 'Of course I can! The offer rose by almost a third this morning.'

Rakel turned around, supposedly to adjust the filter she'd put in the coffeemaker. She was actually looking out the window, trying to keep her mind clear. Disappointment mingled with a sense of powerlessness and probably a little rage. She reached for the coffeepot and filled the mugs.

'Things won't end well if you sell.'

Rúnar snorted and raised a finger to silence Rakel. His voice rose from loud to almost a shout. 'A big flat fee and a permanent job. With catch-based bonuses on top of my salary. I'd be a complete idiot to refuse an offer like that!'

Rakel returned the coffee pot to the warming plate and glanced out the window again. Hildur was still playing down at the shore. She'd taken dried heels of bread from the kitchen for the birds. The younger girls were napping. Rakel drew a breath and joined Rúnar at the table.

Rúnar impatiently waved away her concerns. 'It's my boat. The decision is made. I'm selling. It's a great offer.'

Rakel shut her eyes. It hurt that Rúnar didn't listen to her. How could he be such a blockhead that he couldn't see it, even though she'd spelled it out for him? *Herdís* was a small wooden fishing boat that was past its prime. The name meant 'goddess of armies'. But the name was of little value, and so was the boat itself. At least not ten million krónur. Why couldn't Rúnar see what he was selling?

Rakel took a cookie and dipped it in her black coffee. 'He doesn't care about that old boat; he wants the fishing quotas that come with it. Can't you see that?'

Rakel generally didn't talk much in Rúnar's company, because conversations between them often turned into arguments. But now they were talking about a subject that was important to Rakel and that she knew a lot about. She tapped the tabletop with her forefinger as she spoke.

'Fish are a common resource. It's in our Constitution. But now the backscratching elite are planning on dividing it amongst themselves. Mark my words, those fishing quotas will rise in value. When that happens, you'll have flung them pearls for the price of sheep pellets.'

Rúnar slammed his coffee mug down so hard the coffee sloshed over. The words spraying from his lips were accompanied by droplets of spittle. 'Don't you start talking that commie shit in my home!'

He raised his cap again and leaned in toward Rakel. She instinctively pulled back a few centimetres.

'You're going to give me financial advice? Is that what's happening here? Don't forget who in this family works and puts food on the table.'

Rakel stood and took the dishrag. She wiped up the coffee Rúnar had splashed on the table and returned the rag to the sink. She remained next to the counter and eyed her husband's profile. His broad shoulders and jutting chin.

'He doesn't want *Herdís*. He wants the fishing quota that comes with the boat. If you sell it now, you'll never get it back.' She repeated her claim, hoping this time he might listen.

'So what? I'll still have a permanent job and an income,' Rúnar snapped.

Rakel decided to venture a little further. She said she was sure that before long, the geographical restrictions tied to the quotas would be lifted and the owners would be able to sell them to whomever they wanted. *Herdís*'s potential buyer was far-sighted. Rakel knew him. He was a third-generation fisherman and owned the biggest trawler in the northern Westfjords. It was a handsome boat, and the trawl it dragged netted thousands of kilograms of marine gold: haddock, cod, herring. When you owned a golden goose like that, buying up small wooden boats made no sense.

Rakel had a lot of regular customers, and she made the rounds of local homes delivering her homemade natural ointment. During these encounters, she and her customers would chat at length, discussing everyday subjects, like the weather and the price of hay, but also politics and society. The system of fishing quotas had been a hot topic ever since Parliament had begun preparing the relevant legislation. Limits on fishing had arrived in Iceland a few years before. The goal was to protect the country's substantial territorial waters from overfishing. The Ministry of Fisheries had referenced scientific research in determining the total allowable catch, which was then divided up among those fishermen who owned boats. Each vessel had been assigned a certain quota defining how much fish it could catch.

Not everyone was satisfied with the new rules. The fishing law had caused a lot of dissatisfaction, especially among those who had not been awarded a quota.

In this case, the potential buyer's trawler was so big that he'd been granted a substantial quota that assured him and his family a very comfortable livelihood. But based on what Rakel had heard around the village, he'd grasped something many others hadn't yet.

Rakel knew the old saying held true: the one who sets out rowing will catch the fish. Fish was caught, fish was exported, and fish was sold. The work on fishing vessels was hard and the days were long. When the boat was at sea, no one counted working hours. The endless sea tested the workers' heads, the storms tested their stomachs, and they suffered from a chronic lack of sleep. Boats could be damaged in big storms. Fishing was a dangerous profession. Not all of those who set out necessarily returned to port. Who wouldn't dream of a slightly easier life? And this was the dream a lot of small-scale fishermen had now lowered their nets in hopes of catching.

Rakel vividly remembered a visit she paid the previous summer to a blue wooden house at the edge of a nearby village. It was home to a woman who bought Rakel's ointment to ease her husband's knee pain; he suffered from arthritis and walked with two canes. He also happened to be a leader in the local labour movement. He'd urged Rakel to join the party too. Despite being sympathetic to the cause, she'd politely declined. Rúnar was loyal to the centre-right progressive party popular among farmers and would have had a conniption if his wife had joined the red party. The last thing Rakel needed was another excuse for Rúnar to pick a fight with her. But the man with the bad knee had said something very interesting: he was sure it wouldn't be long before fishing quotas became transferrable. Apparently, the big fishing companies were already scooping up boats to acquire their quotas. Soon it would be possible to use a quota as collateral for bank loans. Iceland's economy would open up when the country joined the European Economic Community. That would mean an opportunity to make fabulous amounts of money for those in possession of something valuable. It drove Rakel crazy that Rúnar refused to understand.

Rúnar stared at her, eyes narrowed, and spoke in a stern voice: 'Stop talking shit.'

Rakel gave it right back: 'He's trying to stab you in the back. Don't put the knife in his hand.'

This was too much for Rúnar. He jumped to his feet so fast the table swayed and the coffee mug toppled. A light-brown puddle spread across the table and trickled to the floor.

Rúnar thrust his face right up in Rakel's. The stench of cigarettes, coffee, and unbrushed teeth made Rakel nauseous.

Rúnar tapped Rakel's forehead with his fore- and middle fingers. 'All you do is loll around the house all day. Cook up your stupid ointments like some crazy witch. You don't even have a job. It sounds to me like you don't have enough to do since you have time to think up all this nonsense.'

Rúnar pulled his ball cap down and hurtled out of the kitchen. Rakel placed her hands at her temples and massaged them in a circular movement. She had to stave off the approaching catastrophe, but how?

Rakel knew everything was for sale if the price was right. Absolutely everything. And that worried her.

Chapter 13

2 May

Hey!

Thanks for your letter. I'm so happy to hear you're not mad at me. I understand why you'd be confused and maybe even a little hurt, and I'm sorry for the distress I caused. My circumstances just changed so fast I didn't have any choice but to leave without saying anything.

I think things will ultimately turn out for the best. I just have to chase my dreams now. I want to get by on my own. I spent too many years doing what everyone else wanted me to do. I let myself be driven by the expectations of others and forgot myself. I can't let that happen again.

I think you understand, even though the way you live your life is different. You want stability. You feel secure in familiar circles. And there's nothing wrong with that.

But people change with time. Maybe we'll be different people when we're old, too? Maybe our paths will cross again someday.

Have a great summer,

R.

P.S. My address is on the other side.

Chapter 14

Ísafjörður, June 2022

Jakob let his book and notetaking supplies fall to the floor, then kicked up his feet on the coffee table and shut his eyes. The cramming he'd done on damages legislation was making his forehead throb. He was too tired to continue.

Every now and again the thought would creep into his mind that finishing this law degree might not be for him. Trying to complete the demanding course in a foreign language was a challenge. He had to work harder than everyone else, because all Icelandic legislation and commentaries on it were in Icelandic. First, he had to translate what he read, and only then understand and memorise. Plus he had a full-time job and a child in primary school.

Jakob opened his eyes. He leaned forward to retrieve his study material from the floor and set it down on the coffee table. His situation wasn't impossible; it just required effort. The thought of becoming a police chief appealed to him. He wanted to accomplish something that felt hard. Hildur had encouraged him from the start and helped him get through the toughest patches.

She'd clearly been offended earlier today, when Jakob had refused to discuss the unpleasant messages he'd received. He trusted her; that wasn't it. He was just running on empty. Jakob knew Hildur didn't brood or hold grudges. He could probably ask her tomorrow to look at the relevant passages on establishing a median income.

Jakob rose from the couch and went into Matias's room. His son had just come home from soccer practice. They'd agreed his screen time began after soccer. Matias was sitting on his bed, watching some children's show on his tablet.

Jakob looked at his boy, so young and yet older with his new haircut. Matias's curled, sun-bleached tips had practically reached down to his chin, but a couple of weeks ago he'd asked to have the sides shaved and leave the top tousled. Jakob had taken Matias to the barber, where his son had pulled out his phone and shown the barber a photo of Neymar. Jakob had a son who wanted to look like a Brazilian soccer star. It was touching.

Jakob pulled a chair over to the bed and asked Matias what he was watching. Jakob and Matias always communicated in Finnish.

'*PAW Patrol*.'

'In Icelandic?'

Matias replied with a nod.

Jakob was pleased. Watching children's shows was how he'd built up his own language skills too. 'Matias, could you hand me your tablet for a second?'

Matias didn't look up, just replied that he had screen time left.

Jakob looked around the room. Posters of soccer players hung on the walls, children's books and Lego boxes filled the bookcase, and a few schoolbooks stood on his desk. Jakob was particularly moved by the soccer cards, which regularly changed. Matias had friends.

'Come on, hand me the tablet. This is important. I'm going to install monitoring software on it,' Jakob said.

Matias lost his temper and flung the tablet on the bed. 'I still have ten minutes of screen time left!'

Jakob kept his voice steady and explained he just wanted to help. The software was for Matias's own safety. 'I'm going to install software on the tablet to help me make sure you don't see things online kids your age shouldn't see.'

Matias popped to his feet and clenched his fists. His entire body tensed like a bowstring.

'You're mean! You can't do this to me!' He grabbed the tablet from the bed, slipped it under his arm, and dashed from the room. 'I hate you! I hate you!'

Jakob heard Matias pull on his shoes, open the front door, and slam it behind him so hard that the keys hanging from the hook jingled against each other.

Chapter 15

The vibrations from the electric drill permeated her body, and the screws fell into Hildur's fist one at a time. She leaned her right elbow against the wall as she loosened the bracket. She had to shift it a few centimetres to accommodate a new black-out curtain that covered the whole window. The roller shade clicked neatly into place. Hildur eyed her accomplishment in satisfaction. When you did things yourself, you could count on first-rate results.

Hildur heard a noise at the front door. That same instant, her phone chimed, indicating an incoming text message. Hildur stretched down to pick up her phone from the floor.

The message was from Jakob:

I guess Matias came over there.

Hildur replied with a thumbs-up. It had become a pattern: when Matias and Jakob got into an argument, Matias would come over to Hildur's side of the duplex to calm down. After an hour or two of hanging around, he went home, often in a better mood than he'd been when he'd stormed out.

Matias walked straight from the entryway to the couch. He and Hildur greeted each other with simple hellos. Out of the corner of her eye, Hildur watched Matias take his *Batman* comic book from the newspaper basket and continue reading where he'd left off.

Hildur put on a pot of coffee and smeared chocolate spread on toast. She wanted things to always be the same at her place.

Matias wasn't allowed to browse his phone or tablet. He wasn't allowed to watch television too loud, and he wasn't allowed to jump on the couch or the bed. Everything else was permitted. Hildur wanted to give Matias the same stability she'd received from her aunt Tinna. And she liked being able to help Jakob.

Hildur took the skyr and cream from the fridge and a banana from the fruit platter. She cut off a bite of banana with her spoon. The taste was off. She took a closer look, and it seemed fine. She quickly finished the bowl and topped off her snack with some coffee.

Her phone began vibrating on the counter. 'Hey, Hildur. I got your message. What did you want to talk about? I have a minute now.'

It was Smári Vilhjálmsson, one of the four Icelandic police officers who focused on human trafficking investigations, which were led from Reykjavík.

Following the visit to the post office, Hildur had looked for more information on Manuel. She'd checked with Interpol to see if there was a possible warrant out for his arrest; they didn't have any information on him. As Venezuela didn't have an embassy in Iceland, she'd called the one in Oslo and asked them to verify the validity of Manuel's passport. Everything was in order. The passport was genuine and hadn't been reported stolen. It was true the embassy didn't have any information on the passport holder's current whereabouts – no travel notice appeared in his name – but the embassy representative didn't think there was anything unusual about that. Many people didn't report their itineraries these days, even when taking a longer trip. Manuel's most recent home address was ten years old. Hildur had written it down just so she'd have it at hand. Last of all, she'd called the hospital, but the doctor wasn't very hopeful about the possibility of interviewing Manuel. His condition had taken a turn for the worse. He was tired and groggy from the powerful painkillers and slept most of the time. The doctor had recommended she not return until tomorrow afternoon at the earliest.

No one from the ship had offered any comment on Manuel. Nevertheless, Hildur, Jakob, and Beta all agreed he worked on the boat. The uniform he'd been wearing and Andri's account suggested as much. Although she wasn't sure why, Hildur's instincts told her it wouldn't be safe for Manuel to go back to the ship. Something about his reluctance to speak had raised her suspicions about the possibility of his being in danger. Manuel was afraid of something. Hildur had sent the baggie Andri had given her to the forensic lab in Reykjavík for analysis. They hoped to have the results by tomorrow afternoon.

Hildur had begun wondering about illegal working conditions or even human trafficking. The topic had received a lot of attention in recent years. The exploitation of foreign workers was an unfortunate and familiar problem on big Icelandic construction projects. Workers were paid irregularly, and worker safety was neglected. There had also been multiple cases of suspected human trafficking at individual restaurants and hotels in Reykjavík, but only a handful of culprits had been charged and found guilty.

Smári was one of the driest police officers Hildur had ever met. That wasn't a criticism. He took his work seriously and thought before he spoke. He saw so much misery on the job that allowing himself to get too emotionally involved would have no doubt put him on a fast track to burnout.

Phone at her ear, Hildur peered into the living room. Matias seemed so focused on his toast and Batman's adventures that he didn't even notice her. Even so, she shut the kitchen door so she could speak privately. She gave Smári a quick overview of everything she knew about Manuel.

'So this Manuel has his passport with him?' Smári confirmed.

Hildur replied he did.

'If he wasn't forcibly kept on board and was, then, theoretically free to disembark – that doesn't exactly support your human trafficking suspicions.'

'I find it really odd that no one from the boat has asked about him,' Hildur said. 'He works there, but officially he doesn't.'

After thinking for a moment, Smári wondered if something less serious could be going on, like issues with workplace safety or being paid under the table. Or both. 'If the victim's injuries are from a workplace accident, the shipping company might wash its hands of potential damages by claiming they don't have any employees by that name.'

'If Manuel is in a dependent position and he's being exploited, then . . .' Hildur pulled a stool under her backside and sat, '. . . there could be just about anything going on.'

She considered the alternatives. Manuel was in the hospital and didn't want to return to his job. But he couldn't stay in Iceland either, because he didn't have a visa.

She heard Smári take a gulp of water. 'There's not really much you can do.'

He added that the Reykjavík police had opened a few investigations into suspected crimes that had taken place on cruise ships, but they'd dried up every time. Simply determining which country's laws applied in each instance was a laborious process. Smári explained that if the crime happened while the boat was at harbour, the Icelandic police had authority to act. But if the crime took place at sea, the nationalities of the perpetrator and victim could impact which country's laws served as the basis of the investigation.

'Employment legislation is determined by the flag the ship sails under.'

Hildur said: 'This vessel is registered in Bermuda.'

Smári didn't find that surprising. Many cruise ships were registered in exotic countries, like Panama or the Bahamas, due to low taxation and wages or, for instance, to skirt national regulations. He said he thought it highly unlikely the captain would allow police from a foreign country onto the ship. If the captain wouldn't let Hildur aboard, there was nothing she could do. The only person Hildur could investigate was Manuel himself.

'Don't take this the wrong way, but you can't be too nice. You'll never achieve anything if you give everyone the benefit of the doubt. Be sceptical. If you have reason to suspect Manuel of a crime that took place in Iceland, you must interrogate him on Icelandic soil.'

Hildur thanked Smári and ended the call. There was nothing to lose by trying to call the captain tomorrow. Or if Manuel's condition improved, Hildur could revisit their conversation the next day. Maybe she'd made an error in judgement from the start. Had she been too naïve, too quick to see Manuel as a victim?

Chapter 16

Kotsdalur, June 2022

As she came up on the T-intersection, Hildur looked left, and because there were no vehicles, she barely slowed as she turned right. Brenda rocked from side to side down the dirt road. At a bigger dip, she shuddered. Brenda had passed inspection that spring, but Hildur had been given a list of necessary repairs.

Rósa had called Hildur late the night before and asked for help installing the septic tank. Hildur had time to help before her 10 a.m. meeting with the team.

She noted the purple pansies growing in a terracotta pot next to the old house. She brushed her fingers across them as she passed, and the soft blooms bowed to her touch. They were probably the only summer flowers that could survive in such a cold, windy yard.

Hildur found Rósa on the slope behind the house. Her sister had on a white shirt, light-blue jeans, and a jacket tied around her waist.

'Goddamn this damn bitch of a—'

Not even the ever-present wind could drown out Rósa's cursing. Hildur smiled as she pulled on a sweater. The string of obscenities was pure Rósa. Her sister had a foul mouth.

Rósa had been hard at work over the past few months. The windows and front door had been replaced. The roof had been repaired, and the peeling paint had been scraped from the wooden siding.

Thirty years had passed since anyone had lived at Kotsdalur. Hildur had never felt much of a draw to her childhood home. There was something unsettlingly bleak about the place. She didn't know how to put it any better than that. Luckily, she had the luxury of choice and could live in the centre of town in her spacious, solidly built duplex. But it was fantastic that Rósa had been inspired to renovate the Kotsdalur homestead and wanted to live here. This was a big opportunity for Rósa. Her first solo home.

Rósa was busy stripping the protective plastic from the septic tank. Hildur offered to help.

'The excavator guy has cancelled twice already. If he doesn't show up today, I'm going to go over there and drag him here with my bare hands,' Rósa threatened.

There was a perpetual shortage of plumbers, electricians, construction workers, and carpenters in Reykjavík, and it was even harder to find skilled workers in sparsely inhabited areas. There was precisely one excavator operator in the Westfjords.

'He's working for the Road Administration basically all summer, building roads. But this shouldn't even take an hour,' Rósa huffed.

Rósa had decided to install a septic tank to store and process her wastewater. In the countryside, almost everyone discharged their blackwater directly into the sea. There was a lot of coast and not many people, so the sewage wasn't viewed as a particularly pressing environmental issue. Now that Rósa finally had her own place, she'd wanted to do things differently. She planned on renting rooms to tourists once the renovation was complete, and she wanted her inn to meet the most stringent environmental standards. She meant to use environmentally friendly paints, install solar panels on the roof, and recycle all waste.

'Shit doesn't belong in the sea,' Rósa said, tossing her knife. It flew blade first into the ground and stuck there.

Hildur and Rósa shared the same build and resembled each other in other respects as well. Rósa's shoulders were as wide as a door. It was clear from her hands that she did outdoor work, even though she also had a customer service job with a telecommunications firm.

'Have you been working out?' Hildur asked.

Rósa laughed and cleared the phlegm from her throat. 'Not at all. I work and eat.' She eyed Hildur longer than usual. 'But you look off somehow. Is everything OK?'

Hildur was perplexed by the question. 'Nothing much to report. Work has picked up a little after a quiet spring.'

The sound of a vehicle carried from the nearby road. The wheeled excavator was approaching at a speed of thirty kilometres an hour, no more.

When the excavator reached the homestead, the driver jumped from the cab and in front of the sisters. He was wearing a golf team T-shirt and worn jeans, and introduced himself as Frans.

Hildur noticed him look at Rósa a few seconds longer than was necessary. Rósa was used to people staring at the damaged half of her face. She took Frans's hand, gave her name in a clear voice, and continued in the same breath: 'A pot full of hot cooking oil spilled on me when I was a kid. That's all.'

Frans started discussing the excavation with Rósa. The septic tank's site had been marked with rocks. He said he'd start higher up the hill, so he wouldn't have to drive the ten-tonne machine up and down the grassy slope multiple times.

'Going down to two metres?' Frans confirmed.

Rósa nodded. If the tank and the pipes were installed at that depth, they wouldn't have to be insulated against the frost.

A cold wind picked up, and the clouds grew darker. The fjord was narrow, the mountains surrounding it tall. When clouds made their way into the fjord, they tended to stay for a long time.

'He smells nice,' Rósa said, indicating the excavator climbing the hill.

Hildur grunted sceptically. Frans had stunk of sweat.

'I like it,' Rósa said, lighting a cigarette.

Hildur and Rósa exchanged the latest news. Hildur was just reporting on her visit with Björk when there was suddenly a loud crunch from the slope. The excavator stopped moving. Frans killed the engine, opened the door, and jumped down from the cab.

'Maybe I saw wrong, but why don't you girls have a look too,' Frans said, gesturing for Rósa and Hildur to come closer.

'Girls?' Rósa snorted, grinding out her cigarette under her shoe.

Hildur felt the unpleasant, nauseating sensation that had been swirling under the surface for the past couple of days return. She gulped it down. The excavator's bucket hung apathetically in the air. Frans stepped over to the edge of the hole and supported himself on the bucket.

'You've got to be kidding,' he exclaimed. His face had gone white, and the small muscles in his jaw stood out clearly. 'It looks like there's a human head down there.'

Frans's hands trembled as he pulled a pack of smokes and a box of matches from his pocket. He lowered his head as he attempted to light his cigarette.

Hildur asked Frans to step back and hurried over. The soft, just-moved earth sank underfoot. When she reached the edge of the hole, she stopped and looked down. She gasped.

Frans wasn't wrong: two black holes, eye sockets, were staring directly at her from a skull. Numerous white bumps split the surface of the dark-brown soil.

'Help me down. I'm going to have a closer look,' Hildur said, extending her hand toward Rósa. She didn't want her feet to touch the edge of the freshly dug hole, because she didn't want to send soil cascading to the bottom.

It was cold outside, but her face felt hot. The sweet smell of warm soil mingled with the sharp fragrance of the neighbouring hayfield.

'Did the excavator hit the bones?' Hildur asked, glancing back at Frans.

Frans shook his head and said he'd stopped the instant he'd seen white. He asked if there'd ever been a church on the homestead in the olden days. 'There would have been a cemetery attached to it.'

Hildur pondered. No, she didn't remember having ever heard anything about an old church.

'Rósa, could you grab me a pair of disposable gloves?' she said. She told her sister she'd find them in the side pocket of Brenda's driver's door.

Rósa ran off to the car. Hildur placed her feet in the deepest part of the hole, as close as possible to the bones while making sure she wouldn't accidentally step on them, and bent down for a closer look. She could feel the bile rise into her throat. Nausea swelled in her abdomen, and hot tears welled up in her eyes. She wiped them away with her sleeve. The discovery was taking her back to a moment from her recent past. She'd experienced a similar situation once before.

A couple of years earlier, when investigating the violent death of her friend Freysi, Hildur had used a search-and-rescue canine to track a suspect. The tracks had led to Ísafjörður harbour, but the dog's handler had turned out to be an old friend.

He'd participated in the search for Rósa and Björk long ago. Following his advice, Hildur had visited an old farm a couple of hours' drive outside Ísafjörður, where an unmarked grave had been found on the property.

'Should I call someone?' Rósa asked as she handed Hildur the disposable gloves.

Hildur pulled on the gloves and told Rósa to wait a minute. Then she bent down again and carefully brushed some soil off the bones.

When investigating that grave on the farm a couple of years prior, Hildur had found bones she'd decided had belonged to a human of small stature. Closer analysis had proven they were bits of calf's leg bone. Presumably a stillborn calf had been buried behind the barn.

But this time there were more bones, and they looked big. Hildur was sure she was running her fingers across the remains of a dead human.

After moving enough earth aside, she stepped forward and dug her fingers into the stony soil again. She could feel the sharp edges of the small volcanic rocks against her fingers and did her best to avoid puncturing her gloves on them. She moved the dirt one fistful at a time, picked out the small rocks, and made sure not to press her hands too firmly against the soil.

Rósa's voice carried down from the rim of the hole: 'Well?'

Hildur waved away the interruption; she wanted to work in peace. This was not the time to hurry.

A moment later, she stood up straight and considered how to express what she was about to say. She didn't have to mince words with Rósa, but she wasn't sure about Frans.

'Um,' she mumbled, using her elbow to wipe the sweat from her brow. She did her best to keep her dirty fingers away from her eyes. 'I'm going to have to call in the forensic investigators. There's no doubt these are human bones, and there are at least two complete skeletons here.'

Chapter 17

Westfjords, early 1990s

Rakel

The grey Nissan Sunny was parked at Ísafjörður harbour. A thick blanket of white clouds spread across the sky. The sunlight filtered through this cottony layer, turning everything silver-grey. Outside the car all was peaceful, but the mood inside it had turned tense.

Rakel pulled a crumpled banknote from the breast pocket of her white summer coat and turned toward the back seat. She tried to give a carefree smile, hoping Hildur wouldn't pick up on her anxiousness. 'Go buy some flour, and I'll make *lummur* for dinner.'

Her daughters loved the small, thick pancakes with syrup and rhubarb jam; it was their favourite treat.

Hildur grabbed the money and slipped out of the car. Rakel watched as her daughter skipped away. Hidur's bright red lightweight sweater was a couple of sizes too big, and the long sleeves swung as she rocked from side to side in her thin cotton trousers. The younger girls were waiting at home with Tinna.

'Tell me you're lying,' Rakel said, eyes on the supermarket door Hildur had just stepped through.

At Rakel's side, Rúnar tapped his thick fingers against the steering wheel. *Da-dum. Da-dum.* The movement produced a march-like rhythm. 'Everything I just said is true. I sold it.'

To confirm his words, Rúnar jerked his head toward the harbour. *Herdís*, the little white fishing boat Rúnar owned, stood at dock. The south-facing harbour was full of similar vessels, each with an inboard motor and a small hold for the catch.

Herdís had originally belonged to Rúnar's father. Rúnar had inherited the wooden tub fifteen years earlier and used it to line-fish for cod, haddock and wolffish. Before the children, Rakel had joined Rúnar on his summertime line-fishing trips. After Hildur was born, Rúnar had done the fishing with a friend, but Rakel and the women from the neighbouring village had helped with baiting the lines. Weights had been attached at either end, along with wire traces at 1.5-metre intervals. Mackerel, mussels, or herring had been hooked to the ends of the traces as bait.

'I have the money here,' Rúnar bragged, lifting his left buttock from the driver's seat. He took the bankbook from his back pocket and unfolded it. A fishing-hardened fingertip pointed at the most recent transaction. Rúnar had a blue-collar manicure: dry cuticles and ingrained grime under the nails.

Rakel glanced at the long figure. A quick calculation told her it would buy two two-hundred-square-metre apartments in Reykjavík and still leave enough for two cars, a new television, and a nest egg that could be deposited in a savings account to accumulate interest.

'From now on, there's not going to be any shortage of cash in our family. There'll always be bread on the table,' Rúnar said, laughing the laugh of a man who's been freed from his cares.

Rakel didn't share in her husband's delight. She sighed and shifted her gaze from the bankbook to *Herdís*.

'What the hell is wrong with you?' Rúnar snapped, shoving the bankbook back into his jeans pocket. 'I've made the deal of a lifetime, damn it! We could drive straight to Reykjavík right now and stay at a hotel. I could buy you the finest stockings from Stella and the most expensive skirt Parísartískan has to offer. And what's your response? You twist up your commie face into a horse's cunt!'

Rakel closed her eyes and did everything in her power to pull herself together. She strained to smile. Then she nodded in approval at her husband's words and suggested they go home. Rósa and Björk were no doubt eager for their return. Hildur briskly exited the store, a two-kilogram bag of flour under her arm.

'Let's celebrate. I'll make *lummur*,' Rakel promised, scratching her husband's thigh.

Rakel projected calm, despite being tormented by strong, conflicted feelings. There was no point in thrashing out the situation any further: what was done was done and couldn't be undone. She could no longer influence the decision to sell the boat, so she'd just have to accept it.

The dirt road leading out of the village followed the shoreline toward the base of Önundarfjörður. They were on their way home to Kotsdalur.

Maybe time would heal her disappointment over the sale of *Herdís*. Maybe things would turn out fine after all. Maybe her doubts were unfounded.

Chapter 18

Kotsdalur, June 2022

The time was coming up on 6 p.m. Hildur stood at the kitchen window in her childhood home, gazing out. Her legs felt heavy; the familiar strength had drained from her hands as they gripped the counter edge. It was as if a cold wave were surging through her, saltwater coddling her insides.

Hildur reflected that they'd been lucky today too. The forensic investigators from Reykjavík had been able to begin their work less than three hours after she'd placed the call. That must have been a record for the Westfjords. A hospital helicopter had just been leaving Reykjavík to pick up a surgery patient in Ísafjörður, and the investigators had been able to hitch a ride.

The front door opened, and the entryway floor creaked. Beta and Jakob took off their shoes and seated themselves at the big farmhouse table.

Beta and Jakob had picked up the forensics team from the airport. While the two of them had monitored the investigators' progress, Hildur had been inside, placing phone calls. The division of labour had suited Hildur just fine. Seeing human remains in the backyard of the old homestead had sapped her strength and intensified her nausea.

Hildur took a painkiller from her pocket and launched into a report of her lengthy telephone conversation with the expert from the Museum Council.

'There wasn't an old church or cemetery in this valley. Apparently, they'd know if there had been. They said they might not have records of individual graves from hundreds of years ago, but they didn't think it was very likely that skeletons would have remained in very good condition for hundreds of years. They said of course they couldn't be completely sure.'

Jakob began to knit. He placed four different colours of yarn on top of his left forefinger; he'd reached the pattern stage of his sweater-making.

'There's no reason bones couldn't be preserved for ages in a cold climate like this,' he said, critically eyeing his handiwork.

Before going to the police college, Jakob had worked as a biologist, so he knew more about bones than other officers. He added that it was possible to tell the approximate age of a person at the time of death from the bones, but not necessarily when they died.

'It could have been eight hundred or eighty years ago. Bones last longer in cold soil than in warmer climates. And there aren't any big predators on the island to dig up bodies in hopes of a meal. Those corpses have been allowed to rest in the earth's bosom in relative peace.'

Hildur grunted in agreement. Things would become clear in time.

'I think the bones belonged to adults,' Jakob added.

Hildur asked how he could be so sure.

'Children's bones are finer and smaller. Of course the forensic pathologist will be able to make more precise observations about their density and so on,' Jakob said, pulling more yarn out of his tote bag.

It was Beta's turn to ask questions: 'You own this property, right?'

'On paper, yes. But Rósa lives here.'

Beta gathered up her curly hair and tied it in a bun at her nape. 'It's not relevant yet, but if it turns out we have to open an investigation, you'll have to recuse yourself. You focus on Manuel, and Jakob and I can take responsibility for this.'

Hildur agreed.

'But let's wait and see what the forensic investigators tell us. It's possible there won't even be a police investigation,' Beta reassured Hildur. Nevertheless, she proceeded to explain what they would do in the circumstances an investigation were launched.

Beta asked Jakob to look up the information on everyone who'd gone missing in Iceland over the past seventy years. That's where they'd begin. They'd reconsider looking into older cases at a later juncture if it proved necessary. Very old missing persons cases weren't high on the police's list of priorities, because even if the disappearance involved a crime, it was more than likely the perpetrator had died.

The outside door creaked. A short, dark-haired woman appeared in the kitchen doorway. In addition to the two forensic investigators, forensic anthropologist Emma Bruun had made the trip. Half-Danish, half-Icelandic Emma had toured crisis areas for years under a UN mandate, examining human bones from mass graves excavated during investigations into war crimes and genocide. The winter before, Emma had received a professorship at the University of Iceland and moved to Reykjavík. Some of her working time went to assisting the forensics investigators and the country's sole forensic pathologist.

In recent years, a few one-off bone finds had turned up at construction sites. As Iceland's population grew, new residential areas were rising rapidly, and it was in no way uncommon to find old graves during excavation. Humans had inhabited the island since the 800s, and knowledge of former gravesites hadn't always been passed down. Any and all bones that were discovered were studied. With Emma's expertise, it might be possible to determine the deceased individuals' ages at death and maybe even time and cause of death. Crimes were rarely suspected in such cases. Once the bones had been examined, they were reinterred at an official cemetery.

But this was the first time a mass grave like this had been found in Iceland. Emma suggested the police officers join her outside. 'We've begun packing up four skeletons. But there are a couple of things it would be good for you to know right away.'

Emma looked at each of them in turn. Hildur immediately liked Emma. She seemed both efficient and captivatingly confident.

The foursome walked over to the excavation site. Emma pointed at a row of skeletons arranged face up. Hildur found them beautiful. The skeletons looked surprisingly complete – like puzzles with every single piece in the right place. But Hildur's assessment wasn't wholly accurate.

'See that? The second and third ones from the left.'

Hildur didn't know what it was she was supposed to be seeing. The bones could have been in the ground for a long time. Maybe some of them had disappeared.

'This one is missing the left hand from the wrist down, and that other one is missing almost the entire left forearm,' Emma said, pointing at the arm bones but not touching them. She shared her observations without resorting to the technical jargon of her field.

'Maybe they're still in the soil?' Jakob suggested.

Emma immediately shook her head. The hole had been cleared of bones. The investigators had unearthed everything there was to unearth.

'I think these people were buried without the missing body parts. All the other bones were easy to find. I venture to guess we're not talking about old fractures that took place well before death. As you can see, the cut is relatively smooth in both cases,' Emma said, extending her rubber-gloved hand toward the bone stubs.

'So what do you think happened?' Jakob asked, taking a closer look.

'I'll have to perform a methodical assessment in Reykjavík. But if you want to know my first impression, I can share it.'

The wind snatched at Emma's smooth, mid-neck bob. She pulled up her hood to protect her head and said she'd seen similar markings in the Congo when examining the bodies of those who'd died in conflicts between rebels and soldiers. Emma picked up one of the bones so the police officers had a clear view of the cut.

'I think this person's hand was severed with a sharp object.'

Chapter 19

6 June

Hey again!

Thanks for the letter. You're right. And you got the address right too. I live and work on Railway Street, but that's all you need to know about that. I've made my choice and that's that.

I'm doing well. I've got a new grip on life. I like my work, I have nice coworkers (we don't work together, but we see each other every day), and I make a decent living. I have enough money to get by and a little extra. Everyone here is really kind to me. And for the first time in years I have savings. I also went to the movies for the first time in years. It was fun.

How are you? Have you done anything special lately?

I hope to hear from you soon,

R.

Chapter 20

Ísafjörður, June 2022

After performing a few muscle-releasing stretches, Hildur set out running alongside the road. The grass felt better underfoot than the hard tarmac. She continued into the residential area built on the slope and the small spruce wood that rose beyond. It was only during her visit to Finland the previous winter that she'd truly understood how big a forest can be. Here in Iceland, she ran through the local woods in five minutes.

Beyond the forest, she cranked out a few uphill sprints to the avalanche barrier. The place sparked a lot of memories for her: this was where Freysi had been murdered in cold blood. Freysi's death had been one of the most difficult investigations of her career, but she'd survived. And although the memories associated with the avalanche barrier stung, Hildur hadn't stopped running here. *It's just one place among many*, she'd kept telling herself. Avoiding it wasn't going to change anything.

The uphill sprints felt unusually laborious today. Hildur's lack of sleep was manifesting as stiffness in her body. The day at Kotsdalur had been a long one, and it had been after midnight by the time she got to bed. To stabilise her breathing, Hildur switched back to walking. The thermometer at home had shown ten degrees, but running had drawn warmth and perspiration to the surface of her skin. Hildur adjusted the straps of her sports top, which were chafing her shoulders uncomfortably. The stretch had gone out of the garment. Hildur glanced at her running tights. The fabric at the thighs was thin to the point of wearing through. Now that she thought about it, it was time to refresh her athletic wardrobe. It must have been several years since she last went shopping for clothes.

Hildur glanced at her watch. She meant to visit Manuel again after her run. The forensic laboratory in Reykjavík had confirmed that the powder Manuel had given to Andri was amphetamine. Small amounts of the substance had been found in Manuel's blood too.

Hildur also planned on going to the harbour to observe the cruise ship scheduled to arrive today. It was owned by the same company as the vessel on which Manuel had been working when he was injured. Hildur's instincts told her she needed to take a closer look at the vessel. Maybe there were shady things going on onboard.

According to her sports watch, Hildur still had an hour before the cruise ship docked. She had time to drop by the nursing home; she'd be running past it regardless, and Helga usually woke early.

Hildur was just walking in through the doors of the nursing home when her phone rang. It was Axlar-Hákon, real name Hákon Bjarnason, the only doctor in Iceland who performed both forensic and medical autopsies.

'I hope I didn't wake you,' his calm masculine voice said.

Hildur gave a summary of her morning. Hákon replied that he had a hard time sleeping late in the summer himself. Might as well go in to work instead of tossing and turning in clammy sheets, hoping sleep would return.

'I'm calling about the infant you brought in a few days ago.'

Hildur stopped and pressed her phone to her ear. Jakob had almost finished the paperwork; all that was missing was the forensic pathologist's report.

'The cot death?' Hildur asked. For some reason she suddenly felt unsure. She'd been under the impression all signs supported the theory of a sudden, inexplicable death of a baby that had been considered healthy.

'It wasn't SIDS,' Axlar-Hákon said. Hildur heard him tapping at his keyboard. 'With SIDS, there's no identifiable cause of death. But with this female infant that's not the case.'

Hildur felt her chest tighten. *Damn it.* Had some detail escaped her that morning?

'Cerebral haemorrhage. I won't torment you with medical jargon, but the long and short of it is the death was caused by a vein that ruptured in the brain.'

'In such a young child?' Hildur asked.

Axlar-Hákon took a moment to frame his words. 'It's highly unlikely but not impossible.'

He added that there had been no external signs of injury on the baby's body. Not a single bruise, no broken bones, nothing. Axlar-Hákon said he'd pulled up the files from the postnatal clinic; they suggested the child's development had been completely normal. She'd been brought in for her appointments, and nothing out of the ordinary had been observed. This information eased Hildur's mind a little.

'A sad statistical aberration,' Axlar-Hákon's voice sighed down the phone.

He said he'd finalise the paperwork, then give permission for the body to be buried. He said he hoped he'd be able to finish up as quickly as possible, if for no other reason than for the parents. They understandably wanted to bury their child without delay.

The forensic pathologist and Hildur exchanged subdued goodbyes.

Hildur wasn't sure what to make of this. She had a hard time believing in coincidence. She craved an explanation, despite knowing full well it wasn't always possible to break down everything into small pieces. Was there any chance the child had been the victim of violence? But when she tried to come up with any detail that would have suggested the child had been abused, she drew a blank.

Her eyes began to sting from the sweat dripping from her forehead, interrupting her reverie. She wiped her face on the hem of her T-shirt.

The nursing home's receptionist greeted Hildur and told her the residents were all at breakfast. 'You're welcome to join them if you're hungry.'

Hildur thanked her and made her way down the corridor to the dining room. The chess players greeted her raucously again. Helga sat at the next table over in an orange knitted top and casual white trousers, reading the newspaper – apparently, the same one she'd been reading the last time Hildur visited her.

Hildur dribbled some cream into two coffee cups and took a roll and a slice of cheese from the buffet. The run had made her hungry.

'Have you already been chasing after crooks this early in the morning?' Helga asked as Hildur took a seat across from her.

Hildur explained that she'd been on a morning run. Helga lifted her coffee cup to her lips and slurped. Hildur realised the old woman's hands never shook when holding a coffee cup.

'Your mother was exactly the same,' Helga said, gazing off into the distance. 'Rakel got things done. Participated in local meetings, sold those salves of hers, and was never too shy to talk to anyone. She was incredibly brave.'

Once again, Hildur was reminded that Helga had known her mother longer than she had.

After a pause, Helga continued: 'She was brave in a special way. She wasn't afraid to ask for help.'

'Did she ask you for help too?'

Helga nodded.

'In what way?'

Helga took the paper napkin from under her coffee cup and wiped the corners of her mouth. 'We took turns helping each other. I gave her a little money, and she paid me back in hay. Practical help, things like that.'

Helga had so much information about Rakel and experiences Hildur knew nothing about. Hildur took a moment to think. These encounters at the nursing home had turned out to be incredibly important.

'I remember Mum being pretty quiet. She was always at home with us. We barely went anywhere except for your place.'

Helga gazed at her coffee cup, suddenly looking sad. 'I know. Sometimes I still wonder . . .' Helga brought the coffee cup to her lips and sipped, '. . . because I saw the marks.'

'The marks?' Hildur asked, mouth full of roll.

Helga shrugged and gave Hildur an enigmatic look. After a long silence, she continued: 'The more children your mother had, the more subdued she got. Maybe life with little children was more tiring. I wouldn't know, since Hallgrímur and I never had kids.'

Hildur tried to return to the subject: 'What marks were you just talking about?'

Helga swatted away the question with a grunt. 'The past is the past.'

Hildur stood to fetch more coffee and asked if she could bring some to Helga too.

'Well, ten drops.'

After returning to the table with the refills, Hildur asked if her mother ever talked about divorcing her father. 'Mum wasn't happy, so why didn't she leave and change her life? If she was so brave?'

Helga appeared to consider, then shook her head. 'It wouldn't have been easy to raise three children alone on the income she made from her ointments.'

Helga picked at her sweater sleeve without speaking. The wiry chess player with glasses walked past them and nodded. Hildur flashed a smile in response. Then she realised Helga's eyes had filled with tears.

'If I'd just . . . If I'd just been enough of a woman to leave with her. Things might have turned out differently.'

Hildur pitied Helga, who'd once made a decision and regretted the consequences since. But Helga was being too hard on herself. There were a lot of ways to live a good life.

'There's no way you can know that. There's never one big decision that decides the entire course of everything that comes after, either right or wrong.'

Hildur stroked Helga's hand. It was the only way she could think of to comfort the old woman. It seemed to do the trick. Helga gave a slight smile.

'You're a little like your mother. She also had the gift of persuasion. I remember attending a meeting with her once. Your father was at sea, and Hallgrímur was working in the fields, so she and I had a chance to go together.'

Helga recounted the speech Rakel had given that day at the Westfjords' Fishermen's Day celebration. Rakel had urged all the fishermen to guard their independence and hold on to ownership of their boats.

'She told them not to work for someone else if they could manage on their own. The problem was that not everyone had a choice. There was a lot of talk back then about women coming here in secret. And the men who left their homelands to work here. There were all sorts of shenanigans . . . Your mother didn't care for it one bit. She felt it was never a good thing if you couldn't get by on your own or couldn't make decisions for yourself.'

Hildur interjected: 'That's how she felt, even though she herself was living a life she wasn't happy with?'

Helga shrugged. 'I guess in the end there aren't many people capable of living according to their own principles.'

After saying these words, Helga's face closed up.

Hildur was hoping to learn what her elderly friend had meant by *women coming here in secret*, but Helga didn't appear to hear the question. She gazed off into the distance and calmly sipped her coffee.

'You sure are sweaty. Have you already been chasing after crooks this early in the morning?'

Hildur didn't let the repeated question throw her; she simply answered the way she had the first time, explaining about her morning run. Helga leaned toward Hildur and lowered her voice. A mischievous, youthful look had sparked in her eyes.

'We need you to catch those crooks. If you only knew! Folks have gone missing. Just like your little sisters. They vanished in that tunnel, and no one knew what had happened to them. Someone should look into that too.'

Hildur conceded that she was doing her best as a police officer to catch the crooks. Hildur had shared stories about Rósa and Björk on plenty of occasions, but it appeared as if Helga had forgotten what she'd heard. Most of the time, Helga had no trouble remembering, but when tired she'd get confused and forget things. Cognitive skills declined with exhaustion. Maybe they'd been discussing heavy topics too long.

'Yes, there are all sorts of things that need looking into,' Hildur agreed.

It was time for her to get going if she wanted to make it to the harbour in time. She gathered up their breakfast dishes. Suddenly, Helga lowered a bony hand to Hildur's arm and squeezed it with unexpected vigour.

'Rakel was here. I saw her again.'

Chapter 21

Hildur had a thing for ports. The smell of fish, the shriek of gulls. The sense of constant movement, that nothing was permanent.

The recent spring had been a hoax, and foolishly she'd gone and believed it. She'd thought peace had finally descended on her life. Months had passed with nothing out of the ordinary happening, and then everything had come crashing down on her at once. An unusually high number of break-ins at cabins had been reported. Bones had been found in the backyard of her childhood home. Jakob was receiving strange messages that upset him. She'd experienced the bad, oppressive feeling again, and she was afraid it portended some major event. Anton was texting good-natured but meaningless messages – but in the end, words didn't matter, actions did. Helga was suffering more and more from temporary memory loss. A cruelly assaulted man lay in the local hospital. Hildur didn't crave any more excitement, experiences, or exploits. Deep down, she just wanted a peaceful life.

As she walked past the biggest warehouse in town, a grim grey colossus, she saw the door to the cold storage was open. A forklift stood in the middle of the warehouse. Men in coveralls were sitting outside on stacked pallets, taking a break.

'The circus is about to start up again,' one of the men muttered, sliding a fat forefinger under his upper lip.

Hildur greeted the forklift drivers. One walked over to her. His upper lip was unnaturally distended from snus.

'You have to go around to get past the fences,' he said, pointing beyond the seafood warehouse.

Hildur thanked him and followed the route he'd pointed out. Movement around the port was controlled by fences and signs to ensure the safety of cruise ship passengers.

Hildur pulled her police ID from her pocket and slipped it around her neck as she melded in with the crowd that had appeared to welcome the ship. About thirty tour guides with placards stood at the harbour. Everyone's eyes were on the docking vessel, the *Petit Arctic Princess*, but Hildur suddenly had the sensation someone was watching her. She let her gaze scan the ten-storey ship. It had a spiral water slide and a few beach umbrellas on the top deck.

The first person to disembark was a woman in a blue skirt suit who shook hands with the lead tour guide. Hildur decided she was the cruise ship officer responsible for the day tours. Hildur heard the woman and the tour guide exchange a few words consisting of formalities and a quick briefing: how many passengers, how many participating in day tours, how many tour guides and buses. The guides held their numbered signs aloft, pointed at the buses, and called out instructions.

Passengers used their mobile phones to take pictures of the harbour buildings, the mountain rising behind the harbour, and the local gulls dipping and diving near the fishing boats in hopes of a meal. Hildur wondered why she'd felt like she was being watched. What had that been about?

She entered the port building through the double doors. The door to the harbourmaster's office was open, and she knocked on the doorframe. Jósef Ragnarsson was on the phone. He greeted Hildur with a nod and gesticulated that the phone call would be ending soon and she should wait.

The office had large windows that looked on to the area where the cruise ships docked. There were four screens of different sizes on his wide desk, some of which showed CCTV camera footage from the harbour and some detailed information about marine traffic in the vicinity. A big houseplant nodded in front of the desk, its heavy stalks bound with a cord attached to a wall hook. Hildur picked up a dry leaf that had fallen to the floor and dropped it into the wastebasket next to the door.

'My mother-in-law gave it to me for my sixtieth birthday. I'm waiting for it to die,' Jósef said, once the call ended. 'The plant, not her,' he clarified with a broad smile.

Hildur glanced at the plant that had lost its will to live, then nodded at the cruise ship outside the window. 'Manuel, the young man who was transported to the hospital from here a few days ago. We suspect his employer might not be completely on the level.'

Jósef's high-backed office chair creaked as he leaned into it. He patted his round belly in apparent satisfaction. 'And what does this have to do with us?'

Hildur was caught off guard by the reaction. An assault victim had stumbled into their local harbour and was lying in the hospital on the verge of death.

'He's too afraid to talk and doesn't want to go back. There's definitely something shady going on. Manuel also worked shifts on the vessel that just pulled in. I'd like to board and have a look around.'

Jósef rolled his chair closer to his desk, lowered his elbows to the desktop, and leaned on his hands. The flesh of his plump cheeks pushed up into Wienerschnitzels.

'You can't just board,' he said between his compacted cheeks.

Hildur began losing her temper. 'Do I look like an idiot? I know I'd need the captain's permission to board. That's why I'd like you to call him. Now.'

Jósef shook his head in frustration but reached for his phone nonetheless. 'Wait outside, please,' he said, waving his phone toward the door.

Hildur yanked the door shut behind her as loudly as possible. She sat in an uncomfortable plastic chair and pulled out her pocketknife to clean the grime ingrained under her nails. If she had time, she'd go plant the rest of the seed potatoes on the slopes of the community garden that evening. It would be nice to bring Aunt Tinna some homegrown potatoes in the early autumn. When she reached her right pinky, the door opened.

'The captain refuses to give you permission to board. He claims everything is in order and then some. They've just been awarded some quality certificate,' Jósef said, before wishing Hildur a better continuation to her day.

Hildur sighed and left. The response didn't come as a surprise, but at least she'd tried.

The doubtful sensation returned: once again, Hildur had the sense she was being observed. She nearly always carried a small pair of travel binoculars, and they were in her pocket today. When surfing she'd use them to observe the waves and look for possible shoals. They were a big help, especially on unfamiliar beaches.

Hildur aimed the binoculars at the ship and spun the focus wheel until the image was clear. Cleaners were washing the deck. Hildur gave particular attention to the head of the cleaning team, who was wearing long trousers and a dress shirt. He was speaking intently to one of the women. The tone of the conversation appeared aggressive on his part. The woman didn't speak, while he bent over her with an angry look, pointing downward. Suddenly, he raised his hands into the air to build up force and pushed the woman. Hildur flinched. She scanned her surroundings through the binoculars to see if anyone else had seen what she had. The other cleaners were nearby; at least some of them must have heard the argument. But none of them were looking in that direction. Everyone seemed to be keeping their eyes on their own work.

Hildur's attention was drawn to movement on the top deck. A man in black was walking at a leisurely pace there. Despite his grey hair, he moved like a young man. His athletic shirt fit him like a glove, and he carried himself with almost military bearing. He leaned against the railing with his hands and monitored the activity in the harbour yard. When Hildur focused the binoculars on his face, she was almost sure she saw him looking at her. Then she saw him shake his head.

A faint wave like an electric shock travelled from the base of Hildur's back to the top of her spine. The gesture had been discreet, almost imperceptible, but she knew she'd just been sent a message.

Stay away.

Chapter 22

Midday, and the police station conference room was stifling. When the sun shone from a cloudless sky, the room immediately turned into a furnace. But as there were only a few such days every year, installing an air conditioner made no sense.

Beta was sharing her summer vacation plans: 'The boys and I are going hiking in Landmannalaugar for a couple of days with Jóhannes.'

Her vacation would be starting at the beginning of July. Jakob had taken his vacation back in May to help Matias with his school and would be handling Beta's duties during her absence. Subbing for the police chief while she was out of the office would be valuable work experience. All such temporary obligations would be to Jakob's credit when he applied for the job down the road.

'Are the boys big enough to hike three days in a row?' Hildur asked.

She herself had traversed the route twice, the second time while participating in a trail-running race. The first leg was fifteen kilometres, nearly all of it uphill. The difficulty of the terrain was etched in Hildur's memory. Beta's children were still in primary school, and the popular hike was fifty kilometres and included two big rivers trekkers had to cross on foot.

'We'll have tents and plenty of food,' Beta said. 'We can take all week if we want. Jóhannes has all the necessary gear.'

Beta had met Johannes, a movie director who lived in Reykjavík, at dance class. *Sounds like things are getting serious if*

Beta invited him to join her and the boys on their summer vacation, Hildur mused as she took a seat next to Jakob. She noticed his unoccupied hands.

'What happened? Did the country run out of sheep?' Hildur asked Jakob. He was sitting there, looking as if he didn't know what to do with his hands without his knitting needles.

Jakob explained that he'd had to drive Matias to the local campground for his school's field day. During the morning rush, he'd forgotten his knitting bag by the front door.

Beta coughed into her fist: time to stop the chitchat and get down to business. 'Shall we start with Manuel?'

Hildur began by reporting on her morning visit to the port. Beta assumed an *I told you so* expression when Hildur got to the part about the harbourmaster's half-hearted attempt to gain her access to the ship. She didn't say anything about the man in black who shook his head at her. While walking to the office, she'd come to the conclusion that she'd probably assigned more significance to the gesture than was realistic. Maybe her suspicions had been aroused by witnessing the poor treatment of the cleaner.

After her stop at the harbour, Hildur had returned to the hospital with an interpreter.

'The narcotics found in Manuel's blood matched the contents of the baggie Andri gave us. I used that to get him to talk,' she said.

Hildur had told Manuel that the police weren't interested in individual users, but if the case involved distribution in addition to possession, they'd have to take a more thorough look. Andri already had a couple of previous convictions for possession. They were old and hadn't resulted in any punishment aside from fines, but they certainly heightened law enforcement's interest. Or at least that was what she'd told Manuel.

'I said if he wouldn't talk, I'd have to investigate Andri. He didn't want to cause his friend any trouble.'

Manuel had said the speed helped him get through long shifts. It was the only way he could stay on his feet. Manuel had admitted to buying the speed on board but refused to say who'd sold it to him.

'And since we can't investigate, I dropped the issue.' Hildur paused long enough to pour herself a glass of water from the pitcher and wipe the sweat from her brow. 'Could we open the window?'

Beta was sitting closest to it. She stood and opened it.

Hildur continued that according to Manuel, the kitchen crew worked incredibly long days. Fourteen hours was a short shift. The reason for the long shifts was simple:

'Debt.'

Hildur said that a couple of years before, Manuel had been offered work by a man whose name he refused to give. This had happened back in his hometown in Venezuela. The man had said Manuel would have clean indoor work that included lodging, food, and a monthly salary that equalled Manuel's annual salary at the time working as a prep cook at a street kitchen.

'There was only one condition,' Hildur said.

Beta guessed the rest: 'He had to pay a fee.'

It was a nasty situation, but Hildur was pleased that in her eyes Manuel was once more a victim, not a criminal. She'd felt protective over him from the beginning. If he'd turned out to be a crook, she'd have been forced to admit her ability to read people was seriously rusty.

Manuel had paid out to the party that arranged the job. This was one element of human trafficking. Someone promised work in exchange for payment in shady circumstances. The fee was sold to the job applicant as a broker's commission of sorts, although in reality it was merely a cruel way to put the worker at the employer's mercy.

'How much did he pay?' Jakob asked, restlessly moving his thumbs around the surface of the long wooden table.

Hildur reported a sum of five thousand US dollars. Manuel had borrowed some of the money from friends and family, and he owed the remainder to his employer. He'd been working on the boat for a couple of years now and still owed over four thousand dollars. Interest and other charges were constantly added to the principal. 'The debt isn't ever supposed to be paid off. It's a leash the employer uses to keep Manuel under control,' she added.

Theoretically, Manuel could have quit. He had possession of his passport, and no one was keeping him prisoner. But quitting would have left him indebted to criminals and the loved ones he'd borrowed money from.

'Was he assaulted because he'd threatened to quit?' Beta asked.

Hildur shook her head. The cuts to his face were the only thing Manuel had refused to say a word about.

'He stuck to his story of an accident. Supposedly fell in the kitchen,' Hildur said. 'But I don't believe him.' She assumed Manuel's unwillingness to talk was motivated by a desire to protect his coworkers who were still on the boat.

Beta tapped the tabletop with a ballpoint pen. 'So Manuel's situation isn't unique?'

Hildur rolled her head; her neck muscles were stiff again. Manuel had said there were dozens of crew members – mostly those who had no direct contact with passengers – who were in the same position. Cleaners, kitchen crew, dishwashers, laundry workers . . . it was a long list. Most didn't speak Icelandic or English. That made things worse.

'Does he have any evidence?' Beta asked. 'Did he give the names of the party extorting him or anything else concrete?'

Hildur shook her head. 'He's too scared to say anything else unless he's admitted to a human trafficking witness protection programme.' Finding witnesses was often the hardest thing, because victims didn't dare talk. They were afraid of revenge.

Beta rapped the table lightly with her knuckles and looked first at Jakob and then Hildur. 'I hate to say this, but we have to look reality in the face.'

Hildur pensively chewed her pinky nail. She already knew what her boss would say.

'None of this sounds kosher. There's a hell of a huge case here for someone to investigate. But not us. We can't dedicate any more time to this. When Manuel is released from the hospital, he'll have to return to his workplace.'

Hildur was chastened, but she understood. If Manuel had money, he might be able to get permission to stay in Iceland, at least for a little while. But the immigration laws for people arriving in Iceland from outside the European Economic Community were stringent: you had to have a pile of documents, an invitation from an employer, and a large chunk of change in a bank account to prove you could support yourself. Even then, getting a residency permit wasn't a given. If the party that recruited Manuel caught wind of his communication with law enforcement, his problems would multiply. When it came down to it, Manuel had nothing but lousy alternatives. Hildur's heart ached that he'd asked her for help. It felt awful to tell him that although he was the victim of a crime, there was nothing that could be done.

Beta roused Hildur from her reverie: 'Are you OK? You're white as a sheet.'

Hildur said she was in need of lunch.

Beta said that she'd spoken that morning with someone from the forensics lab about the excavated bones. 'Sorting them is going to take some time. Apparently, some bits of rubber were also found in the hole and are being analysed too.'

The pieces of rubber piqued Hildur's interest, but Beta knew nothing about them yet. She'd learn more by the end of the week at the earliest.

'Have you had a chance to have a look at the missing persons register?' Beta's question was directed at Jakob.

He opened the plastic document protector in front of him and pulled out a few printed pages. The list included all those people who'd been reported missing over the last seventy years and never been found. Because the skeletons had clearly been those of adults, Jakob had only included adults on the list.

Beta and Hildur listened to Jakob's summary.

There were a couple of hundred names in Jakob's document, the majority of whom had gone missing over the past fifty years. Icelanders made up the lion's share of the list, but there were also about thirty foreigners. Most of the missing people had been last sighted on the southern coast or in Reykjavík. That made sense, because that was where most Icelanders and tourists spent their time.

'Once the forensic anthropologist puts a little more meat on the bones, I'll go through the names with a fine-tooth comb,' Jakob said, immediately apologising for his bad joke.

Next he reported on the latest developments in the investigation into the cabin break-ins. He'd spoken with nearly all the cabin owners and was waiting for the lists of stolen items they'd promised to deliver. After that he meant to go through the biggest Facebook marketplace groups and a popular website where Icelanders could sell used items. Unloading the stolen goods would be fastest online.

'I've been in contact with the other police districts just about every day. It's possible it's one and the same group, because the break-ins seem to cluster in one location, then cluster at the next location. I'll keep you up to date.'

Jakob added that he'd be meeting one of the cabin owners when she arrived to spend her summer vacation in the Westfjords. 'Saga Maríudóttir, a cardiologist from Reykjavík. For some reason she wanted to meet in person.'

Chapter 23

Do you have time to bring me a pizza? Ham, onion, and blue cheese please.

The text message was from Helga. Lunch had been served at the nursing home a little over an hour ago. A second message followed on the heels of the first: the baked fish had been watery and Helga hadn't cared for it.

Hildur smiled. She rose from the conference table and said she was stepping out to get herself a bite.

The local pizzeria was right next to the police station. A man in a brimmed hat was jabbing at the slot machine in the gaming corner that was prohibited to minors. Other than that, the place was empty.

'Everyone's at the handball game,' the freckled salesperson said as she wrote down Hildur's order. Apparently, the local team was playing one of the many teams from Reykjavík.

'What do you think? Who's going to win?' Hildur asked, flashing her credit card at the payment terminal.

'I couldn't care less. I think handball is insanely boring.'

Hildur sat down to wait for her order. She glanced at her phone and saw she'd received a couple of new messages from Anton. The first was a photo of a reindeer. In the second, Anton asked if everything was all right since he'd never got a response to his previous message.

Hildur sighed and started tapping out a reply. What exactly did Anton want from her? He wasn't interested in visiting Iceland, that was clear. So what was it, then? Going on and on about feelings? Feelings were like cream: when you whipped it too much, it turned into butter. When you did the same with an emotion, it changed too. The attempt to understand another person almost always resulted in a jumble of confused assumptions.

The freckle-faced girl handed Hildur the pizza boxes and wished her a nice day. Hildur thanked her and tapped out the rest of the message to Anton. She apologised and said something vague about being busy at work and, a moment later, added a heart-eyes emoji. When she thought about it again, she decided the emoji was stupid, but it was too late. The message had already been sent.

A few minutes later, Hildur walked into Helga's room carrying the steaming pizza boxes. The place was a little stuffy. Hildur opened a window and left the door ajar to get the air moving.

'Should I put a pillow under the box so it's easier for you to eat?' Hildur asked, opening the pizza box.

Helga waved away the idea and gestured for Hildur to set the box down in her lap. 'I don't have any pillows. I don't use them: they make my neck stiff.'

Helga grabbed a slice of pizza and took a big bite. After devouring a few mouthfuls, she profusely praised the taste.

Hildur picked up the newspaper from the floor next to her chair and took a closer look. *Bæjarins Besta* was still the Westfjords' local news source, but it had been years since it had appeared in print. The paper was ten years old. Part of the back page had been torn off.

'Why on earth are you reading such an old newspaper?'

Helga chuckled. 'It's all the same stuff, year in, year out. The price of lamb, fishing quotas, and how many tonnes of shrimp some guy named Einar is allowed to bring into the harbour.

Besides, I like old news, because I remember those people and times a lot better.'

Hildur set the paper back down on the floor.

Helga said she'd brought the old papers with her from home. 'It drives the cleaner crazy, because my wardrobe is full of them. She says she doesn't have room to dust.'

They spent the next few moments focused on their pizzas. Helga's room felt cosy. The walls were decorated with a few Icelandic landscapes and one colourful cross-stitch. Animal-themed tchotchkes and two framed photographs stood on the windowsill. One was a traditional black-and-white wedding portrait of Helga and Hallgrímur. The newlywed couple looked solemnly at the camera. The other was in a silver frame. In the picture, Rakel was leaning against a wooden fence in her work overalls. There were sheep on the other side of the fence.

'Rakel came by again yesterday,' Helga said suddenly.

Hildur decided to play along with Helga's chatter. She figured it couldn't do any harm.

'How do you know?'

Helga took another bite of pizza, then shifted her gaze to the open door and the hall beyond. 'I can always hear her coming.'

'How do you know it's Rakel?'

'When people tiptoe in wool socks, it makes this whispering, shuffling sound. In her final years, your mother always walked cautiously like that.'

Hildur nodded. There was nothing else she could do.

'When she enters the room, I can instantly tell it's her. I get this warm feeling whenever Rakel's around.'

Helga ate one more slice of pizza and asked Hildur to hand her a glass of water. Hildur turned on the tap and waited for the water to cool. She took a glass from the cupboard and filled it.

'I could be wrong,' Helga said, as she accepted the glass.

Hildur looked the old woman in the eyes, and what she saw there was the gaze of a lively young woman. Her eyes moved quickly, and the furrows in her forehead formed waves. Helga breathed heavily for a moment. 'Maybe it's one of those missing people. No one has investigated those cases,' she sighed, then drained her glass.

A gust of wind blew in through the open window, chilling the room. Hildur walked over to the window and shut it.

'What cases?' Hildur asked in a neutral voice as she took the glass from Helga. She washed it, laid a paper towel across the edge of the sink, and set the glass down on it to dry. She tried to humour Helga, because she wasn't sure if Helga was remembering something accurately or if she was getting tired and slipping into her imaginary world again.

'The ones who disappeared without a trace. There's a story about them there on page three,' Helga said, pointing at the old paper.

Hildur picked up the paper again. She read the page three headline and said out loud: *'Disappeared Like a Dewdrop in the Sun. Polish citizen Jan Nowak has yet to return home. Jan's wife is dissatisfied with the efforts of the Icelandic police.'*

The article reported on a Pole who'd come to Iceland to work, quit his job at the fish processing plant, and planned on returning home. But he never arrived in Poland, and his family and friends couldn't reach him. Jan had vanished. The Icelandic authorities believed he'd done so voluntarily. Jan's wife was sure something had happened to him.

'And he wasn't the only one,' Helga said, closing her eyes and munching on the last slice of pizza with evident relish. She continued:

'But Rakel was the most important one. Always. I'm sure that's why she came back. Every bit of her will come back in the end. On the last day at the latest.'

Chapter 24

Jakob was sitting in the bleachers at the soccer field. Forty primary-school boys were following the example of their three coaches, warming up. Jumping jacks and a light jog in a rectangular area bounded by plastic cones. Matias had begun playing soccer in early spring. Back then, the boys had practised ball handling indoors. In summer, training was held outside on the local pitch. Jakob had been able to leave work earlier than usual today, because no new information had come in on the bones and no urgent action needed to be taken in the cabin break-in investigation. So he'd gone home to change clothes and grabbed his knitting bag from the entryway while he was there. For the first time in a long time, Jakob had time to watch his son's soccer training. It felt nice.

Jakob took a new skein of yarn from his canvas tote and changed colours. At the moment, he was knitting his first summer sweater from lightweight Einband yarn. The 2.5-millimetre needles felt as slender as toothpicks in his hands. He was knitting it as a present for Guðrún. Her birthday was in mid-July, so Jakob still had a few weeks to finish. The sweater would be light and airy. Jakob had thought of himself as a fast knitter, but the delicate yarn demanded slow, methodical work. He'd begun three weeks ago and had only finished the sleeves and part of the yoke.

Jakob tried to hold the yarn loosely so it wouldn't chafe his fingers bloody. Knitting was an important hobby and mind-clearer for him. As he knitted, he calmed down and difficult thoughts momentarily faded into the background. He was able to keep a better handle on his nerves when he steadily and dutifully repeated the same movement over and over. The more he knitted, the better he got at it. And yet every garment was different, so he learned something new every time. Besides, knitting was ultimately as unpredictable and chaotic as life. Even if you were the one manning the needles, holding the yarn, and following the instructions, the outcome was never guaranteed. Sometimes it was better to follow a pattern, sometimes not.

After the boys warmed up, the coaches divided them up into three groups. Matias's group began playing owl and mouse under their coach's direction. Jakob didn't need to look at the needles, so he was able to watch the practice. The boys in their matching coloured jerseys and shorts dashed enthusiastically around the grass. Everyone had their own ball. When the coach held up a yellow card, the boys were allowed to dribble the ball down the pitch. When the sun set and the owl showed up, it was night and then the mice had to stand perfectly still. The game helped the boys practise moving and stopping the ball. When the card lowered, Matias stopped the ball with his feet and froze in place. He glanced proudly at his father. Jakob nodded at Matias in greeting, but Matias just smiled. He didn't move: it was night now, and the owl was on the hunt.

Jakob was proud of his son. He felt the happiness as a warmth spreading through his body. The two of them had gotten off to a difficult start, but Jakob believed they'd rounded the bend. They'd make it. Matias's difficulties adjusting would no doubt pass; Jakob would make sure of it. No one was ever going to come between father and son again.

Jakob's phone vibrated in his pocket. He straightened his legs to pull it out and unlocked it. One new message.

It saddens Martti and me that you don't trust us. You don't answer our calls or messages. We were happy to hear you and Matias are living together in Iceland now and you have a good job. Imagine: you're a police officer! I still don't understand why we can't finally meet. We'd love to see our grandchild. It's been a long time. Kaisa.

Jakob sighed and jammed the phone back in his pocket. He had no intention of replying. He hadn't answered his parents for years, and he wasn't about to start now. Jakob didn't want to have anything to do with them.

Relations with his mother and father – or, as Jakob had always referred to them, Kaisa and Martti – were distant, to say the least. His parents had worked abroad for nearly the entirety of their careers, and Jakob had been forced to move a lot. His mother had been a diplomat in service of the Foreign Ministry; his father had lobbied on behalf of Finnish companies and been involved in promoting exports. Any time a better position had opened up somewhere in the world, or some country had appeared interesting from the perspective of Finnish business interests, they'd moved. Sometimes they'd changed homes more than once a year. When Nokia had been at the top of the mobile phone industry, they'd moved to India, where Martti had helped the company find local spare parts manufacturers to contract with. When Nokia had begun talking about taking over China, the family had decamped to Shanghai. Then to South America for a position in the Foreign Ministry, then the US, then back to Europe . . .

Jakob had been raised by an ever-changing cast of nannies. He'd spent summers with his grandmother in Finland, in the western Lappish village of Äkäslompolo. His parents had always been at work, and on the rare occasions they'd been at home, they'd had guests. Jakob couldn't remember a single moment from his childhood when he was alone with his parents. As soon as Jakob had been able to look out for himself, he'd moved out and back to Finland, gotten a job, and begun earning his own money. His parents hadn't even commented on his decision.

When he'd moved to Oslo, fathered a child, and landed a research job at the university, his mother and father had galvanised. To Jakob, the reason was clear: Martti and Kaisa were interested in their grandchild. Their careers were winding down; their days were no longer so consumed by work.

In a moment of weakness, as the father of a newborn child, Jakob had allowed his parents into their home for a visit. Since then, his parents had sent Matias gifts, and after each gift reminded Jakob that good manners demanded a thank you note. But the gratitude was never enough. The card was either too brief or his thanks hadn't been sufficiently sincere. Jakob had found Martti and Kaisa's attempts at bossing him around incredibly irritating. He was heartbroken his parents wanted to stay in touch with their grandchild but had never given a damn about their own son or his life.

When things had deteriorated between Jakob and his Norwegian wife Lena and he'd been forced to move out of their shared home, his parents' attempts at contact had abruptly stopped. When Jakob had asked them for financial support with the custody case in Norway, they had refused. A grown man had to clear up his messes on his own; that's what they'd said. At that point, Jakob had decided to never be in contact with his parents again. For him, they didn't exist. It was that simple.

His parents had clearly had their ways of finding his contact information. It presumably hadn't been hard, since he'd always worked in the public sector. One Google search was enough to find it. But Jakob had systematically deleted all messages from Kaisa and Martti without replying. One couldn't choose one's parents, but there was no need to automatically respect them either. *They're just getting what they deserve*, Jakob reflected, shifting his gaze back to the pitch.

Matias was skilfully moving the ball down the grass. He was fast and agile. If only Matias's problems at school would resolve themselves. If things didn't look any better in the autumn, Jakob would have to look for professional help for them.

A small cloud floated past the sun, casting a little shadow on the pitch. Jakob thought about the text message he'd just received and his parents' unpleasant way of pressuring him. Would he be like them when he grew old? Or was he already? Matias was just in primary school and had already had to live in three different countries and lots of different towns. Was he repeating the same patterns with his son that he'd been forced to endure as a child? Would Matias be sitting in the bleachers some day, watching his own children, hoping the phone in his pocket wouldn't chime? Jakob shivered at the thought, and sorrow and fear weighed on his arms.

Chapter 25

A faint bleat carried from somewhere in the distance, followed by another, louder noise. The sounds followed each other in waves. Maybe it was a snipe diving earthward, performing its mating display.

The state of restful unconsciousness was disrupted. Light muscled its way into the darkness. The blanket fell to the floor.

Before long the sound changed. The gentle bleat transformed into a wave crashing into a rocky shore. The surge became a whitehead, the dragging sound intensified. Something powerful was approaching. The water that had amassed far out to sea had gathered strength and was surging over her. Her feet kicked at an invisible opponent, and her heavy head began to sink beneath the surface. A rushing filled her ears. She was surrounded by murky water. Then gradually, one calm stroke at a time, the panic began to ease. Her strength ebbed; the time for struggle had passed. The drowning itself was silent.

Hildur started awake. She could feel the beat of her rapidly pounding heart. A few slow, deep breaths did a little to steady her pulse. The room was hot, but her skin was clammy. Hildur picked up the blanket from the floor and rose to sitting on the bed. She pulled her knees to her chest and tried to recreate the dream she'd just had. She'd thought she was about to die. She'd never had a dream where panic over drowning morphed into a light sense of surrender.

Hildur lay back down.

The gnawing sensation in her gut felt new. It wasn't the familiar angst she experienced as tightness in her chest which made it hard to sit still, the oppressiveness that settled over her before an accident or tragedy. That she could evade by running or lifting weights. But moving wasn't going to do any good now. She was seasick in the middle of a tempest. Waves rocked the boat back and forth for hours, her legs went limp, and her stomach began to roil with vomit. The cold metallic taste in her mouth was nauseating; the seeping powerlessness in her muscles paralysed her.

Hildur lay naked on her bed and focused on breathing. The sounds of a snipe's mating display carried in through the open window. The tail feathers played the song of an Icelandic summer night.

After lying there for a while, Hildur accepted she wouldn't be falling back asleep. She pulled on her clothes, ate a bowl of granola with sour milk and honey, and tied her thick hair back in a braid.

Just as she was stepping out, her phone rang. Jódís Grímsdóttir introduced herself in a delicate voice. 'I'm calling from the nursing home. I apologise for calling so early. I hope I didn't wake you. I'm calling with regard to Helga Ingimarsdóttir.'

Hildur was struck by the strangeness of hearing Helga's patronym for the first time in ages. She'd always simply referred to her elderly friend as Helga. If it was necessary to clarify, she added the name of the farm Helga and her husband Hallgrímur had once owned, Kotsdalur Efri.

Hildur tossed the braid over her shoulder and stood there in the middle of her bedroom floor. Her dream hadn't boded well. Jódís said she'd found Hildur's phone number in Helga's address book.

'It was the only number in it,' Jódís added softly.

Hildur nodded, despite understanding Jódís couldn't see her. She cleared her throat with a feeble cough: 'I visited her yesterday. Has something . . . Has something happened since?'

'Unfortunately, I have bad news,' Jódís said. She gulped. 'Helga died last night. We called you because we thought you might want to come pay your respects. She hasn't had any other visitors for years.'

The clock over the doorframe was ticking faithfully. It wasn't even seven thirty yet. Hildur had to steady herself against the wall. She tried to digest what she was hearing. A nightmare and a phone call. A moment that changed everything.

'I'm on my way. I'll be there as fast as I can.'

Chapter 26

Jódís was waiting for Hildur in the nursing home lobby. She was sucking on a cough drop and shifting her weight from foot to foot. The bun at her nape was tied so tightly you could pluck it. She had prominent veins in her forehead.

'We've already changed her clothes. We'll move her after your visit. I thought you might want to say your goodbyes to her.' Jódís pinched her lips at the end of every sentence and waved her hands to give weight to her words.

At the door to Helga's room, something about the surroundings set off Hildur's spidey senses. The clean, hard plastic floor creaked underfoot more loudly than it had during her visit the day before. There were two nurses with breakfast carts further down the corridor. The coffee cups clinked against the metal tray as the shorter nurse pushed her cart.

'I'll leave you here for a moment. You can find me down there in the staff break room. Out the door and right. It's the last room,' Jódís said, then exited.

Hildur took a few steps. Her heartbeat accelerated when she reached the bed. She looked for a moment, then drew a sharp breath. A sound reminiscent of a whine emerged from her throat.

She'd seen countless dead bodies. But one never grew fully inured to death's presence. Encountering it reminded Hildur of the feeling of showing up late: someone stronger than her had beaten her to the punch, leaving behind a sense of final departure. There would be no thrill of reunion, no future letters or calls. The corpse was an empty shell; the person had vanished.

Every time she was in the presence of death, Hildur experienced the same struggle of contradictory forces within her. She felt powerless upon seeing the end that could not be postponed. At the same time, she felt peace. Facing finality reinforced the contours of the world. Death was obvious and straightforward.

Helga looked so small. Her eyes were shut; her hands had been crossed over her chest. A single yellow tulip had been slipped between them and the blanket beneath. The flower was from a bunch Hildur had bought from the florist a few days before. The colour had drained from the dark green leaves.

Hildur touched the jaundiced hand. The skin under her fingers felt thick, like a rind. The hand was cold. Hildur couldn't help thinking about her mother, how she had touched this same hand. Helga had asked Hildur not to reveal her relationship with Hildur's mother to anyone. It had always remained a delicate subject for her. The secret had only grown heavier with time, as Helga came to regret the decision she'd made. *Everything would be different, perhaps better, if I'd had the courage to leave.* So Helga had said to Hildur on multiple occasions. Hildur had listened and kept it all to herself. She hadn't told anyone, even her sisters, about their mother's affair with Helga. These were the kinds of promises Hildur kept. Always.

Helga's curls had spread wildly across the pillow, and Hildur tucked them tidily behind her ears the way she liked. Suddenly, her hand stopped moving. She took a quick step backward and eyed Helga's body from a short distance. That's all she needed. Hildur had realised something. She needed to speak with Jódís immediately.

Judging by the place names punctuating the conversation, the nursing home staff were discussing their plans for their summer holidays. When Hildur knocked on the break-room doorframe, the conversation died. All eyes turned to her.

'Could you come with me to Helga's room?' Hildur asked Jódís. The nurse assumed a look of empathetic professionalism and followed Hildur into the corridor.

'The hospital chaplain is close by if you want me to give her a call. It doesn't usually take her long to get here—' Jódis said as they made their way to Helga's room.

Hildur thanked her and said she didn't need a chaplain.

'Can you tell me about the moment Helga was discovered?'

Jódis's head twitched backward. It was as if she didn't understand the question.

'I'd just like to hear about her final moments,' Hildur explained.

'I came in after six and found her.'

'Was she lying in bed?' Hildur asked.

They stepped into the room.

Hildur repeated her question. 'Did you find her lying in bed like this?'

Jódis shifted her gaze from the dead Helga to Hildur. 'I already told you that over the phone. I could immediately tell she was dead.'

Jódís said she'd called the hospital immediately, and a doctor had come right over. Even though Helga hadn't been breathing, hadn't had a pulse, and her skin had been cold to the touch, a doctor was necessary to pronounce her dead. Jódis said it appeared as if Helga had had a peaceful end.

Hildur registered small details in the room. The newspaper Helga had been rereading was still folded up on the floor. The wedding picture and photograph of Rakel were in their usual places on the windowsill. The glass Hildur had left on a paper towel to dry was still there on the edge of the sink.

Hildur felt her fingertips tingling. 'What about between the time the doctor left and the time you called me?'

Jódis touched her ring finger at the spot where a ring would be. Hildur noticed a strip of paler skin there. *Recently divorced*, she decided.

'We changed the sheets and dressed the body. The last thing we did was put that flower there. We can dress her in something else if you'd like. Had Helga expressed any wishes, do you know?'

Hildur said there was no need; the clothes Helga was wearing would do just fine.

The beeping of a reversing truck carried from the distance.

'That pillow,' Hildur said.

'What about it?' Jódís asked, still stroking the ringless finger.

'Did you bring it in when you were dressing her?'

Jódís took a moment to think. She lowered her hands to the edge of the bed and shook her head. 'It was next to her when I found her. We just changed the sheets. We didn't move anything else.'

Hildur felt a sharp, tiny twitch in her diaphragm. Helga had said she didn't own any pillows, because she preferred to sleep without.

Chapter 27

Westfjords, early 1990s

Rakel

Rakel turned on the water and rinsed the dirty bowls one by one, then stacked them on the counter for washing later.

The weather was often rainy toward the end of autumn. This week a wet wind had been blowing off the sea for days. The salt it carried had crusted the windows, smearing the view.

The glasses, utensils, and coffee cups would pass under the lukewarm water next, followed last of all by the big soup pot. Rakel was careful not to bump anything against the edge of the sink. She stacked the dirty dishes slowly to make sure they wouldn't bang into each other by accident. She was trying to stay as quiet as possible.

A little over a year had passed since the sale of *Herdís*. For the last six months, Rakel had been walking on eggshells at home.

Rakel had plenty of dishes to do after every meal these days. The dishwasher had broken down a couple of months ago. A plumber of their acquaintance had told them it was beyond repair. They couldn't afford a new one.

Rúnar's wheezing breaths filled the kitchen. Rakel turned her head slightly so she could see Rúnar sitting at the table. He was still scribbling notes with a ballpoint pen on the edge of an envelope. She assumed he was counting the money they no longer had.

Rakel turned on the water and began rinsing the glasses.

Rúnar's fist instantly struck the table. The saltshaker toppled from the force of the blow.

'Do you have to let the tap run? Hot water is expensive.'

Rakel turned off the tap and continued washing the dishes with the old water. Arguing would have simply made things worse.

They had just finished dinner, but Rakel was still hungry. She'd only had a small ladleful of fish soup in order to ensure the others could eat. They wouldn't have any money until next week, when Rúnar was paid. *If* he was paid. Over recent months, there had been all sorts of problems with getting his salary. This hadn't come as a surprise to Rakel. She had guessed it would happen. Rúnar had blown through the money he'd received from the sale of the boat in six months. He'd been south to gamble and wasted money on the most expensive hotels in Reykjavík and who knows what else. Rúnar claimed the money had gone to the roof repair the spring before, but it wasn't true. Besides, only part of the roof had been fixed. He'd been promised a good, permanent job with a regular monthly salary and healthy bonuses. But nothing about these conditions had been written down on the deed of sale. The lack of a written record made it hard to complain.

Rakel reached for the pot and started scrubbing. As she soaped it, her elbow hit the stack of glasses on the counter, knocking it over. The clatter alerted Hildur, who was watching television in the living room. She ran to the kitchen doorway: 'Is everything OK?'

Rakel quickly restacked the glasses and dried her hands on the dish towel. She squatted down in front of Hildur and rolled up the sleeves of the too-big sweater the girl was wearing.

'I'm just washing dishes. Go back to the living room. Make sure your sisters are OK too.'

Rósa and Björk were playing in the corner of the living room.

Rakel rinsed and dried the glasses and put them away. Then she returned to the pot.

'Are you deaf? Hot water isn't free on this part of the island.'

Rakel turned off the water and clenched the pot scrubber. Her fingers were wrinkled from doing the dishes. It was still raining outside.

'Did you hear me?' By now Rúnar was almost shouting.

Rakel nodded. She was more occupied with her worries about tomorrow than Rúnar's tantrums. Rakel didn't want to ask Helga for a loan, but she couldn't think of any other alternative at this point. They were out of money, and she'd sold her stores of ointment. She had to go grocery shopping tomorrow. There was nothing in the fridge but half a cabbage and a carton of milk. Luckily, Rúnar would be headed out to sea that evening. The second he left, Rakel would head straight to the neighbours'. With money she'd be able to buy not only food but more beeswax so she could make more ointment. She just had to sell ten jars of salve and she'd be able to pay Helga back. Rakel clenched the pot scrubber until her knuckles turned white. If that cursed boat had been even half in her name, she never would have sold. When something seemed too good to be true, it usually was.

In addition to anger, frustration, and fears about the future, Rakel – to her own surprise, she had to admit – also felt sorry for Rúnar. He laboured long days at sea, but his paycheque didn't reflect his efforts. He piloted the old boat that no longer belonged to him. Brought in hauls of fish that no longer belonged to him. Rúnar had lost everything.

Rakel set the pot scrubber on the counter and left the pot in the sink. Before long, Rúnar would head outside for his post-dinner cigarette. Rakel decided to wait.

There was a sudden screech of bench against wooden plank as Rúnar jumped to his feet. He flung the pen to the table and crumpled up the old envelope. The balled paper rolled across the table to the floor. Rakel shot a discreet glance toward the living room. Hildur was sitting as rigid as a pillar of salt on the couch, facing the television, but Rakel could tell she was monitoring the situation unfolding in the kitchen.

Rakel hoped the moment would pass. Why was time moving so slowly? She shut her eyes and pinched her lips. Rúnar took a step and walked right next to her, blocking the view to the living room. He stood there for a second, wheezing. And then he marched into the entryway and pulled the door shut behind him.

The rain fell for weeks.

Chapter 28

Ísafjörður, June 2022

The sound of a car door slamming carried inside. Hildur could tell from the way Beta was walking that her boss was upset about something. Her gait was clipped and quick. Jakob was following at a half-run.

'Let's hear it, Hildur. I hope you've got a damn good excuse,' Beta shout-whispered once she was inside the nursing home lobby. She kept her voice low, but there was no mistaking the tone. The tight phrasing popped from between her pinched lips.

Hildur had had to call Beta and Jakob and ask them to come to the nursing home. It was rare that her suspicions were completely unfounded. Hildur's alarm bells had been going off since she realised the significance of the pillow at Helga's side.

Hildur told Beta about the pillow. Her boss's jaw muscles continued tightening. Jakob had hung back a few feet.

'Hildur, you're skating on thin ice. This is a nursing home. They see one death here every three weeks on average. The fact that someone uses a pillow when they're sleeping isn't exactly—' Beta didn't finish the sentence. She rubbed her face and muttered something about a waste of time and approaching vacation.

Hildur didn't react. She had the sense something was off, and she was sure she would soon have evidence too.

'Come and see for yourselves,' she said, starting down the corridor toward Helga's room.

Fortunately, the hall was empty. There was no sign of anyone.

‘The media will be here as soon as word gets out,’ Beta said.

The reporter from the local paper would no doubt dash right over if they caught wind of police officers buzzing around the nursing home, investigating a possible homicide. Beta and Jakob had intentionally come by unmarked vehicle.

‘The story will immediately spread to the national media,’ Beta continued peevishly. ‘I’m sure someone from here has already been in touch with our local reporter.’

Hildur held the door open so Beta and Jakob could enter Helga’s room first. Jakob was carrying the kit bag Hildur had asked him to bring.

Hildur repeated her account of that morning’s events and the fact that Helga never slept with a pillow. ‘She didn’t even have a pillow in her room. I was looking for one yesterday.’

‘And your theory is someone killed her?’ Beta asked. She turned to look at Helga, who lay on the bed, the wilted tulip under her hands.

‘I’m not sure about that yet. It needs to be investigated.’

Beta sighed. ‘Your suspicions sound far-fetched. And we have plenty of other things that require attention – cases under investigation, the patrol officers’ summer vacations about to begin, not to mention the tourists are just starting to roll in.’

Hildur knew all this.

‘Even so, you want to investigate this,’ Beta said. She glanced at Helga and her expression softened. Hildur thought she sensed understanding in her boss’s voice.

‘I do.’

Hildur took the camera Jakob held out to her and started photographing the room and its details. If this was a crime scene, it had to be documented. First, she took a shot of the view from the doorway. She eyed it from the camera screen critically, then took the next picture. 'During my most recent visits, Helga said someone would visit her room at night. It might have something to do with this.' She turned around and shot again, facing the door.

'So she felt threatened?' Beta asked.

Hildur shook her head. 'She said she'd hear sounds out in the hallway and that . . . someone would come in from time to time. At the time I thought she was imagining it, but I'm not so sure anymore.'

She wasn't any more explicit about what Helga had said: that Helga believed Rakel visited her at night. That would have sounded too strange.

'Regardless, we need to investigate. It will take a few hours to collect and record the evidence. If anything comes up in the autopsy, we continue. OK?'

Beta looked Hildur long and hard in the eye and took a couple of deep breaths. She tapped at her mobile phone. 'OK. You have today – and we're not calling in forensics for this.'

Hildur nodded. No forensics team. There was no need. Hildur was capable of leading a simple crime scene investigation. Jakob pulled carbon powder and fibreglass brushes from the bag and prepared to collect fingerprints. Hildur kept taking pictures.

'But if what comes up doesn't substantiate your suspicions, you will stop investigating then and there. We need you on the cabin break-ins.'

Hildur promised. Before Beta and Jakob's arrival, Hildur had spoken with the night nurse who'd been on duty. He'd done his rounds around 10 p.m., and Helga had been sleeping peacefully then. He'd heard her snoring lightly.

Jakob pulled on a pair of disposable gloves and started in on the room's surfaces. The room was pale, so he decided to use a dark powder. He started from the aluminium bedframe.

'Hildur, come photograph this,' he said.

The bed's hard surfaces were covered in fingerprints. Hildur photographed all of them as a precaution. At least they would have pictures if the fingerprints themselves were destroyed in the next phase of processing.

'I'm sorry I snapped when we arrived,' Beta said in a conciliatory tone. 'I know you two were close.'

Hildur glanced at Beta over the camera and nodded. Small disagreements between them had never turned into lasting grudges in the past, nor would they this time either.

'Maybe there's a natural explanation for the pillow,' Beta said, mostly to herself.

Maybe, maybe not, Hildur reflected. She focused on a fingerprint and pressed the shutter button. They could use the record of the prints to identify the culprit and exclude others.

They wouldn't be able to take fibre samples, but there was no need. Helga's clothes and sheets had been changed right after her death anyway. Apparently, that was the usual protocol when one of the residents died. The bed linen and clothing were already in the washing machine, and in addition to the doctor, at least three nurses had been by to look in on the deceased.

'The cleaner had already mopped the floors before I got here,' Hildur remarked.

Jakob began pressing lifting tape over the next fingerprint. He massaged the air bubbles out of the tape with his gloved forefinger. Then he pulled up the piece of tape, fixed it to a fingerprint card, assigning it a number and noting the location where it had been found.

Autopsies were not automatically performed on people who died in nursing homes. Under normal conditions, the body would have been transported to the morgue at the hospital and then moved from there to the chapel closer to the day of the funeral.

'Will you order a forensic post-mortem?' Hildur asked Beta, as she watched Jakob work.

'Of course,' Beta said. 'Otherwise taking these fingerprints would be a waste of time.'

Helga's body might reveal something to the forensic pathologist that they were unable to see with the naked eye: a stranger's DNA under the fingernails, internal bleeding, or other signs of violence could come out during his examination. Beta would arrange to have the body transported to Reykjavík.

'Let's send one of the patrol officers – say, Gylfi – to fly with the body. I'll go and submit the paperwork,' Beta said, pulling out her phone and heading back to the station.

A couple of hours later, Jakob and Hildur were standing in the nursing home lobby. Hildur had briefly spoken with all the residents, and the results had been slim. Everyone but the night nurse had been asleep, and no one had seen or heard anything. Nor had the night nurse noticed anything out of the ordinary.

Now they were waiting for the hospital's head of security to bring them the CCTV recordings for the last twenty-four hours. The nursing home had two entrances: the main one, and a passageway that connected it to the hospital. Hildur had asked and learned that the main entrance and reception closed at 6 p.m.

Jakob checked the time from his phone, then slipped it in his pocket. 'So after dinner, the only way to access the nursing home would be from the hospital. Then again, all the rooms are on the ground floor and each one has a private patio . . .'

Hildur had asked about the rooms' patio doors and had received the same response from everyone. 'The residents' patio doors were checked during the last round of the evening and any that were unlocked were locked. It would have been impossible to enter through one without being noticed.'

Just then, the head of security strode into the lobby. He had broad shoulders, naturally curly, shoulder-length hair, and a long, thick beard.

'Aron,' he said, extending a hand. The arms under the short-sleeved shirt were tattooed to the wrists.

'Which one of you wants this?' Aron's boyish voice was in stark contrast to his manly demeanour. The USB stick looked tiny in his paw.

Hildur slipped the memory stick in her pocket.

The corners of Aron's mouth drooped slightly beneath his beard. 'I watched the recording at high speed. There's not really anything until morning. The recording from the passageway camera is in a different folder. You guys have a look with fresh eyes just to be sure,' he said, pushing his business card on both of them.

Hildur and Jakob hadn't told anyone they were investigating Helga's death as a possible crime. It was to everyone's advantage to wait to announce the suspicions. They didn't want to cause uncertainty and distress among the residents. They'd told Aron they wanted the camera recordings to check whether Helga might have left her room without anyone noticing and, for instance, hurt herself.

The main doors opened automatically as they approached.

Hildur planned on picking up some lunch for them from the grill so they could get right to work. Jakob had said he had a meeting that afternoon with the bone specialist. By then, Emma Bruun would have answers that could be of use to them in their review of the missing persons register.

A snipe cry carried from somewhere in the distance. The familiar sound of summer. Hildur strode down the flagstone path toward the space where she'd parked that morning. She suddenly realised Jakob was lagging behind.

'Come look at this.' Jakob was gesturing for her to join him where he'd squatted at the nursing home's entrance. The doors remained open. He pointed near the lock. 'Do you see?'

Hildur bent down to look. 'Boy, you're not kidding.'

The metal edge was warped about three centimetres. The door had been forced open with some hard implement. The door opened automatically via motion sensor, so Hildur hadn't noticed the damage earlier. Luckily Jakob's eyes had been sharper.

Hildur stroked the twisted metal. It felt sharp under her fingers. The damage looked relatively fresh; there was no sign of wear. Hildur pulled out the camera and took a few close-ups.

Why would someone want to break into a nursing home?

Chapter 29

Jakob knew it was going to be a long day. He stretched his neck and refocused his eyes on his computer screen.

The empty kebab containers and soda bottles from lunch were waiting to be cleaned from the corner of the desk. The room was dim. He and Hildur had closed the blinds so they'd be able to see the video more clearly.

Hildur had spent well over an hour reviewing the CCTV recordings. Big, bearded Aron had been right: at least so far, she hadn't come across anything interesting.

After Jakob spotted the signs of a break-in at the main entrance to the nursing home, they'd returned inside and reported their observation to the staff. None of the nurses or cleaners could tell them anything about possible missing objects or anything else out of the ordinary. Nevertheless, Jakob and Hildur had taken fingerprints from the staff and residents for comparative purposes. They said something vague about the possibility of a break-in and its investigation, although they really wanted the fingerprints for their investigation into Helga's death.

Jakob was uploading the fingerprints to the automatic fingerprint identification system – or AFIS. The final comparison between the prints they took from the residents and staff and the prints found in Helga's room would be left to the forensic laboratory. Jakob would be getting the results tomorrow at the earliest. After successfully saving the last set, Jakob got up to go and get himself some coffee. He grabbed the kebab containers and shoved them into the wastebasket under the desk.

'Want something?' he asked, making a drinking motion with his hand. Hildur was hunched over her computer and didn't immediately register her colleague's question. Jakob rapped the desk with his knuckles and repeated the question.

'Yes, please. And a glass of water, if you don't mind,' Hildur said.

Jakob measured out the coffee and pulled the mugs from the cupboard. He spooned two teaspoonfuls of sugar into his. While waiting for the coffee to brew, he read the message he'd received from Emma, the bone specialist. It was an apology: she had to postpone their meeting until later in the day because she was so far behind. Jakob glanced at the clock. There was no way he was going to make it home by three thirty, so he texted Guðrún. His spoken Icelandic was pretty good these days, but writing proved more of a challenge. When speaking he could adjust, use indirect expressions, but written text left less wiggle room. The mistakes were immediately obvious. Nevertheless, he tried:

> I can't make it home to evening. Would you be good if you take Matias from a soccer practice when the time is up?

The message was a little slapdash, but Guðrún understood. The reply came immediately.

> It would be really good. I'll take him for a burger and ice cream. See you tonight, if you're not too tired ;-)

Jakob replied with two emojis: a flame and an eggplant. Right now he was a lucky, happy man. He had a partner and a child, a home and a job. Five years ago he'd been homeless in Oslo. A father who wasn't allowed to see his son. A man with a past but no future. He felt like he'd been given a new lease on life.

Jakob's gaze grazed the old newspapers and advertisements piled up on the break room table. The same ad appeared on the front page of two papers: the cruise ships that toured Iceland were now marketing their cruises to Icelanders too.

PAMPER YOURSELF – EXPERIENCE YOUR COUNTRY LIKE NEVER BEFORE. THE LAST LUXURY CABINS OF THE SUMMER ON SALE NOW! the advertisements proclaimed.

Something about the dates of the cruises caught Jakob's attention.

He quickly poured coffee into the mugs and filled a glass with cold water.

'In what version of hell does that make sense?' Hildur snapped. 'There's no security camera in the lobby?' She rubbed her temples in frustration as Jakob set down a cup of coffee and the glass of water next to her keyboard.

The damaged nursing home door and the investigation on his desk had set Jakob's thoughts in motion. He'd just tried to call Aron, but the hospital's head of security hadn't picked up. His second call had gone to reception. The receptionist had promised to pass on the message. Jakob had left his name and number and emphasised it was urgent. He set his phone down on the desk and rubbed his temples. He'd caught hold of a thought and didn't want to lose it . . .

Cabin break-ins were relatively rare in Iceland. Jakob had come to learn the traditions surrounding summer cabins were different here in Iceland than they were back home in Finland. In Iceland, some of the year-round cabins were houses owned by consortiums or employers that consortium members or employees could rent for a week or two. Summer cabins were often only used in the summer. Then there were the wilderness cabins that had no electricity or running water, which primarily served as shelter when driving sheep or hunting. Because most cabins were rented week by week or only used occasionally, no one kept valuables or anything else worth much in them. A typical Icelandic cabin break-in was generally the handiwork of substance abusers. Those on the fringes of society who were looking for temporary lodging, something to eat, or anything to steal that could be quickly turned into cash or the next fix.

Or so Jakob had thought. He glanced at the cruise ship ad he'd taken from the break room and leaned it against his computer. There were many more break-ins being investigated this year than in years past. Their numbers had risen sharply in the spring. The winter had been quiet, but starting in May cabin owners had reported broken gates and front doors that had been forced open.

Jakob had a few things he needed to check. Over the past few weeks, a surprising number of cabin break-ins had been reported around Akureyri. Jakob had heard about them from his local colleagues there. In Iceland, break-ins and thefts were investigated by the local police district, but there'd been so many cabin break-ins over the past six weeks that the districts had established a group to exchange information and report on the progress of investigations. The free-form group was being coordinated out of Reykjavík. Establishing a structure for information exchange had been a good idea. If a criminal gang circling Iceland was responsible, all investigative teams were after the same perps. So far there had been no major breakthroughs. No fingerprints had been found, not a single cabin had had a security camera, and none of the cabin owners had been able to identify any valuables that had disappeared, other than two bicycles and one bracelet. The forced gates and smashed locks had spoken of uninvited guests, but it was strange that almost nothing had been stolen.

Some neighbours of the vandalised cabins had reported to the police that they'd seen an unfamiliar car in the vicinity, usually a white or grey passenger vehicle. Someone had wagered a Toyota Yaris, someone else a Dacia. No one had written down a licence plate number. Most of these sightings had been made in the vicinities of Reykjavík and Akureyri. There were so few cabins in the Westfjords that there had been no eyewitness sightings there. At least not yet.

Jakob slurped down more coffee. The combination of caffeine and sugar gave him a kick. And in that instant, his eyes caught on something in a police report that made him choke on his coffee. The dates were so perfectly matched that it couldn't be coincidence. He was coughing so hard his eyes welled up with tears. Hildur slapped her colleague on the back. Jakob raised his hands to signal he was OK.

'It'll pass,' he said as he hacked, adding that Hildur might want to hit him a little more lightly next time. Jakob rubbed his back and returned to his screen.

Finland had seen a big criminal business spring up around stolen goods, because it was possible to transport the goods across frontiers to black markets. Before the war in Ukraine in particular, hot goods had been exported to Russia, but also through Estonia to Central Europe or across the northern border into Sweden. But transporting stolen goods from Iceland was so expensive it made no sense in terms of making money.

That's why he found it strange the break-in crews – or crew, if one and the same group was responsible – were so well organised. He felt his body tense as he pulled over the open almanac from the edge of the desk and flipped back several weeks. He'd struck on a repetitive pattern, and it couldn't be coincidence.

'Well, I'll be double-damned,' Hildur cried suddenly, turning her laptop toward Jakob. 'You have to see this right away,' she added, starting the video. 'This is from the passage between the hospital and nursing home at two in the morning.'

Jakob watched the empty corridor for thirty seconds. Then a shadow appeared at the bottom of the shot. Hildur slowed playback. All that could be seen of the thin figure in hospital pyjamas was dark hair and the back. The figure seemed to have a hard time walking and kept looking around. The face wasn't visible.

Jakob looked quizzically at Hildur.

'Wait, they come back in fifteen minutes,' Hildur said, fast-forwarding through the recording.

First there was a shadow, then a man wearing light-coloured hospital pyjamas appeared on the screen, carrying a small bundle under his arm. He was unsuccessfully trying to avoid the cameras. The curls that spilled partway down his forehead wouldn't have served alone to identify him, but the face – or the little that could be seen of it – did.

Chapter 30

Kotsdalur, early 1990s

Rakel

Rakel's fingers wrapped around the phone cord. After three rings, someone picked up at the other end.

Rakel's voice was dry from nervousness. She didn't want to humble herself to ask yet again.

'Hi, Rakel.' Helga's constricted voice revealed her alarm. 'It's his heart. I have to drive him to the hospital.'

Helga's husband had heart trouble. He needed regular care, and sometimes the pains came on suddenly.

'How are things ...?' Helga's question was tentative. She didn't want to pry.

'I ... ' Rakel began, then cut herself off. She was afraid her voice would crack, and she didn't want to worry Helga. Rakel gripped the phone receiver more tightly. The pinky being strangled in the cord was turning blue.

'Did something happen to the girls?' Helga asked in a panic. The words came out faster toward the end of the sentence.

Rakel assured her the children were fine. 'I need a little money, just a little money for groceries,' she said, and felt her stomach lurch.

Helga sighed empathetically, without the tiniest hint of *I told you so*. The only people who'd demonstrated any schadenfreude had been Rakel's parents, back when they were still alive. They hadn't much cared for Rúnar, but Rakel had ignored their advice, done what she wanted, and married the handsome rascal. Rakel had been in love with Rúnar and decided to bear the consequences of her actions. For better or for worse. As she'd vowed before the pastor.

Rúnar had never been an easy person. Rakel tolerated her husband's mistakes and outbursts of rage with gritted teeth. Lying she wouldn't have been able to tolerate, but she'd never caught Rúnar lying, not even once. Besides, of the two of them, Rakel was the one who was lying and living a double life. Rakel wanted Helga, who secretly wanted her, but Helga wasn't available to be a life partner.

Rakel considered her situation. Rakel wanted to divorce Rúnar but couldn't: she wouldn't be able to take care of herself and her children. And she would never leave her children. She wouldn't be able to manage with the girls on her own. After Rúnar had sold the fishing boat, spent the money, and brought the family to the brink of bankruptcy, Rakel had been forced to save anywhere she could. She always bought the cheapest alternative at the store, mended worn clothes, and brewed her coffee weak to make the beans last. She made as much ointment as she could and did her best to sell it. Rúnar's wages were insufficient and irregular, but at least they provided some income.

Rakel meant to hang on in the marriage long enough to find a way to earn more money and change the direction of her life. She'd planned on preparing more ointment, and she could make foot and hand creams too. They would definitely sell. She'd pick the herbs in the mountains and turn over every stone in her search for the beeswax honey. She'd do anything.

She looked out the entryway window. There was no sign of Rúnar. The girls were playing outside. She uttered her next words to Helga quickly.

'I'm ashamed to call and ask for money again. When I asked last month . . .'

There was utter silence at the other end of the line. Helga knew the truth. The two of them had discussed this before.

'I wish I could help, but right now things are hard. All this month's money has gone to Hallgrímur's medication. I'll be getting some more in a week's time. Can you wait that long? Or I can ask my mother—'

Rakel cut Helga off. No. She didn't want to mix up any relatives in this. 'I'll be fine. Don't give it another thought. Say hello to Hallgrímur.'

And with that Rakel hung up, so Helga wouldn't hear her crying.

She wiped away her tears, pulled herself together, threw on her winter coat, and walked to the paddock. Rúnar was scattering feed. The girls were in the corral, scratching the horses. The smell of hay wafted through the air. The harvest had been good the previous summer; they had enough hay to last them the whole winter and then some. Maybe she could sell the excess to the neighbours? It would be better to sell it and make money that way than ask for money without offering anything in return.

'I could drive over to Hallgrímur and Helga's later this week and ask if they need more hay for their sheep.'

There was a sudden shift in Rúnar's demeanour. He stood up straighter and his arms stiffened. His face hardened. 'I know why you go over there,' he spat, flinging the last of the hay to the horses. Then he climbed out of the corral and walked up to Rakel.

'We have extra hay. We could use the money,' Rakel said.

Rúnar took a tobacco pouch, and taking papers from his pocket, began rolling himself a cigarette with twitching hands.

Hildur ran over to Rakel. Her little sisters followed on short, unsteady legs.

'Mum, Mum. I'm hungry. Can we go inside and eat?' Hildur asked, fixing her dark eyes on Rakel. Thick, dark hair cascaded from under her heavyweight beanie; the winter humidity had curled the tips.

Rakel thought feverishly. There was oatmeal in the cupboard and milk in the fridge.

'In just a moment. I'm going to talk to Dad for a second first,' Rakel said, despite knowing any sparks of hope were dying.

Rúnar lit the cigarette and sucked on it, cheeks concave. He batted his eyes; his hand shook back and forth. Then he calmly said: 'Go inside, girls. Your mother will be right in.'

It was plain Hildur found the situation unpleasant. She wasn't sure what she should do. But the girls knew they were supposed to obey their father, so Hildur started walking toward the house and told Rósa and Björk to follow her.

Once they were gone, Rúnar turned to his wife. He blew out smoke between his teeth and clicked his tongue against his palate.

'Are you saying Hallgrímur would pay to fuck you? That's why you're always over there.'

Rakel closed her eyes and gathered her strength to face what was coming.

'I'm going there to sell hay. We have to get money somewhere.'

Rakel had tried to apply for public assistance at the municipal social services office, but it had been a pointless visit. Rakel and Rúnar wouldn't be getting any assistance because they owned assets. They owned the farm in Kotsdalur. The social services representative had put a slip of paper in Rakel's hand with information on food banks.

'Sure you are,' Rúnar said, stubbing out his cigarette on the fencepost. 'You'd better go, then.' And with that, he raised his hand and struck.

Silence fell between them. Every few moments, one of the horses would snort, then continue eating.

Rúnar opened his mouth. He wiped his palm on his trousers and said: 'I'll go in first. You can come later.'

Rakel watched her husband go. It wasn't the first time he'd hit her, and it surely wouldn't be the last. Rúnar had apologised for the first blow. Not for any that had followed.

There were people who never apologised for their behaviour, they just did what they wanted and moved on without any care for other people's feelings.

Rakel thought back to something she'd heard at one house the previous week. Katla, the wife of the chair of the labour movement, had invited the local women over for a sales evening. She'd baked a delicious trout tart and a wedding cake filled with rhubarb jam. One of the other women, a shop clerk whose name escaped Rakel, had said something about a Polish man who'd left a big bill unpaid. Over a period of a couple of weeks, he'd shopped on credit, but when the time had come to pay up, there had been no sign of him. He'd simply left town without ever settling the bill. The women had spent some time guessing what might have happened to him, where he'd gone.

When listening to them, Rakel had begun considering her own circumstances. What if she just abandoned her debts and obligations one day? Could she just simply leave too? Take the kids and vanish?

Chapter 31

Ísafjörður, June 2022

'Can we go into the conference room? There's something you ought to see,' Hildur said to Beta, who had just arrived at the station.

Hildur led the way into the conference room and walked over to the flipchart. Now things were starting to move. The new electricity and urgency felt good. They dulled the keenest edge of the crushing grief resulting from Helga's death. Beta took off her summer coat, hung it on the back of the chair, and took a napkin from the table to pat away the beads of sweat that had formed on her brow.

Jakob reiterated the basics of the spring and summer's break-in investigation. He took a black-and-white map from a folder on the table, with the locations of the break-ins noted on it in red marker. Meanwhile, Hildur wrote the dates on the flipchart.

'I noticed something interesting about those dates today. The dates of the cruise ships and the cabin break-ins are an exact match.' Jakob paused and looked at Beta, then nodded at Hildur. 'The break-ins in our district took place on the exact days a cruise ship docked in Ísafjörður. Not at any other time.'

Hildur had double-checked Jakob's observation and arrived at the same conclusion. There was no way it could be a coincidence.

'So all the local break-ins took place on those days?' Beta confirmed.

Jakob nodded. 'In May, there were just under a dozen break-ins near Ísafjörður. The same number in June. And all the dates match.'

Beta frowned. Her eyes narrowed slightly. 'So the break-in crews are travelling by cruise ship?'

Hildur noted that transporting stolen goods through the passenger entrance to the cruise ships would be difficult, because passengers had to go through a security check when reboarding. 'On the other hand, food, beverages, and other supplies are brought on board all the time. When I was at the harbour this morning, I saw goods being loaded onto the ship. The stolen goods could be transported that way.'

Beta nodded, looking thoughtful. All three of them knew freight wasn't monitored very carefully at small ports. People trusted each other, and that trust was easy to exploit.

Hildur shifted her weight from her heels to her toes and back. The rocking movement helped her concentrate. 'But there's another scenario.'

Hildur explained that she and Jakob had also considered the possibility that the criminal gang had nothing to do with the cruise ships, but was simply taking advantage of the masses of tourists who arrived by boat. Most small towns were only accessible by a single road. Anyone arriving could be seen coming for kilometres. Plus, unfamiliar cars were easy to distinguish from those of locals.

'When a town is teeming with strangers, it's easier for the break-in crew to blend in to the crowd. No one would remember having seen anyone nefarious or anything out of the ordinary, because the whole town is full of lost-looking tourists.'

Beta agreed. 'That sounds a lot more realistic.' She studied the map Jakob had produced. 'Have you had a chance to consult with the other police districts yet?'

Jakob glanced at his notebook and nodded in satisfaction. 'Our colleagues in Stykkishólmur, Seyðisfjörður, and Akureyri checked the dates and made the same observation. There's a clear pattern.'

With the addition of Reykjavík, the towns Jakob listed were the country's most popular harbours on the cruise ship circuit.

Beta took a closer look at the map and mused that the gang of thieves could have moved from town to town by car before the arrival of the cruise ship. The distances weren't too great. 'Damn good work.'

Jakob said that he'd been wondering why none of the cabin owners had yet supplied a detailed list of stolen items. The cabins had been broken into, but there seemed to be no sign of anything being taken.

'I'm going to continue working on that. The summer season for Icelanders begins next week. When people return to their cabins, they'll probably start noticing things missing.'

Beta stirred in her chair and glanced at Hildur, who launched into the next topic.

'Moving on to the nursing home, because at least judging by the damaged door, it seems to be related to this string of break-ins.'

Hildur had drawn a square on the flipchart and marked two Xs on it. She told Beta about the signs of a break-in at the nursing home and pointed at the Xs she'd drawn. One represented the damaged door, the other the passageway connecting the hospital to the nursing home.

'Nursing home residents have a surprising amount of property in their rooms: jewellery, decorative objects, watches . . . A lot also still keep cash on hand in their dresser drawers,' Hildur said.

Beta nodded in agreement, but a hint of scepticism had crept into her eyes. Hildur set the marker down in the tray and continued, despite sensing Beta might not be very enthusiastic about the theory she and Jakob had come up with.

'We believe thieves entered the nursing home. Helga woke up at the wrong moment, spooking the thief, who killed her to avoid being caught.'

Beta rubbed her temples and appeared to think. 'But Helga died during the night. The cruise ships are only at harbour during the daytime.'

Hildur shook her head. This time Beta was wrong. On the night Helga died, one of the smaller ships had remained at port. Hildur said she'd spoken to a tour guide acquaintance of hers who'd taken fifty passengers for a two-day hike in a nature reserve. The ship had been at harbour that night.

Beta took the scrunchie from her wrist and tied her hair back at her nape.

'But there's a third possibility too,' Hildur said. She explained about the CCTV camera footage from the passageway connecting the hospital and the nursing home. Hildur and Jakob had just watched the recording a third time to be sure. Hildur had taken a still image of the recording and zoomed in on it. She showed the close-up to Beta now.

'Last night at 2 a.m., someone we all know was in the passageway. He walked from the hospital to the nursing home and returned fifteen minutes later. We recognised him from the gauze covering his head.'

The colour drained out of Beta's flushed face and she sighed: '*Jæja*.' The legs of her chair scraped the floor as she popped to her feet. 'It doesn't look like our Venezuelan friend's condition is as bad as we thought. I want you two to get to the hospital. Now.'

Chapter 32

5 September

Hey!

I moved and changed jobs. I just started here this week. My new address is on the other side. I still live near the sea, and it's gorgeous here in autumn! As summer comes to an end, the green fades and the landscape turns red.

I'm sorry I didn't have time to answer your letter over the summer. Work has been really busy. I've been working day and night, but it's been worth it. I've paid off my debts. Amazing! Yay for me!! I trusted the wrong people and took that stupid loan. I never imagined I'd be able to pay it off so soon, but I did. I'm sure I'll be able to handle this new adventure too.

I also met someone . . . He's quite a bit older, but that doesn't bother me. He's wonderful. He has his own company and offered me a job. A better job than the ones I've had so far.

He has a huge house: three storeys and a big balcony. And a garage where he keeps his new car. And plenty of money. So I went to work for him, and then something else happened very fast. We grew close. I'd never imagined I'd have a stroke of luck like this.

Write if you feel like it!

Have a great autumn,

R.

Chapter 33

Ísafjörður, June 2022

The sunlight filtered through the blinds covering the tall windows, painting stripes on the white hospital walls. Hildur and Jakob strode quickly toward the nurses' office. Hildur could feel her surfacing disappointment testing her nerves.

The door to the nurses' shared space was open. A clock ticked on the wall, and notes regarding the day's duties had been jotted down on the whiteboard. Hildur saw Lára, the nurse who spoke Spanish, standing at her workstation. She was entering information into her computer with a look of concentration. She seemed to have surprisingly little trouble using the keyboard with one hand. Hildur coughed.

It took Lára a moment to recognise her. 'You're the police officer. Is there something I can do to help?'

Hildur asked Lára to step aside with her and Jakob. Lára clicked the mouse a couple of times and logged out of her computer. As soon as they were in the corridor, Hildur got to the point: 'We need to speak with Manuel immediately, but he wasn't in his room.'

The unmade bed and the hospital socks suggested Manuel hadn't gone far, but Hildur had begun to suspect the worst.

'Is he in X-ray or something?' Jakob asked.

Lára shook her head in confusion. 'He left this morning.'

Damn it, damn it, Hildur swore to herself. They were too late. 'What do you mean, left? Ran off?'

Lára took a more solid stance and stood up straighter. 'No one just runs off from here. Foreigners have to pay their bill when they check out.'

Lára explained that the hospital treated a lot of foreigners every summer. Tourists who'd fallen off a horse, hikers who'd twisted an ankle, or children who'd got an ear infection on vacation generated a lot of work for the caregiving staff. Icelanders were mailed their bills, but foreigners had to pay for treatment before being released, because experience had shown invoices sent to addresses abroad went unpaid. 'The international collections process is arduous and expensive.'

Lára reminded Hildur and Jakob that any information the hospital had about Manuel would be considered confidential. After her lecture, she took a breath and stated she couldn't turn over a patient's medical records to anyone just like that, not even the police.

Hildur sighed. *Dear holy lamb.* Who was this data protection hardnose who was telling her what she could and couldn't do?

'Listen here. We're investigating Manuel's possible connection to a death, so I'm going to ask one more time. When did he leave and who paid his bill, seeing as how he didn't have a wallet on him when he arrived?'

Lára softened at the mention of the death. She smiled as she explained the doctor had given Manuel permission to leave the hospital at around ten, because he'd recovered surprisingly well.

'There's no need for us to keep healthy people here. We're short of beds as it is.'

When in Manuel's room, Hildur had noticed hospital pyjamas in a heap at the foot of the bed.

'What was he wearing when he left, do you remember?' Jakob asked.

Lára thought for a moment, then shook her head. But she was able to provide them with more information about how the bill was paid.

'It was paid in cash. I was just coming from my rounds when I saw Manuel standing with his blond friend at the cashier. When I told you about the friend last time, I'd mistakenly assumed it was a woman, but it was the man who paid the bill,' Lára said. She nodded toward the office. 'If you don't have any more questions, I have to get back to work . . .'

Hildur thanked Lára and asked her to be in touch if she had any news about Manuel or remembered anything else about him.

She and Jakob had come a few hours too late. Hopefully, Manuel hadn't made it far.

It took one phone call for Hildur to get Andri's home address. Ten minutes later, she parked the car halfway up Tangagata Street.

Andri lived in the basement of a bright yellow, corrugated metal house. A couple of bicycles and a toy tractor stood out front. The entrance to the basement apartment was around the rear, so Hildur and Jakob made their way there. A trampoline took up almost half the back yard. Children's toys were scattered around. Hildur lifted a plastic wheelbarrow and leaned it against the wall.

Jakob rang Andri's doorbell, and he and Hildur waited.

Hildur remembered what she'd meant to tell Jakob. It had slipped her mind during the morning's excitement. 'That list of missing people and the conclusions of the bone expert,' Hildur said, looking at Jakob. 'I saw in an old newspaper that Helga had been hoarding that a Pole named Jan Nowak disappeared in the Westfjords in the 1990s. Apparently, the police didn't have much interest in looking for him. Check to see if his name is on the list of missing people.'

Jakob promised to check as soon as they got back to the station.

He rang Andri's doorbell again. They could hear the bell ringing through the open ventilation window, but no one came to answer. Hildur shielded her eyes with her hand and pressed her face to the window. The open dishwasher told her she was looking into the kitchen. There was a box of cold cereal on the table.

'Is anyone home?' she called.

Hildur heard sounds coming from a window above. A cranky-looking old man was staring at her and Jakob. He snapped: 'What's with all the noise?'

'We're looking for Andri,' Hildur said, flashing her police ID.

The man immediately calmed down. The way he shook his head suggested the police showing up at Andri's door didn't surprise him in the least.

'You mean make-up man? What's the weirdo done this time?'

Hildur ignored the prejudice and went calmly to the point. The old man seemed like the type who actively monitored the lives of his neighbours.

'We need to speak with him. Have you seen him?'

The old man opened the window wider, placed his hands on the windowsill, and leaned forward. Hildur hoped he wouldn't topple all the way out.

'He left around eight this morning and I haven't seen him since. It's an unusual time of day for him. He usually goes in at six to deliver the mail and comes home around two.'

Hildur grunted. Her guess about the neighbourhood watch had been right on the money. So Andri hadn't been home all day.

She continued questioning: 'How does he get around?'

As far as she knew, Andri didn't own a car. But maybe the nosy neighbour knew more about the vehicle register.

The old man pointed around the corner. 'He parks out front. He's got a red 1970s Volkswagen bus. He's let it get into sad shape. Rusty as all get out and makes a terrible racket.'

Hildur smiled as widely as possible at the man. 'This was very important information, thank you. Have a nice day!'

The man mumbled to himself for a moment, then drew the window shut behind him.

'There can't be many VW hippie vans registered in Iceland,' Jakob wagered as they circled back around to the street.

Hildur waited for Jakob to buckle his seatbelt before she pressed the gas. Next they needed to find out who owned the bus, and if things went well for once, they might learn other useful things while they were at it.

Chapter 34

Hildur tapped the printer impatiently. Her irritation would morph into a headache if she weren't able to get some exercise soon. The printer spat out two sheets of paper. Hildur grabbed them and collapsed at her desk. She glanced at the printouts in relief. There were only a couple of dozen Volkswagen buses registered as still in use in Iceland. Not a single one of the owners lived in Ísafjörður or even the Westfjords. She would have to call through every name on the list. The nosy neighbour had said the bus Andri drove was red, but it could have been painted since it was registered.

A young woman's voice answered the first call using her first name. Hildur introduced herself.

'You own a 1972 VW bus. Do you know where the vehicle is at this moment?'

The woman's voice at the other end of the line laughed. 'With me here in Þórsmörk. I came here to go hiking and left it parked on the other side of the Krossá river. It's so big I didn't dare try crossing it in that tin can . . .'

The woman went on and on about her travel plans for the upcoming summer and sang the praises of her minibus. She didn't seem at all thrown by the phone call from the police. Hildur thanked her for her help and wished her a pleasant day.

The next few calls didn't generate any useful information either. A couple of buses were currently in for repairs, and a few were stored in garages in the Reykjavík area. Nor was Hildur able to reach every name on the list; some of her calls went to voicemail.

Hildur glanced at Jakob, who was sitting across from her and talking on the phone with Emma the forensic anthropologist. Hildur waited antsily for him to finish the call.

Just then Axlar-Hákon called to report his team's results. Four sets of fingerprints had been found on the bedframe in addition to Helga's. Two belonged to nurses who'd been on duty, one was Hildur's, and one remained unidentified.

Unidentified fingerprints. The first thing to come to Hildur's mind was the missing Manuel. They needed to get fingerprints from him as quickly as possible and have them compared to the prints that had been found.

'What about Helga's autopsy?' Hildur asked.

Not all results of the laboratory tests were in yet. What Axlar-Hákon could tell Hildur already was that Helga's heart had been in very good shape for a woman her age, and nothing else had come up in the examination that would have explained her passing, no cancerous tumours or such like.

'Hildur, that's why this next thing I'm about to tell you is so important. There were small blood vessel ruptures around the deceased's nose and mouth. They weren't very prominent and there weren't many of them.'

Hildur didn't comment. She figured the forensic pathologist would continue. Axlar-Hákon was in the habit of clearly noting when the most germane points were being communicated.

'I found a little feather in the deceased's windpipe.'

Hildur instantly knew what that meant. She was pleased that her hunch had been correct. And yet she felt a pang of grief somewhere near her hip. Someone had pressed a pillow to the old woman's face and invited death prematurely.

The news about the feather also caused a slight disappointment. Hildur had heard from a member of the cleaning staff that all residents used the same kinds of pillows and blankets. Hildur had fetched one from the linen cupboard and sent it along to the lab for analysis. She wanted to know for sure whether the weapon that had taken Helga's life was from the nursing home.

'The nursing home doesn't use down comforters or pillows. The fabric is organic cotton; the stuffing is polyester,' Hildur recited from memory.

Axlar-Hákon told Hildur to take it easy. 'The feather will be sent in for closer analysis. We'll compare it to the pillow you sent.'

Hildur thanked Axlar-Hákon for the information and ended the call.

Jakob was still on the phone, and the conversation didn't show any signs of ending soon. Hildur felt restless. She scratched out a note, set it down in front of Jakob, and exited at a half-run. She had to get outside to calm down.

In the car, Hildur called the remainder of those VW bus owners who hadn't picked up yet. They still didn't.

Hildur sighed and put her phone back in her pocket. She'd spoken with Andri's employer, but they had no information about his possible whereabouts. All they had was the address of the basement apartment on Tangagata Street. Andri had no siblings, and according to the national registry, his parents lived in Denmark.

A short run would do her good. A few days ago, Hildur had gone running in the woods to the south of town. There was plenty of beautiful terrain in the Westfjords, but not many options for running. The bike path that hugged the main road led in two directions: toward Reykjavík or west, toward the village of Hnífsdalur. The road to the southern Westfjords left from the base of the fjord and entered a tunnel a few kilometres long.

The tunnel connecting Ísafjörður with the southern villages wasn't a pleasant place to run, due to the darkness and poor ventilation. Hildur's gaze circled the mountains surrounding the town. The slopes were difficult for runners, but the views were spectacular. Besides, she knew it would do her good to squeeze out a few drops of sweat.

Hildur drove to the Naustahvilft trailhead. The highest point on the route was called 'the seat', because seen from a distance the hollow in the slope looked like a chair. According to the old story, a troll on a nocturnal excursion had sat on the edge of the mountain to admire the view. It had settled its feet on the ground and its rump on the mountainside. The earth that spilled between its feet had created Eyri, the peninsula hooking inside the fjord, where Hildur's home stood. A round dell had formed under his backside.

When she got to the top, Hildur reached into the metal box at the highest point of the path and pulled out the guestbook, found the latest entry and wrote her name beneath. Those who roamed the wilds were in the habit leaving a record of themselves. Hildur flipped back through the book. She noticed familiar names in the entries from early May: Jakob, Matias, and Guðrún had been here.

Hildur sat on a rock and looked down at the town. She tapped the toe of her shoe against a white dryas, sending its bloom swaying. The stalk was short but strong; it bent but didn't snap. Hildur could make out the police station down in the town and her house close by it. The school, the pool, the church, the daycare centre, the seafood warehouses, the car repair shop, the gym, the hospital, and the nursing home. This was her world, here before her. She had spent the majority of her life in these parts. The world was like this here, but would it be different somewhere else? She grunted at her reflections. She felt satisfied with her life here in this fjord; that was enough.

Just then Hildur felt her phone vibrate in her pocket. The number was one of the VW bus owners she'd just tried to call.

'Skúli here from Selfoss. You called?'

Hildur explained about the vehicle she was looking for. For a moment there was only rustling at the end of the line. Then the voice returned.

'I moved into the other room. I don't want my wife to hear; she loses it every time I talk about this. Family drama, you know . . .' Skúli said with a chuckle.

Hildur said she knew a thing or two about family conflicts.

'My cousin Andri has always been sort of a free spirit, the black sheep of the family. He's a good kid, if a little different.'

Skúli said he'd helped Andri out now and again, including arranging a job for him at the Westfjords post office. 'I also lent him my bus. Was that a mistake? Has something happened?'

Skúli would have been happy to keep talking, but Hildur cut him off. She put Skúli's mind at ease; this was nothing serious. The police were simply trying to locate the vehicle.

'It doesn't necessarily have anything to do with the matter under investigation, but we have to check out every detail,' Hildur said, asking if Skúli happened to know where Andri might spend time when he wasn't at work or at home. Did Andri have any hobbies or the like?

'I have a little cabin on the outskirts of town,' Skúli replied and gave the address.

Chapter 35

Hildur steered Brenda out of Ísafjörður's sole roundabout and onto the shoreline road. The local summer cabins stood at the base of the fjord, a few kilometres outside town. Their use was prohibited in winter due to the danger of avalanches. Hildur had informed Jakob as to their destination when she picked him up at the station. The investigation had taken a big leap forward, but neither one was in the mood for conversation.

They drove side by side without speaking. The silence was pleasant, not awkward. Hildur considered it a sign of mutual trust, not having to talk in another's presence without either person finding it uncomfortable.

Children of all ages were kicking balls around the soccer pitch. Past the playing fields the speed limit rose to sixty. Hildur hit the pedal as the shrieks of the children faded. School was out for the summer. Jakob had told Matias about the soccer club, and his son had been excited. Practice, playing, and eating lunch would fill Matias's weekdays for the next couple of weeks.

At the base of the fjord, Hildur turned right. The dirt road leading to the cabins entered into a climb. The gravel from the road's surface stuttered against Brenda's chassis. The road narrowed. Hildur slowed to twenty.

'Matias likes Batman.'

Hildur replied that she'd noticed the same thing. He read the comic book every time he came to hers.

Jakob drummed the dash with his fingers. 'He's just like you.'

Jakob's unexpected comment made the hands on the steering wheel lurch. With a quick correction, Hildur recovered control of the car.

She knew the story of Batman. Bruce Wayne's parents had died when he was a boy. After witnessing their death, he'd trained like a madman and made it his life's work to bring criminals to justice.

'In his free time he's a hedonistic playboy. Are you saying that doesn't sound familiar?' Jakob said, glancing at Hildur. Their eyes met.

'A traumatised hero who fills his lonely life with action, violence, and one-night stands. There are quite a few people who match the description,' Hildur noted drily and returned her eyes to the road.

A big tractor hauling a trailer had stopped up ahead. The driver was fetching something from a nearby field. There wasn't room to pass. Hildur gave the horn a tap. The farmer waved from the field, pointed at his watch, and raised the fingers of one hand. Five minutes. Hildur turned off the ignition. They weren't in a huge hurry. This was the only road leading to the cabins. If Manuel was where they thought he was, he wouldn't be able to escape. Now they just had to wait.

'What did Emma say about the bones?'

Emma's work as a forensic anthropologist fascinated Hildur. After muscles, organs, skin, hair, and everything else had turned to dust, bones remained. Bones offered a flash of how the individual had lived their earthly life.

'Emma has constructed biological profiles of all the skeletons we found. She's still refining them, but she already has a solid foundation that will allow us to move forward with identification.'

Hildur asked Jakob to tell her something: 'Are they all women?' It was the first question to pop into her mind.

Jakob shook his head. 'No. Two of the skeletons are male, two female.'

Hildur felt the heaviness inside evaporate like morning dew in the sunshine. This bit of information was a relief. She wasn't sure why the suspicion of female victims had crept into her mind. Maybe it had its source in the tropes of crime-based entertainment, where a young woman found naked and dead was the most typical victim of a homicide.

But Hildur knew she was lying to herself. She had no doubts as to where the image originated. Although no one knew the timing of the burials yet, Hildur's thoughts had started up a path that led to her father.

She'd seen the bruises and sensed her mother's skittishness when Dad was at home. Rúnar had never beaten their mother in the girls' presence, but one didn't need to see everything with one's own eyes to know what one knew.

Helga had said that Rakel had never spoken well of Rúnar. Had Helga known about the abuse? Presumably. Helga wasn't stupid. She'd mentioned the bruises herself. Hildur had witnessed plenty of instances of domestic violence being kept secret. Decades ago, attitudes had been even more repressed. The tendency had been to view family matters as private; outsiders were not supposed to intervene.

Dad had never been violent toward Hildur, but Hildur remembered her mother's flinching and aloofness. Her voice had lost its force and her games had slowed when Dad entered the house. Hildur didn't know the whole truth, but she knew enough. Upon discovering the bones, her first thought had been that her father had done something to women and buried the bodies in the backyard.

'Is Emma sure about the genders?' she asked.

Jakob nodded. 'The men are about fifty, which means one of them could be the Jan Nowak who disappeared in the Westfjords and was mentioned in that old newspaper article. The females had both died at a clearly younger age, but as adults nonetheless.'

Jakob said children had about three hundred bones at birth. The bones fused over the years; at around the age of twenty, the number of bones stabilised at 206. Two of the skeletons were missing the bones from the left hand, but the other two were complete, so there were no questions as to the bodies' ages or genders. The teeth of the male skeletons were worn down, those of the females weren't. This was what had led Emma to deduce the women were in their twenties when they died, the men older.

'How can she be sure about the genders?' Hildur insisted.

Jakob placed his hand on Hildur's neck. 'The neck bones attach to the skull here at the hairline. You don't have a bump,' he said.

Hildur felt the moving hand at her neck, shivered, and turned her head. The touch felt too intimate.

Jakob quickly pulled back his hand and laid it on his own neck, talking fast: 'Men have a bump here at the back of the head; women don't. It's also possible to tell the gender from the brow ridge. It's more prominent in men.'

He continued by explaining the process of decomposition. Bodies decomposed faster in warm climates. In Iceland the climate and soil were cool, but there was nothing left of these Kotsdalur bodies but the bones. That meant they couldn't be that fresh. But they could have been buried two decades or two centuries ago. According to Jakob, radiocarbon dating wouldn't be of any use in this instance.

'When a person dies, the amount of carbon isotope decreases as the isotope breaks down. The half-life is several thousands of years, which means carbon dating isn't useful for younger bones. Besides, analysing bones of that age would make no sense in terms of pursuing criminal justice. The perp would already be dead regardless . . .'

'I'm going to start decomposing right now if that farmer doesn't get over here and move that tractor,' Hildur huffed, turning on the ignition to hint to the man marching around the field that it was time to get a move on.

A few minutes later, she and Jakob pulled up outside the place they were looking for: a modest, old-fashioned summer cabin. One storey, slanted roof. A small gas grill and a couple of plastic patio chairs stood on the wraparound porch. Hildur parked by the wooden fence and glanced out of the corner of her eye at Jakob, who struck her as uncharacteristically stiff.

'Hey, bump-at-the-back-of-the-head, are you ready?' she said, slipping the car keys into her pocket.

Jakob relaxed. He gave Hildur a gentle shove in the shoulder. 'Ready. And I promise not to fondle your neck again.'

They both laughed. The moment that had briefly thrown them out of whack had been restored.

'Looks like we found what we're looking for,' Hildur said, nodding toward the cabin. The rear bumper of a red VW bus was visible behind the building.

The boards creaked as they stepped onto the porch. Jakob knocked on the door. Hildur could hear music inside but couldn't make out the words. Jakob knocked again, this time more loudly and on the glass pane in the door. Hildur said she'd go around and check if there was a back door.

There was no back door, but there were big windows in the rear façade. The view of the mountain rising behind and its cascading waterfall must have been spectacular from inside.

Hildur could hear the music more clearly now. She walked over to the uncovered window and peered in. What she saw stunned her. She delicately withdrew.

'Knock more loudly,' she said to Jakob upon returning to the front door. In response to Jakob's inquisitive look, she explained the guys were occupied and that was why they couldn't hear. 'They're clearly a couple,' she clarified.

Jakob caught the hint and pounded the cabin's wooden wall twice with his fist.

The music was turned down. The door squeaked open. Andri had wrapped a grey linen towel around his waist. Hildur gestured that they were coming in. Andri nodded. He seemed displeased by the arrival of law enforcement but didn't resist in any way. Just the opposite: he took a couple of steps backward and made room for them in the entryway.

'I've been trying to call you, but you haven't answered,' Hildur said. 'And you weren't at work today.'

'No, I wasn't,' Andri replied. 'I wasn't feeling well this morning.'

Hildur said they were looking for Manuel, who had checked out of the hospital. Andri's eyes widened slightly. The glance he shot toward the room down the hall said all that needed to be said.

'He left the hospital this morning. Someone brought him clothes and paid his hospital bill in cash. We have a strong suspicion it was you.'

Hildur waited for her words to have the desired effect. Jakob started exploring the small cabin one room at a time. The look on Andri's face grew increasingly embarrassed. Hildur figured he knew he wasn't going to be able to wriggle his way out of the situation.

Andri swept the hair out of his eyes and adjusted the towel, then nodded toward the door at the end of the hall. 'He's in there.'

Hildur looked at the kitchen in front of her. There were two benches and a narrow wooden table.

'Get Manuel. We can all talk in the kitchen,' Hildur said to Jakob. She turned to Andri, who was still standing in the entry-way, looking lost. 'And you: put on some clothes first.'

A moment later, four people were sitting in the tiny kitchen.

Hildur said she would call for an interpreter, but to her surprise, Manuel asked her not to.

'I speak English,' he said, abashed. He admitted he'd been playing for time when he'd pretended he didn't. 'I'm sorry. I was just trying . . . I was just trying to make sure I didn't have to go back to the ship.' Manuel had to search for the words, but Hildur had no trouble understanding his English.

He said he'd wanted to stay at the hospital longer, but then the police had found the speed. 'I knew it was probably going to cause me problems . . . That's why I had to leave.'

Hildur said there was no need for an official interrogation yet. At this point she just wanted to talk to Manuel and Andri. Find out what had been going on and hear about last night's events in particular. Then she would see what steps needed to be taken. The bedroom scene Hildur had witnessed a moment ago twisted things into a slightly different shape in her mind.

'So you two are dating?' Hildur asked, looking each man in the eye.

Andri glanced at Manuel, who nodded discreetly. 'Yeah. We met on the boat. We were both working on it, like I told you last time.'

Andri said they'd stayed in contact, sometimes more frequently, sometimes less. They called now and again but texted more often. The long-distance relationship had been a difficult time for both of them. Hildur's thoughts flitted to Anton, who lived in Lapland. She could empathise.

'At first, I thought we'd never see each other again. But then . . .' Andri paused and gave Manuel a dazzled look that put Hildur in mind of being served a delicious dessert without a spoon.

Manuel smiled and said: 'I was so happy when I heard I'd be working on a cruise ship that circled Iceland. I knew I'd be able to see Andri again and that felt . . . it felt amazing.'

Manuel explained that they'd seen each other that spring and summer every time the ship had stopped in Ísafjörður. They were supposed to meet this time too, but there'd been a change in plans.

Manuel had lowered his gaze, and his voice was thick as he spoke. 'I don't want to go back to that ship. I had to come up with something. You guys kept coming back to the hospital. I wanted some time to think. That's why I came here.'

Hildur eyed the painful-looking bruises clearly visible under Manuel's white T-shirt. 'Tell me about the ship. Why don't you want to go back?'

Andri wrapped a protective arm around Manuel and stroked his shoulder.

'There's no way you can understand,' Manuel said. 'It's hot and cramped. And you can't make any mistakes.'

Hildur waited for him to continue. A moment later, he raised a hand to his face and pointed at his injuries: 'Mistakes are punished.'

The tiny kitchen had grown hot. Hildur stood and cracked the window, took off her long-sleeved top, and set it on the bench at her side.

'Start from where you got those injuries.'

Manuel said he'd been chopping up chickens. He described the work, which demanded speed and precision. Manuel had only got a few hours' sleep the night before, because he'd been woken up in the middle of the night to work the breakfast shift; the omelette cook had come down with stomach flu. After the morning shift, he'd had to go straight to carving up the broilers.

Manuel explained that he'd taken a short break from the butchering. He'd leaned against the wall so he wouldn't faint from exhaustion. A moment later, the boss had emerged from his cubicle, reached into his breast pocket, and pulled out a baggie containing white powder.

'Frying Pan Face gave me some speed. You can't say no if you want to stay awake.'

Hildur cut in: 'Who's Frying Pan Face?'

'The shift lead, Juan Lopez. His face is so flat it looks like someone whacked it with a frying pan. He's a bad man. He answers to his bosses for all the kitchen workers.'

Now Jakob interrupted: 'To his bosses? The captain?'

Manuel laughed, semi-amused. 'No, not the captain. To his bosses back in Venezuela. The Venezuelans run the kitchen. The cleaning crew is from Asia. Thailand or somewhere. Or Cambodia. I'm not sure.'

Manuel explained that the subcontractors had to submit a bid every year. Or so he'd thought when he was hired. The

Venezuelan employment agency had received an order from the shipping company to manage the kitchen staff for the cruise boats. Manuel had run into a man who worked for the agency one night when he was out at a bar. The salary, living expenses, and job description had sounded excellent, so Manuel had taken the job and paid the broker's fee.

'Five thousand dollars?' Hildur confirmed.

'I can't believe I was stupid enough to believe his bullshit,' Manuel said.

Hildur didn't think Manuel was stupid. If a person in a hopeless situation was offered even the tiniest opportunity for something better, they would jump at it.

'I was cutting off a breast when I made a mistake. The knife accidently hit the bone. My grip slipped, I lost my balance, and tripped. I was half-lying across the counter. As soon as I felt a warm trickle on my face, I knew it was bad.'

A pool of red liquid had begun to spread where Manuel was sprawled. The knife had rolled under him, blade up, and he'd cut himself at the temple. His face had throbbed with pain.

'I started to scream. It hurt so bad.'

Manuel held a pause and took a sip of his soda. The cruise ship crew included a couple of trained nurses, and all employees – or at least the ones that existed on paper – had received first aid training. A patient requiring more intensive care was transported to the closest hospital on land.

'I knew I had to get to the hospital and get stitches. There was so much blood. I knew we were about to dock in Ísafjörður.'

But going to the hospital hadn't been an option. Frying Pan Face had taken Manuel to the infirmary and tried to clean the wound and bind it with tape. Manuel had protested and said he'd walk to the hospital if he had to. Juan had been infuriated and assaulted his subordinate with a pocketknife to the point he lost consciousness. Judging by the cuts, the assault had lasted a long time and been extraordinarily aggressive.

'One of my coworkers risked everything to help me,' Manuel said. The coworker had got his hands on a maintenance key and opened the locked infirmary from the outside. He'd shaken Manuel awake, and Manuel had staggered off the boat.

Hildur had one more question: 'Tell me . . . What were you doing at two in the morning on Tuesday in the passageway that runs between the hospital and the nursing home?'

Manuel started. 'I was trying to escape. I woke up in the middle of the night, and I was nervous. I took my clothes. I wanted to sneak out without anyone seeing, but there was a guard at the entrance to the hospital. I followed some exit signs to that other lobby. Those doors were locked. I couldn't get out. I went back to my room.'

Manuel said he knew citizens of Venezuela could stay in Iceland for three months without a visa. Any longer than that and you had to apply for permission to stay temporarily in the country. That permission wouldn't be granted if the applicant couldn't demonstrate they could provide for themselves.

'I want to stay here,' he said softly.

'Do you, or I mean you guys, have money?' Hildur asked.

Manuel and Andri both shook their heads. 'We've been thinking about ways I could stay. But we don't have the kind of savings required by the Foreign Ministry.'

Hildur sighed. She had to call it like she saw it. 'You've been the victim of a crime, and in principle we should help you. There's just one big problem.' She paused before continuing. She had to be honest. 'Even if you reported what happened in detail and acquired evidence of the problems on the boat, and even if you agreed to testify against the wrongdoers, I can't do anything as a police officer, because Icelandic law doesn't apply on cruise ships.'

To Hildur, Manuel's story had the ring of truth. But she still couldn't know if he'd killed Helga. Maybe he'd stolen from the old people at the nursing home to pay his debts.

'According to the security camera footage, you were over in the nursing home for about ten minutes. Maybe you went into one of the resident's rooms?'

Manuel's jaw dropped. Hildur studied his expression. The reaction seemed genuine.

'Which resident's room?'

'I'm asking the questions here,' Hildur said.

Manuel closed his eyes and seemed to think. The summer breeze blew into the kitchen through the open window and stirred the wooden beads that hung between the kitchen and the entryway. Birdsong carried in from outside.

Manuel coughed and made himself more comfortable on the bench. He said he'd spent some time in the lobby, at the locked doors, considering his alternatives.

'Probably a few minutes. I don't know exactly. Then I walked back to my room. I didn't go anywhere else.'

Hildur studied Manuel's face. He seemed sincere. Even so, she was uncertain. She nodded at Jakob, who began pulling the fingerprinting kit out of the forensics gear he'd brought with him.

'We need your fingerprints so we can compare them to those found in Helga's room.'

Manuel seemed momentarily flustered, but Hildur didn't read fear or resistance in his eyes. He rolled up his sleeves and did as Jakob instructed.

When Jakob was finished, Manuel looked pleadingly at Hildur. 'Is there anything you can do to help me?'

Hildur looked at the downcast young man on the narrow wooden bench. Andri's arm was still wrapped protectively around him.

Hildur sighed. 'I'll try to think of something. Things usually work out somehow.'

Manuel visibly relaxed. A hopeful look kindled on his face. It tore at Hildur's heart.

'But right now I have to arrest you.'

Chapter 36

Westfjords, early 1990s

Rakel

After the school bus had picked up the girls, Rakel had combed her hair, put on some lipstick, and climbed on her bicycle. The dense cloud cover was breaking up, and the sun's rays slipped through the cracks and into the valley. Dark, cloud-shaped shadows splotched the terrain. Rakel pedalled down the middle of the dirt road, dodging the shady spots. She wanted to feel the sun on her skin. Her hair and the hem of her knee-length skirt fluttered as she rode; the thrill of anticipation had pinched dimples in her cheeks.

The road had been levelled earlier that summer, but thanks to the rain, a small, tight washboard had reformed on its surface. The rack of Rakel's three-speed bicycle clattered on the bumpy stretches. She didn't care. She was grateful she had the bicycle. It gave her freedom on days like today when the children were at school, Rúnar was at sea, and their car was in the garage yet again: a second hole had formed in the exhaust pipe, which they couldn't afford to replace. Luckily their car repairman had said he'd be able to weld-patch the second hole too and likely get at least another year out of the old exhaust pipe that way.

But where will we get the money for it next year?

Rakel had no idea, and just now she didn't want to think about the future, at least if doing so involved worries or woes.

She leaned her bike against the greenhouse. There was no need for her to knock, but she still rapped on the door with her knuckles before she stepped in. That was polite.

'I'm here.'

Rakel took off her shoes and went into the kitchen. The room was filled with bright light, and the rays of the sun turned Helga's backlit hair into a shimmering halo of gold.

'How are you?' Helga asked, stepping closer. Her robe had fallen open.

Helga's husband Hallgrímur had set out that morning for Reykjavík to buy feed and spare parts for the tractor. He'd be gone for two days. A new medication had kept Hallgrímur's heart trouble at bay for months, and he'd been able to work at full capacity.

'Better now,' Rakel said, pressing her body against Helga's. Their mouths opened. For a moment, the two women breathed in each other's lips. Now that they were together, they clung to each other like they were drowning. The moment of salvation and their delight at seeing each other again set their skin tingling.

The robe dropped to the floor. Rakel took off her dress. Pressed against each other, they wobbled across the kitchen to the guest room. They never went in the main bedroom. That unspoken agreement had formed between them from the start. They'd never discussed the issue, yet they'd still made the decision. Hallgrímur was a good man, and they didn't want to hurt him. Besides, Helga had admitted that she loved both of them.

Rakel writhed on the open sofa bed beneath Helga. They laughed, then fell silent. First one, then the other. There was exuberance in the moment but also sadness, because they knew it would soon be over. Every time they saw each other was also the first moment of impending separation.

Helga stroked Rakel's left shoulder. The palm-width bruise had faded to yellow but remained plainly visible. Helga looked questioningly at Rakel.

'I took a salt lick out to the pasture,' Rakel said, turning away. 'One of the horses bit me.'

'Are you sure?' Helga asked calmly. Rakel's long chestnut hair was fanned out on the bed, and Helga was running her fingers through it.

Rakel nodded, and Helga didn't insist.

They lay there on their backs, the crocheted bedspread pulled halfway up to warm their feet. Between them, even silences felt meaningful.

A fly was buzzing at the window. There was a knock every few seconds as the poor creature tried to punch through the glass to freedom and the green meadow beyond. Time seemed to have stopped, although both Helga and Rakel knew it hadn't. The sun no longer shone into the room. It was well after noon.

Rakel turned her head just far enough to see Helga. 'It's a bad moment to ask, but . . .'

Helga rolled onto her side. 'It's the best moment.'

There had never been any one-upmanship between Rakel and Helga. They owned farms in the same valley. One had three children; the other didn't have any. One had a decent man for a husband; the other didn't. One loved two people; the other loved one. They each had a driver's licence, a bicycle, and a bank account where they could deposit money. They'd always been relatively evenly matched financially too. Neither one of them had been looking for anything, and yet they'd both found someone. They hadn't needed anything from each other except each other.

So Rakel didn't have to swallow her pride when she said: 'I need a little cash again. Just a little. For beeswax. I know I've asked so many times already; I don't want to—'

Helga placed a finger to Rakel's lips and smiled.

She whispered, although there was no one else nearby. She said she was driving into town that afternoon to go to the post office. 'I'll drop by the bank and transfer the money into your account.'

Rakel thanked her, then quickly added: 'I'll pay you back as soon as I can.'

Helga shook her head. 'It all comes out in the wash; trust me.'

The fly was still buzzing at the window.

'You mean so much to me.'

Chapter 37

Ísafjörður, June 2022

After Hildur and Jakob's visit to the cabin, grey clouds had begun collecting in the sky again. They wrung out their first drops as Hildur gazed out her office window. The intensifying shower drummed rhythmically against the glass. The rain lifted Hildur's spirits. Jakob was currently uploading Manuel's fingerprints to the database so the forensic laboratory would have access to them. Manuel was in the holding cell and would be there at least until tomorrow, when the results of the fingerprint analysis were confirmed. He had his passport, so leaving the country would be easy enough if the opportunity arose.

Hildur hadn't wanted to jail the traumatised Manuel among strangers in Akureyri or Reykjavík. Generally, detainees were transported to larger cities, where there were more cells and more staff. Hildur had wanted to make an exception for Manuel, and Beta had given her blessing, because Hildur had promised to pull guard duty and spend the night. Summer vacations meant there wasn't a single extra colleague they could have called in.

'Let's circle back to that thief angle. If it wasn't Manuel, it could have been some outsider,' Hildur said.

It was critical to keep an open mind during an investigation. You never knew beforehand which path would lead you to your destination. If you set out following the wrong path, you had to retrace your steps and start over again. Besides, a failed break-in was the scenario that had originally occurred to them in the first place.

'Damn it,' Jakob huffed, lightly knocking the side of his fist against his desk. 'I completely forgot. Aron, the security head at the hospital, still hasn't returned my call. There was so much else going on.'

Hildur glanced at the clock. It was late.

'I'm going to have in-depth conversations with all the residents of the nursing home. We need to know whether anyone is missing any valuables.'

Jakob stretched his arms and yawned. 'Should we get back to this in the morning? Aron isn't going to be at work anymore, and there's no point talking to older people this late in the day. Plus, I'd been thinking I'd take Matias swimming tonight . . .'

Hildur nodded. She had to get down to the holding cell anyway, as the patrol officer who handled customer service and permits had gone home for the day. The station was empty.

Once Jakob left, Hildur went downstairs to bring Manuel a bite to eat. She'd set a bottle of orange juice, a cheese sandwich, and some cookies on a tray.

'We hope to have the results of the fingerprint analysis tomorrow,' she said as she entered the cell.

Manuel was wearing clean clothes and he'd slicked back his wet hair. Not long before, Hildur had brought him a change of clothes and soap and shampoo and told him the sheets on the bed were fresh: it had been months since anyone had spent the night in the cell.

'Do you have everything you need?' Hildur asked as she was about to leave.

Manuel thanked her for the food and then cast that pleading look again. 'Do you really think things are going to work out?'

Hildur let her gaze circle the cell's barren walls. Then she considered Manuel's frail presence and nodded lightly. 'I do. That's really the only way to get through life.'

They wished each other good night. Hildur locked the door and walked into the neighbouring cell, tossed her trousers and top on the chair next to the bed, and slipped between the sheets in her underwear. There weren't any other beds at the station, so the cell would have to do. Then she turned off the reading lamp.

Hildur cursed herself for having lied to Manuel. Things didn't always work out, after all. But she'd had to give the Venezuelan a smidgen of hope. When you were running out of faith, hope could help you keep going a little longer. Thinking such thoughts, she fell asleep.

Chapter 38

Early the next morning, Jakob and Hildur were standing in the nursing home lobby, waiting for the head of security. The receptionist had called him, and it wasn't long before Aron was ambling toward them. He still looked like a middle-aged guy who'd wanted to be a rock star but never found fame as a guitarist and ended up working at a hospital.

'Damn it. I forgot to call you back. Summer staffing means things have been busier than usual here.'

Hildur inhaled her frustration. Aron had given the police the security camera footage, but it hadn't occurred to him to mention anything to them about the damaged door.

'Have the hospital or nursing home premises been broken into lately?'

Aron looked at them, perplexed.

Jakob stepped in: 'We never received a report, but we noticed signs of damage on the front door.'

Hildur tried to ignore the shower of dandruff that rained down on Aron's black band T-shirt as he scratched his head, looking confused.

'The front door is broken and you don't know anything about it, even though you're head of security?'

Jakob tried a more conciliatory approach. He asked if there was anyone else at the hospital who might be aware.

Aron pulled his phone from his pocket and made a call. After a few sentences and uh-huhs, he turned to Hildur and Jakob.

The hospital's COO had just informed Aron that the damage to the door had been noticed over a week ago, when the maintenance man had oiled the locks after the first week of June.

'But no one gave it any more importance than that. Probably some local boys up to no good. Last summer, grass was shoved into the downpipes. Sometimes they throw water balloons at the windows. The kinds of things boys do to get rid of excess energy.'

Hildur let out a quiet sigh. 'You don't have an alarm system?'

'We haven't needed one,' Aron said, adding there were nurses and doctors on duty around the clock and at least one guard on duty every night. Cash was banked every day, and prescription drugs were behind locks. Inventories were regularly conducted of the pharmaceuticals on hand. 'Someone would notice if anything was missing. I'd put my money on local boys.'

The head of security was on the defensive; his voice had risen slightly. He told them a new door had already been ordered but wasn't scheduled to arrive until August.

'Are you sure it was over a week ago?' Hildur confirmed.

'As sure as a snowstorm on the first day of summer. My boss remembers the day exactly, because there was a Liverpool match on television. Besides, there's a record of the maintenance man's visit. It was over a week ago.'

Hildur and Jakob reiterated their request for Aron to get in touch if anything else arose. After he had vanished down the corridor again, Jakob glanced at Hildur. They were both disappointed. The theft motive was falling apart. Hildur meant to talk to all the nursing home residents regardless. They'd begun investigating Helga's death as a homicide, but Hildur didn't mean to reveal that yet. She would only ask the old folks about anything that had possibly gone missing. They didn't want to cause a stir among the residents.

Jakob had mentioned Saga Maríudóttir, the cardiologist whose summer cabin had been broken into. She had driven up from Reykjavík late the previous night and still insisted on seeing a police officer face to face, so Jakob would head out now to have a look at the damage and any clues.

Hildur walked into the nursing home wing. A break-in could have still happened without any of the hospital or nursing home staff noticing. And even if said break-in had happened weeks before Helga's death, that didn't mean someone couldn't have broken in again. As a matter of fact, it would be a lot easier the second time, because the thieves would be more familiar with the place and would have had a chance to scope out valuables beforehand.

No one had reported anything having gone missing. But how carefully did the nursing home residents look after their jewellery and cash, in the end? Hildur thought about Helga, who had begun to mix up present and past events.

Hildur glanced at her watch. If chatting to the nursing home residents didn't take too long, she'd have time for a short run before a meeting she had scheduled with Beta and Jakob that afternoon.

She started her rounds from the staff break room and Jódis. Hildur explained about the break-ins at local cabins and the nursing home's wrenched front door and stressed that the police needed to ask residents about possible missing items.

'No one has noticed any uninvited visitors around here. I would have heard about it,' Jódís said, pouring steaming hot coffee from a Thermos. 'Would you like some?' she asked, offering Hildur a tray of chocolate-covered wheat buns.

Hildur smiled and said: 'That's kind of you, but I don't have time for coffee right now.' She explained they'd just spoken with the head of security. No one at the hospital had noticed anything missing either. 'I assume at least some of the residents have valuables in their rooms. Maybe something has gone missing.'

Jódís shook her head vigorously. 'Those are private matters.'

The reaction caught Hildur off guard. This was one response she hadn't been expecting.

'People who can't look after themselves or their belongings have a guardian. Not a single one of our residents does. Their heads all work fine.'

Hildur had a hard time believing it. Some residents no doubt suffered at least some degree of memory loss. Helga had, after all. She didn't think it was at all impossible that someone might not necessarily notice if money had been stolen from them.

'Do you mind if I have a word with the residents regardless?' Hildur asked.

Jódís continued eyeing Hildur penetratingly. 'You don't need my permission. Ask the residents themselves.'

The clutch of men had gathered to play chess again. Two were arranging the pieces on the board. A man in a green flannel shirt and glasses asked Hildur what sort of move she would make. He had the white pieces.

Hildur had played a lot of chess, especially during her time at the police academy, but it had been a while. She looked at the board and the players. Then she said: '1. C4.'

'Ah, you'd do an English opening,' the man said, apparently satisfied with Hildur's reply.

'I'd like to ask all of you a question too,' Hildur said. She told the men about the damage to the nursing home door and the cabin break-ins. 'Have any of you lost any personal property recently?'

The men looked at Hildur, intrigued but clearly perplexed.

'When my wife was still alive, all my money vanished every payday,' quipped a vigorous-looking old fellow watching the game, with a nudge to the shoulder of the fellow next to him.

When the burst of laughter quieted down, the men said no, they hadn't noticed anything.

The conversation flowed with every resident. They all said the same thing: nothing had gone missing. Hildur reassured the elderly people who wondered why she was asking questions and reiterated that the police's suspicions were likely unfounded. They just wanted to be completely sure no other thefts had taken place in addition to the recent cabin break-ins.

Hildur was on her way out when she spotted a stout woman advancing slowly along the edge of the corridor with her rollator. A thin, light-blue scarf was tied over the rollers in her hair. Hildur said hello and introduced herself.

'There's no need to shout; I have a hearing aid,' the woman whispered, pointing at her ear and the device attached to it. She introduced herself as Katla and asked Hildur to open the door to her room.

Hildur followed Katla in. Hildur savoured the older woman's name. A no-nonsense, strong-willed woman, a volcano spewing lava. Hildur presented the same litany to Katla that she'd presented the others, but before she could ask any questions, Katla waved a hand in rejection.

'I don't want any visitors in here. You can't trust visitors.'

Hildur shifted her weight to her other foot and tried a softer approach. 'I was just thinking, if you're missing anything, I could help . . .'

Katla shook her head firmly. 'No police. No one. Nothing has been taken. I have nothing to say. I don't trust the police. Could you please leave?'

The old woman seemed determined. She pushed her rollator into the corner of her room and took a seat in her armchair. Hildur sighed. Katla didn't want to talk, and Hildur couldn't force her. She politely wished the old woman a nice day.

As she walked to her car, Hildur sank into her thoughts. The nursing home's residents hadn't given her any useful information. Even so, she felt like she'd got hold of something that contradicted this impression. Something in Katla's attitude had caught Hildur's attention. She climbed into her car and buckled the seatbelt. Hildur thought there was more to Katla's reaction than a mistrust of law enforcement. Something about the old woman's suspiciousness had sparked Hildur's doubts too. Something was off; she could feel it.

Chapter 39

It was about a thirty-minute drive to cardiologist Saga Maríudóttir's summer cabin. Jakob had never been in this part of the Westfjords before. Skálavík was situated in a small bay to the north-east of Ísafjörður, at the foot of a tall mountain known as Bólafjall. The narrow dirt road, only suitable for summer driving, wound through gorgeous highland terrain. The small, colourful wooden cabins on the shores of the bay reminded Jakob of Finnish allotment garden cabins. That's how small they were. The bay was so remote and enveloped by mountains that there was no mobile phone coverage.

Saga had described her cabin as a pink dollhouse. Jakob pulled into the drive. Saga rose to standing from some foliage growing next to the cabin and gestured for Jakob to approach. 'I'm picking rhubarb. I'm going to make juice,' she said, walking over to shake Jakob's hand.

Jakob glanced at the greenery growing along the wall. Dozens of stalks of rhubarb were strewn across the lawn. 'This is the only plant that grows at my cabin,' Saga laughed, ripping the leaf from the stalk she was holding.

Jakob asked Saga about the process of making rhubarb juice and was given a long answer about how the rhubarb was soaked in sugar water spiked with sodium benzoate and tartaric acid for a few days. Jakob nodded in interest. He had rhubarb growing in his yard too and was curious about making juice from it.

Jakob pulled a notebook and pen from his pocket and told Saga about the ongoing investigation into the spree of break-ins.

Saga set the stalk she was holding on top of the pile and wiped the sweat from her brow. 'My father owned this cabin, and I'm an only child. When he died, the cabin came to me. I spend a couple of weeks here every summer. Other than that, the place is empty.' She nodded at the neighbouring property and said the neighbour had been there the week before. He was the one who'd noticed the signs of a break-in at his place and Saga's too.

'He checked those other ones, those cabins a little further over there, but didn't notice anything,' Saga said, pulling her mobile phone from her pocket. She showed Jakob the pictures the neighbour had taken.

The gate at the head of the drive was locked with a padlock. The chain that held the lock had been severed. Jakob took a closer look at the photo. It was a smooth cut. Probably bolt cutters.

Saga swiped to the next photo. It was of broken porch planks hanging from a few nails. The pink cabin had a wraparound porch at least twice the size of the cabin itself, with space for storage underneath.

'I had the porch planks replaced right away. I can't stand the thought of having to do any repairs here during my short summer vacation,' Saga said apologetically, and looked at Jakob so long it almost felt indecent.

Jakob asked Saga to show him the photo again. The broken boards had been on the sea-facing side of the cabin. Jakob walked over to the spot and squatted to look under the porch. Saga squatted down at his side.

'What's under there? What might the thieves have been after?'

Saga shrugged and smiled innocently. 'What are you after?'

Jakob laughed at the shameless attempt at seduction. 'I live with my partner.'

This information didn't seem to faze Saga at all. 'I have no idea what bad guys want. I prefer nice men.'

Saga was disconcertingly direct. She didn't hide her intentions. *You have to give her credit for that*, Jakob thought to himself, although the frank flirtation felt like a little much under the circumstances.

He shifted places and crouched down again to get a view of the empty space under the porch. 'You're not storing anything down there?'

Saga shook her head. 'No. There's no way to get under the porch; there's nothing there. Nothing has been taken from the cabin, not even the Kitchenaid mixer on the kitchen counter.'

Jakob eyed the cabin. Something about this string of break-ins wasn't adding up. Saga's neighbour and all the other cabin owners had said the same thing as Saga: someone had clearly broken in, but nothing had been taken.

There was nothing in the space under the porch. A couple of metres from where the porch planks had been torn up, the soil looked a little darker than the surrounding earth. That could be due to natural differences in soil composition or, say, dampness. Maybe a glass of water had spilled on the patio.

'Is it OK if I pull up these planks if I nail them back afterward?' Jakob asked. 'I'd like to have a look under the porch.'

'You can look wherever you want,' Saga cooed.

Jakob thanked her and asked her if there was a spade or something else to dig with on the premises and a hammer. Saga was visibly delighted at being able to help. She disappeared inside and returned carrying a hammer and a short-handled garden hoe.

Jakob glanced at his watch. He'd make it to the station on time for the meeting if he was quick about this. He took off his shirt so it wouldn't get dirty.

Saga stood on the porch and looked on with interest.

'I'll get you a glass of rhubarb juice, if you'll allow me? You'll get hot,' Saga said and vanished inside when Jakob didn't refuse.

Jakob took the hammer and began pulling up the planks. He had to know whether the hunch that had just occurred to him was true.

Chapter 40

That afternoon, Beta, Hildur, and Jakob, who had returned from Saga's pink cabin, had gathered for afternoon coffee in the station's conference room.

'This is insanely good,' Hildur said, after tasting the rhubarb juice the cardiologist had sent home with Jakob.

A moment ago, the forensics laboratory had confirmed the unidentified fingerprints at the foot of Helga's body were not Manuel's.

'This confirms Manuel is innocent,' Beta said, 'so we have to release him.'

Hildur agreed. She would handle the matter right after the meeting.

Beta asked Jakob to show them some of the photos he'd taken the morning Helga was discovered dead. 'The ones of the fingerprints on the bedframe.'

Jakob pulled the printed photos from his folder and pointed at two spots on the bed with his pen.

'Those fingerprints at the foot of the bed and there on the lower right belong to Jódís, a nurse on the nursing home staff. It appears they came from moving the bed,' Jakob said. He grabbed the arm of the chair at his side. He kept his eyes on the photograph as he shifted his hand into various positions that corresponded to someone pushing or pulling the bed.

'The other nurse's fingerprints grazed the edge of the bed. She was presumably changing or arranging the sheets.'

Hildur added that the third set of prints – in other words, hers – came when she'd taken a cream toffee from the nightstand drawer.

'And the unidentified prints . . .' Jakob said, demonstrating the movement again, this time on the back of his chair. 'The left hand is wrapped around the edge of the bedframe. The killer could have supported themselves with their left hand while they used their right hand to smother Helga with the pillow. It's also possible the killer was wearing gloves, which would mean we wouldn't find their fingerprints at the scene at all.'

Hildur nodded. They could make no assumptions. The mobile phone on the conference table vibrated twice. The incoming message sent everyone's adrenaline racing.

'That was fast,' Hildur gasped.

The forensics laboratory had compared the stuffing from the pillows used at the nursing home to the feather that had been found in Helga's windpipe.

The contents of the message surprised Hildur. Axlar-Hákon had been right after all: although the material discovered in Helga's windpipe had looked like a feather, it wasn't one. Hildur read the message out loud:

'*Based on the results of the analysis, it is highly likely the fibres are a match. The fibres from the pillow and the fibres found inside the deceased are both polyester. A more detailed lab analysis is attached.*'

'Polyester?' Jakob repeated.

Hildur nodded and clicked the link the lab assistant had attached to the email. The synthetic material made from polyester looked and felt like down. It was used as stuffing in the thinnest coats, blankets, and pillows, as it was easier to wash and dry than feathers.

It was looking likely a nursing home pillow had been used as the murder weapon.

'There's one thing that bothers me,' Hildur said.

The vertical furrow between Beta's eyes deepened as she listened to her subordinate.

No one had seen any outsiders. Nothing else had appeared on the security cameras either. Everything pointed to the perp being someone from inside the nursing home.

'None of the residents reported anything missing. I mean anything, ever,' Hildur said, doubt in her voice as she poured herself more juice and diluted it with water. She wiped away the drops that had dribbled onto her chin, and pointed out that some of the nursing home's residents had lived there for years. 'It's odd that no one has *ever* lost *any*thing. I don't think they're telling the whole story. Or maybe they don't remember.'

Hildur said she'd checked the residents' patio doors. All the locks had been undamaged.

'But I'll have another look when I go back to talk to the residents again,' Hildur said.

Jakob thought it was important to take a close look at the backgrounds of the staff. He asked if there had ever been instances in Iceland of caregivers being found guilty of homicide.

'I don't remember any . . . I don't think so,' Beta said. 'Are you saying there have been in Finland?'

Jakob nodded. He said there had been a couple of cases in recent years. Nurses had murdered their patients by, for instance, intentionally misdosing their medication.

'Why?' Hildur asked.

Jakob shrugged. 'Some had stolen money from their victims and were covering their tracks. But for some the motive remained unclear. The perp was mentally ill or something.'

Beta asked Hildur to look into the backgrounds of the staff.

'We need to be very careful with this. Go through all the permanent and temporary staff but be discreet. I don't want this leaking to the media. That would be a PR catastrophe.'

Hildur understood. The longer a suspected homicide stayed out of the papers, the better. At least at this stage of the investigation.

'Jakob, did you have anything to report on the cabin break-ins?'

'Nothing was taken from Maríudóttir's cabin either. It's looking like the break-ins are literally that. They don't involve theft.' Jakob paused before explaining he'd spoken with all the owners of the cabins, as well as those who managed the consortiums' properties. 'No one could specify a single stolen item. Just broken doors, windows, gates, and porches.'

One curious thing was that someone had done some digging under Saga's porch.

'There was a small patch of looser soil. Half a metre deep and about the same width,' Jakob said, indicating the approximate dimensions with his hands. 'There was nothing in the hole, but the soil had clearly been disturbed.'

'I've seen it all. Organised vandalism,' Hildur said. 'What is going on?' She was starting to get a strange feeling about the spree of break-ins.

Beta rubbed her face. 'Then we have that bigger hole. The old grave at Kotsdalur. Hildur, I know you're recused from that investigation, but you don't have to leave the room. Jakob, give us an update on that too.'

Jakob cited Emma's findings about tooth wear, the shape of the hip bones, and the pelvic joints in the female skeletons.

'I went through the list of missing people and noted all the names that would be a match for Emma's observations. Two men around the age of fifty and two young women,' Jakob said, pulling two sheets of paper from his folder. One he gave to Beta, the other he kept for himself.

'The Jan you mentioned is on the list,' he said to Hildur.

'Who's Jan?' Beta asked.

Hildur explained about the conversation she'd had with Helga, and slid two printouts across the table to Jakob and Beta. She'd made a copy of the archived newspaper article from the 1990s on Jan's disappearance and of the police report indicating that Jan had been reported missing. No official investigation had ever been launched into the case.

Beta eyed the printouts, then Jakob's list.

'Emma said she'd take a closer look at possible fractures in the bones, so there'll still be more information coming later,' Jakob said, stretching his fingers.

The sound of his cracking knuckles sent shivers running up Hildur's spine. She asked him to stop.

Jakob lowered his hands to the table and added the information he'd just received from Emma on textile remnants to his list. A more detailed analysis would be conducted on them as well. Based on the information about the bones, he'd culled his list to ten names. Jakob read the list out loud, one name at a time, including the age when the individual went missing and the month and location where they'd last been seen:

Anna Hildur Tómasardóttir, 20. February 1991. Staðarskáli.
Annie Kolbeinsdóttir, 19. July 1985. Akureyri.
Arnar Lárusson, 48. March 1996. Patreksfjörður.
Catherine Martin Ruiz, 21. September, 1992. Flateyri. (Spain)

Davíð Jónsson, 54. August 1992. Vík.
Ólafur Eggertsson, 49. December 1975. Reykjavík.
Haraldur Valdimarsson, 54. April 1989. Ísafjörður.
Una Magnusdóttir, 23. August 1969. Heimaey.
Daníel Sverrisson, 55. October 2009. Stokkseyri.
Jan Nowak, 50. July 1992. Flateyri. (Poland).

'In theory, the bodies that were excavated could belong to any four of these people,' Beta mused.

Jakob clicked his tongue against his palate and shook his head. 'Emma has already gone through the dental records of all missing Icelandic citizens born in the 1900s.'

Calls to the health centres and dental clinics near the most recent address on record of the missing Icelanders had produced results. The dental records had been retrieved already.

Hildur listened to Jakob's report with interest. With maybe a handful of exceptions, all Icelanders had been to the dentist at some point in their lives, which meant dental records existed for them. Hildur felt her forehead break out in a cold sweat.

'There were no dental records for any of the skulls,' Jakob said.

'But then that means . . .' There was no need for Beta to finish the sentence.

They all knew what it meant: if the buried bodies had belonged to Icelandic citizens, the dental records would have been easy to find. Dental visits were expensive, and many people skipped them because of the high cost, but every Icelander under the age of eighteen received dental care for free. That meant dental records of some sort existed for just about everyone.

The skeletons weren't those of Icelanders.

'That means we can cross eight names off the list,' Jakob said.

Beta read the old newspaper clipping. 'Do you know whether this Catherine on the list was here as a tourist, or did she live here? At least, according to this newspaper clipping, Jan lived in the fjords,' she said, rereading the article more closely.

Jakob said he'd look into that next. Then he'd reach out to the Polish and Spanish embassies. If they found dental records for Catherine and Jan, at least two of the bodies would be positively identified. Both might have living relatives who would finally be able to bury their missing loved ones.

Hildur saw Beta circle Catherine's and Jan's names on the list.

'These two disappeared from the Westfjords. Both had been seen here last. They went missing within a few months of each other. It would be quite the coincidence if the incidents weren't related.'

'I learned they both worked for the same company, Hagfiskur,' Jakob added.

Beta finished her rhubarb juice, pushed the glass away, and commented on her own remark: 'Even so, let's not start making assumptions. But the time window and shared employer will facilitate further investigation.'

If dental records pinned Catherine and Jan as two of the bodies, it was likely the other two bodies had been buried around the same time. Emma had precise information about where each skeleton had been discovered. The one detail Hildur remembered about placement was that the bodies had been buried separately.

'Can I participate in the conversation enough to share what I remember about the day the bones were found?' Hildur asked. Beta nodded, and Hildur continued: 'Three skeletons were stacked on top of each other, but they hadn't been buried together. The body at the bottom was found at a depth of a metre and a half, the next at a little over a metre, and the one on top at a depth of under a metre, maybe seventy-five centimetres. Emma had said there was about half a metre of soil between the skeletons. The fourth was a metre away from the other three.'

All three police officers knew seventy-five centimetres wasn't much for a grave. Even a shallow grave was a minimum of 180 centimetres deep. A metre was enough to bury a dog, but not a human.

'Maybe they were buried hastily?' Jakob suggested.

'Or maybe the bones are really old, and there was a lot more soil on the slope centuries ago,' Beta remarked.

There were too many questions they didn't have the answers to yet.

'I wonder if more skeletons are going to turn up?' Beta pondered. She had the list of names Jakob had prepared in her hands. She kept folding one corner of the printout.

Hildur felt her nausea returning. Why couldn't the past leave her in peace? Every time she thought she'd settled accounts with some long-ago event, the next ghost appeared. Deep down, Hildur knew the grave was somehow associated with her past. Some instinct told her this case wasn't about bones that had been buried centuries before nor about coincidence.

'Not at that site, at least,' Jakob said.

One of the crime scene investigators had gone through the nearby terrain with a spade. In nearly every instance, the spade had struck volcanic rock at a depth of under half a metre. In their estimate, the area consisting of softer soil was about five metres by two metres. A closer survey of the terrain would no doubt be conducted at some later time, but at this point they had to go with the assumption that the yard at Kotsdalur was mostly rock and now clean of bodies.

Hildur thought back to her childhood. Grass had always grown on the slope behind the house. She hadn't known there was rock so close to the surface. Nor had Rósa, who had ordered the excavator. She'd need dynamite if she wanted enough room for multiple septic tanks. Digging into the soil for wastewater pipes might be really difficult, if not impossible.

'If we go with the assumption that the bodies are those of foreigners, why have so few of them been reported missing?' Jakob asked.

Hildur thought she might know the answer. 'Foreigners are more invisible. They usually live alone or in shared apartments where people are always coming and going. There aren't any relatives or long-term coworkers or teammates or friends who'd notice if someone was missing from the group. You can also use invisibility to your advantage if you really want to disappear.'

Hildur explained about the meetings she'd had with the heads of the Reykjavík police and the capital's fire and rescue unit over the last year to discuss suicide tourists. There weren't many, at most a few a year, but they kept volunteer rescuers busy.

'You mean they come to Iceland to die?' Jakob asked.

Hildur confirmed that this was exactly what she meant. 'Iceland is a surprisingly big country; disappearing here is easy. Some people want to commit suicide without their loved ones knowing what really happened. Disappearing in nature feels more merciful.'

For a moment no one spoke. Hildur rose to her feet and walked over to the window. The meeting had gone on so long that her focus was no longer at its sharpest. Gazing out over the familiar landscape was soothing. The mountains rose skyward, scraping the cloud layer, the sea pressed the land down.

Suddenly, a thought occurred to her: 'What's the date today?'

Chapter 41

The walk from the meeting to the pharmacy and from the pharmacy home had felt incredibly long, even though Hildur had made the whole trip at a semi-run. As she jogged down the summery street to her front door, she thought about what Helga had said about Rakel valuing her independence. Hildur could identify with her mother. But how could one hold on to one's independence and yet be bound to someone else for decades? Maybe Rakel had never wanted children. Maybe the three of them had come into the world by accident. Maybe that was why her mother had been so unhappy. Maybe she'd been living a life she didn't want to live. Hildur felt a deep yearning to discuss all this with Helga, but now it was too late.

Suddenly, she'd seen the past two months in a different light. The old athletic top that was too small hadn't shrunk in the wash. She'd grown. But she hadn't paid much attention to the change. Due to lacklustre surfing conditions, she got less exercise in the summer than in the winter. But she ate the same amount year-round. She always ate whatever she wanted. Putting on weight in the summer had been totally normal for her.

Hildur pulled out the small cardboard box that tore easily in half. She read the instructions, lifted the lid of the toilet seat, dropped her sweaty trousers, and tried to aim for the stick. Then she washed her fingers and waited.

Time was a mercy. Nothing ever stayed completely the same. Time swept away just about everything. Except life being good and easy, but also it being bad and hard. Just now the minutes felt like they were dragging. Hildur placed her hands on the floor and sprang onto her arms, feet against the bathroom door. She knocked out ten handstand push-ups, no problem. After four sets, she glanced at her watch again. And then the white stick. Time was up.

She didn't have to reread the instructions. She knew. Two lines.

What sort of swan song was this, supposedly? She was over forty. Besides, she'd used contraception. And Anton had said he couldn't have children. He'd tried for years with his late wife, in vain.

The astonishment made way for a surge of panic. Hildur felt like she was losing control. It hurt. Her pulse accelerated, her hands began to sweat. Too many thoughts were pushing their way into her consciousness all at once. Hildur leaned her head against the bathroom wall and tried to digest what she'd just learned.

She'd never wanted a spouse or children. Hildur listed all the curse words that came to mind, stepped on the wastebasket pedal to open it, and dropped in the stick and the box. She had to wrangle her feelings, reassert control over them. That was her way of bearing responsibility. Nothing was going to change right this instant, so at least for the moment she meant to forget the whole thing. She would worry about it when the ongoing investigations had been resolved. Clinging to the safety that thought entailed pushed the panic into the background and calmed her. She briefly considered texting Anton. But the impulse passed so fast she didn't even have time to look for her phone.

It was better that way. This was her decision.

Chapter 42

Hildur and Jakob had spent the morning at the nursing home, speaking to all the residents one by one. Hildur had been her usual professional self during the interviews, but when she and Jakob had been alone, she'd been unusually subdued. On the walk back to the station, Jakob asked Hildur why her energy seemed so low. Hildur grunted a one-syllable response, the meaning of which remained open to interpretation.

Jakob glanced in both directions and started across the crosswalk. A Toyota Corolla turned from the roundabout toward them at a dangerous speed. There was a screech as the driver slammed the brakes. A thumping bass boomed from the car. The driver gave an apologetic smile and waved at the pedestrians. Jakob shot the driver a warning glance for not using his signal when he exited the traffic circle. But Jakob didn't think it was necessary to write a ticket or give him a warning. He and Hildur were in a hurry to get back to the station to work.

Jakob glanced at his phone. He had yet to read the message that had arrived from Kaisa a couple of hours before. Seeing the accusatory tone of the first couple of lines – *it's nearly midsummer and you won't even reply* – was enough. He deleted the message without reading it. Swiping the red trash can icon felt good. *This must be what it's like to set boundaries*, he thought to himself.

'A chocolate bun for your thoughts. Two if they turn out to be a good lead,' Jakob said to Hildur, slipping his phone back into the breast pocket of his coat. They had reached the street-level door of the station building. Had something happened during their gig that Hildur didn't want to talk about? 'Did something happen at the nursing home?' he continued.

Hildur pulled her braid over her shoulder and looked sternly at Jakob. 'It's nothing. It'll pass.'

Jakob made his way straight to the break room to make them coffee. He took two chocolate-covered buns from his satchel and placed them on a tray.

'You get your bun anyway,' Jakob said, setting the tray down on the desk.

His next task was looking up the phone numbers for the embassies and tracking down more information on the Spanish woman and Polish man who'd gone missing in Iceland.

Hildur appeared to be engrossed in her notes. After a good hour of silence, she pushed her chair back from her desk and stretched her arms.

'Those Finnish nurses who were serial killers . . . How did they get caught?' she asked.

Jakob looked up from his computer and took a moment to think back. He hadn't participated in the investigations. But the cases had been discussed in class during his law enforcement studies, and he'd followed the stories on the news.

'At least in two instances, the suspicions of the victims' family members prompted the police to investigate. More cases and more victims came out over the course of the investigation,' Jakob said.

'So without active family members, the crimes wouldn't have been discovered?' Hildur confirmed.

Jakob wasn't sure, but he didn't think it was impossible. Death was such a constant presence under hospital conditions and in nursing homes that the possibility of a homicide didn't automatically come to mind. Especially if the body showed no signs of violence.

'Today the residents were interested in talking about how dirty the windows are, politics, the rising cost of drugs, whether the morning coffee should be a light roast or dark roast, and relatives who never come to visit anymore,' Hildur said.

Jakob listened to Hildur's report. The residents had wanted someone to talk to, and when Hildur had focused on each of them individually without any hurry, she'd heard a great deal.

'All sorts of things have gone missing, but no one remembers when,' Hildur said and sighed.

Cash had disappeared, but the sums were pretty small. That made sense, because cash wasn't used much. The entire country paid for purchases with credit cards, and asking for extensions on credit card payment deadlines was by no means unheard of.

'What about valuables?' Jakob asked.

Hildur read from her notes: 'Three wedding rings, two gold necklaces, one Rolex watch, a couple of Iceland-made Gilbert watches, and a few small pieces of glass art that could be classified as designer objects.'

Jakob quietly calculated the value of the missing objects. By now they were talking about big sums, at least tens of thousands of euros. It could be the work of an organised crew of thieves. Valuable watches in particular had fast-moving resale markets.

'Why didn't they remember the missing objects the first time you asked?' Jakob wondered.

Hildur grunted. She figured she was to blame. The first time, she'd asked the elderly residents whether they'd *recently* lost any valuables or money. 'I wasn't patient enough. No one had lost anything recently. I took what I heard at face value and moved on. I should have dug deeper and listened better.'

Jakob appreciated his colleague's self-reflection.

'Maybe the sticky fingers belong to one of the nursing home employees,' Hildur continued. 'Opportunity makes a thief.'

Jakob nodded. That wasn't at all impossible. 'Should we call through the residents' family members just to be sure and ask them about the missing items? We'd get precise details to enter into the database,' he mused out loud.

Hildur looked at her computer screen and rapped her desktop with her short nails. 'I was thinking the same thing. But I have to get to the gym first. Otherwise my head is going to explode.'

Chapter 43

Hildur finished the drinkable skyr she'd taken from the gym fridge, tossed the carboard carton in the trash, and went into the locker room. She changed into her workout gear and flat, rigid-soled weightlifting shoes.

The gym had been renovated from an old dairy. The small windows high up in the wall didn't allow much daylight in. That was perfectly fine with Hildur.

As always, she jumped rope to warm up. A hundred simple jumps followed by two minutes of double-unders. When the rope travelled underfoot twice during a single jump, the pulse rose and the lungs got to work. After three sets, that morning's fatigue was nothing but a faded memory.

Hildur noticed a familiar figure. She generally didn't want to talk to anyone at the gym, but today she was delighted to see her old schoolmate, Selma. A few years had passed since they'd run into each other, even though they both lived in the Westfjords.

'I haven't seen you for ages,' Hildur said.

Selma had on a sleeveless athletic top, a generous dash of freckles, and two short pigtails. She recognised Hildur immediately too.

'I'm going camping with the women from the farming association. Our boat to the nature reserve leaves in a couple of hours. I decided I had time to get a workout in before we sail,' Selma said, launching into an enthusiastic description of the five-day hike she was about to embark on. She owned a big sheep farm in the southernmost Westfjords that she'd inherited from her parents.

'Will Greipur be watching the place while you're gone?' Hildur asked. She remembered she'd often heard local farmers complaining how hard it was to get substitute farmers out to the Westfjords.

Selma shook her head. 'My cousins came to help. Things with Greipur didn't work out.'

Hildur remembered Selma had met Greipur in the stands at an Icelandic horse competition, and the two of them had fallen in love. But Greipur owned a sheep farm in southern Iceland. Due to scrapie, a disease that bedevilled sheep farms, Icelandic law didn't allow sheep to be moved from one county to another. The incubation period of the slowly advancing affliction of the central nervous system was at least two years. Humans didn't catch scrapie, but it was very contagious among sheep. It was possible to contract the infection from a pasture years after sick animals had been present. If a single sheep were determined to have scrapie, all the sheep in the vicinity had to be slaughtered and their carcasses destroyed. The sheep barns were disinfected and the pastures were banned from use. Scrapie was a sheep farmer's number-one nightmare, because it nearly always meant the ruin of one's life work.

'In the end, neither one of us was willing to give up our sheep,' Selma said, explaining the break-up, adjusting the barbell to the optimal height. A few years had passed since the break-up. 'I don't know if the decision to split was a hard one, but at least it was ours.'

Hildur reflected that if Selma and Greipur lived in the same country and the distance had proved too great, the distance between her and Anton was impossible. She and Selma exchanged a few more words about their plans for the upcoming summer before moving on to their workouts.

After some quick, short stretches, Hildur set the bar at trap-lifting level. Bringing her elbows into her ribs helped the upper back muscles support the movement. She did the first set with the twenty-kilo bar, no weights. Hildur planted her feet at shoulder width, turned her feet slightly outward, and drew her lungs full of air to establish solid support in her core.

After the first couple of sets, Hildur added weights to the bar. Ten reps with fifty kilograms, then eight reps with seventy kilograms. Sweat began to trickle from her forehead to her throat and chest. When there was ninety kilograms on the bar, she did two sets of five reps. She used the big mirror across from her to check her form. After returning the bar to the rack, Hildur glanced at her midsection in profile. She wasn't sure why she looked, because of course nothing was visible yet.

While she was working out, the assistant from the police station, Kata Leósdóttir, had pulled up the contact information for the family members of the nursing home residents and sent it to Hildur. Each name and number was neatly listed on its own line. *Kata rocks*, Hildur thought in satisfaction and sent a quick reply, thanking Kata for the list of names and asking her to check one more detail.

First Hildur called the oldest son of a resident who'd lost their wedding ring. The man answered, out of breath, from the treadmill. Hildur quickly briefed him on the details of the case but mentioned nothing about the investigation into Helga's death.

The son's story confirmed what his elderly parent had said. A wide, solid gold ring had disappeared a couple of months before. The next couple of calls followed the same pattern. Hildur was able to confirm details about the missing items, and the story she heard from family members was similar in other ways: they'd all noted the valuable missing during their most recent visit, which had been anywhere from a few weeks to a couple of months earlier.

None of the family members had initially considered the possibility of theft. They were sure their parent had misplaced the items in question. Most Icelanders lived a safe, secure existence, and disturbances like theft felt very distant. Hildur hadn't wanted to fan the flames of fear, and so she'd played along and agreed it could well be a matter of forgetfulness or carelessness.

Hildur turned to the last number on the list. Reykjavík resident Hinrik Rökkvason answered the phone quickly with his whole name and asked in the same breath what the call was about. *Busy guy*, Hildur thought to herself, and repeated the now-familiar spiel about the theft at the nursing home. His father, Rökkvi, had lost a valuable Rolex watch.

'Rökkvi couldn't remember the watch model off the top of his head. Do you happen to remember? We're trying to catalogue the missing items as precisely as possible so—'

Hinrik didn't let Hildur finish, interrupting rudely instead: 'I don't have time for this.'

Hildur tried again: 'This won't take long, I just need—'

'I have a company to run, half my workers are on strike, and I have a mountain of other problems waiting on my desk. Can you call back some other time?' Hinrik said and hung up.

Hildur snorted. Now that was strange, that the loss of a watch worth millions of krónur wasn't of interest. Hinrik either had too much money or too little sense.

As she returned the phone to her pocket, she noticed a new email in her inbox. Kata had already looked into the matter Hildur had asked her to. The contents of the email made Hildur's eyebrows rise. Her instincts had been right on the money.

Chapter 44

Hildur left her gym bag in the car parked outside the station and continued through town on foot toward Urðarvegur, one of the streets on the hill. The nursing home had said Jódís had the day off today.

Hildur had no trouble finding the right rowhouse. There was a bicycle and a car parked outside, but no one answered when she rang the bell. Hildur circled around to the back. It was such a warm, beautiful day that people were spending it outside. The spacious yards were protected from the wind and had been planted with flowers. Outdoor kitchens had been built, hot tubs installed.

Hildur noticed Jódís crouching on the grass. She was uprooting dandelions with a small hoe and tossing them into a wheelbarrow. Apparently, she registered Hildur's arrival, because she stopped working and stood. She placed a hand on her lower back and arched her body backward.

'I've got back pain. But I can't leave these dandelions here.'

Jódís set the trowel in the wheelbarrow and wiped her hands on her trousers. She looked questioningly at Hildur.

The pale strip on her left ring finger was still visible.

'You're married, aren't you?'

Jódís didn't seem fazed by the question. She took hold of the trowel again and began working on the next dandelion. 'Is that why you're here?'

'At first, I thought you were divorced, because you're not wearing a wedding ring. You knew we were investigating possible thefts at the nursing home. Why didn't you say you don't have the ring anymore?'

The hoe sank into the soil. Jódís didn't look at Hildur as she answered. 'I took it off when I was washing my hands. Then it just . . . Well, it just disappeared. That was a few weeks ago.'

Hildur had been expecting something like this. But why hadn't Jódís said anything about the missing ring before?

Jódís tossed the dandelion and a bit of root into the wheelbarrow and turned her attention to digging up the next one. She seemed to grasp what Hildur was thinking.

'It's because of my husband,' Jódís said, eyes locked on her work.

'Aron?' Hildur asked. The nursing home nurse was married to the hospital's head of security, Aron.

Jódís nodded. Hildur had just received confirmation that Aron and Jódís had been married for several years.

'He's, um . . .' Jódís searched for the words, 'he's a little short-tempered. He gets angry if I lose things. That's why I didn't want to say anything to him.'

Jódís looked from the hoe to Hildur and blinked a couple of extra times. 'That's how it is when you're married for a long time. You know what topics to leave alone if you want to keep the peace.'

Hildur had no comment on this. She simply asked if Jódís wanted to report the ring missing. Jódís shook her head. There was nothing else for Hildur to do, so she said goodbye and wished Jódís a nice day.

Hildur thought about Aron. He'd seemed calm and easy-going. But the conversation with Jódís had demonstrated how hard it was to say from the outside what people carried inside. She reflected that Aron had seemed maybe even a little too relaxed.

She turned from the path into the front yard and was just stepping onto the pavement when she heard noise behind her. The garage door opened, and Aron stepped out, toolbox in his hand.

'You're that police officer. What has Jódís done now?'

Hildur returned to the garage and shook hands with Aron. 'I just came by to check a detail about the nursing home,' she answered, dodging the question.

Aron narrowed his eyes and looked suspiciously at Hildur. 'Does this have anything to do with her financial troubles?'

The question caught Hildur off guard. This was something she had not expected. 'Why would you ask that?'

Aron lowered the toolbox to the garage floor and crossed his arms. His sigh blew through the long curls framing his face. 'Because she has money problems she refuses to deal with.'

Hildur thought back to the summary Kata had sent her. There hadn't been any mention of payment issues or collections. As Hildur remembered, Jódís had a clean credit record.

'Because I've saved her multiple times,' Aron said with a dry laugh. He said he'd taken on some of her debt in his own name, and the sum had grown to the point that paying the interest alone was getting unmanageable. 'I always take any overtime available. And I do renovation gigs on my days off,' he added, nudging the toolbox with the tip of his shoe.

Hildur said her visit didn't have anything to do with debt: 'Just a routine query.'

And then she smiled warmly at Aron.

Chapter 45

Hildur could still feel yesterday's workout as a state of physical calm. The visit with Jódís had instilled in her a fresh faith that she wasn't losing her grip. It was too soon to say how things would eventually turn out with Jódís. Hildur had to confirm a few more things before it was time to draw any definitive conclusions.

Nevertheless, Hildur was most troubled by Manuel. Her desire to help the young man wouldn't leave her in peace. Manuel had become an obsession of sorts for her. And Hildur believed she'd come up with a solution during the hours she'd lain awake the night before. She wasn't sure it would work, but it was worth trying, because there was no other option. She had just communicated to Manuel through Andri that he should stay at the cabin and maintain a low profile.

The *Diamond Adventure of the Seas* had pulled into Ísafjörður that morning. Hildur had asked the police patrol on duty to keep an eye on traffic at the hospital junction all day. It was a spot where people tended to ignore the speed limits and right-of-way indicators, and a police car was a familiar sight there. But Hildur's real reason was a patrol car near the hospital might scare off any potential spies from the ship.

After a morning coffee and a cheese sandwich, Hildur dressed for the weather and set out for the harbour. Bluish smoke rose from the funnel of the docked vessel, and since there wasn't much wind, the trail of fumes hung over the centre of town.

The cloud of emissions looked grotesque against the green mountain slope and the sea's placid surface.

Hildur had never thought of herself as a particularly political person. She voted if she remembered there was an election.

All Hildur wanted was to do her work as well as possible. It wasn't acceptable to look past anyone when one should have looked straight at them, for good or for ill.

After what Manuel had told her about the events on the cruise ship, Hildur hadn't been able to look away. She'd left her police ID at home that morning, because she was acting of her own accord now. Luckily, she'd taken guitar lessons at the local music school and bought herself an acoustic guitar back in the day. Hopefully they would come in handy today.

Hildur stopped at the gate controlling access to the vessel. A straight-backed young man stood there with a hard-backed folder, monitoring disembarking and returning passengers. He looked at Hildur quizzically from behind his glasses. Hildur unzipped her leather jacket a little. She was going to have to rely on her charms.

'I'm from the band,' she said, holding up her guitar case. 'We're playing in an hour.'

Manuel had said local entertainment was provided in the mornings for those passengers who didn't want to leave the ship for whatever reason. The entertainment always followed the same schedule: a magician performed in Akureyri; a local band played in Ísafjörður.

'I'm a little late. Everyone else is already here, but silly me, I forgot my guitar. I had to go get it. So here I am!'

A coy, slightly helpless smile was usually all the diversion that was required.

'What did you say your name was again?' the young man asked, opening the folder.

Hildur knew everyone who boarded the ship was monitored. The passengers had credit-card-sized cabin keys that also served as payment cards on board and had to be flashed at the gate when disembarking and returning to the boat. All other visitors needed to register beforehand, and their name and phone number had to appear on the list.

'Elín Elíasdóttir. My artistic name is Evil Elín. I'm not sure which one the guys gave. The name of the band is Wild Runners.'

Hildur eyed the man standing before her. Starched trousers, polished leather shoes. A sports watch at his wrist.

'Do you ever get to spend any free time on land? There are gorgeous running paths here in the fjord. If you turn right once you leave the harbour and circle around to that mountain you see overlooking the town, the views are . . .' Hildur kissed her pinched fingers to underscore how gorgeous the views were.

The man lost his grip, and the folder dropped to the floor. Hildur bent down to pick it up. She stepped in closer and slipped the folder into his hand. Then she laughed helplessly: 'I'm filling in for the usual guitarist. He's going through a terrible marriage crisis. The idiot went and screwed his wife's cousin, got caught, and hasn't been able to play since. The guys called me last week. Luckily, I was free to step in at the last minute. I've already been here twice. I know my way around.'

The young man opened the folder, flipped through the pages and shook his head. 'I don't see any Evil Elín here. But your band . . . the other members boarded a second ago. And there's not anyone here I could check with.' He looked around hopelessly.

Hildur glanced at her own sports watch. 'I probably need to get to the stage or I'm going to be in trouble and there'll be another crisis. We're on in half an hour.'

The young man pressed a button, and the red light at the side of the gate turned green. 'OK, just go.' He nodded at Hildur like she'd better hurry before he changed his mind.

Hildur stepped through the gate and right up to the security check. Her guitar and full tote bag were X-rayed for blades or other prohibited objects.

'It's on Deck 7,' the young man said as he handed Hildur her guitar and tote.

Hildur gave him a helpless smile. 'I thought the music bar was on Deck 8?'

The man winked at her. 'I know. I was just testing you.'

Hildur waved, hiked the guitar case onto her shoulder, and headed for the stairs.

The band would play for a good hour, and Hildur would have time to snoop around for the duration of the set.

Manuel had given her a lot of useful information. First, Hildur looked for a certain little-used restroom. It had an unlocked cabinet used to store toilet paper. The cabinet was exactly where Manuel had said it would be. Hildur took the turtleneck she'd folded up and stashed in her jacket pocket and slipped it over her thin top. Then she shoved the guitar and tote into the toilet paper cabinet for safekeeping.

Hildur pulled the hem of her turtleneck straight and tied her unruly hair into a ponytail. She took a paper towel, dampened it under the tap, and wiped off her lipstick.

She would start from the lowest desk, where most of the ship's maintenance areas were located. Manuel had explained that ordinary crew members didn't care who they saw moving around down there. Presumably the only people who would ask any questions were the managers in more formal uniforms. For any tricky situations, Hildur had a story ready: she was an aide for travellers with limited mobility and had boarded that morning to help wheelchair-bound passengers. She was afraid she'd lost her little purse in the crush.

A pleasant if somewhat artificial floral scent wafted through the common areas of the vessel. Soothing elevator music played from the speakers. The windows were spotless, the carpet felt soft underfoot. Near the elevators she found gold-framed information sheets announcing the day's schedule.

Hildur descended the stairs. On Deck 2, the carpet gave way to vinyl. The close air didn't smell of freshener but of sweat and grease. Pots were clattering, equipment was running. The air felt damp.

Hildur cracked the first wide door she came across, and hot, wet air slammed into her. She'd found the laundry. The gloomy space had an eerie ambiance. Big baskets of white bed linens waited, in a row, in the middle of the floor. Two dozen large washing machines were constantly churning through grime. The noise was deafening. The machines along the far wall looked like dryers.

Nothing in the room struck Hildur as interesting. She exited and shut the door behind her. The further she advanced down the corridor, the stronger the smell of grease grew.

She peered through the plastic panes in a pair of big double doors. At the rear of the kitchen, food was being sauteed under massive exhaust hoods. A few cooks were flipping food in pans. The equipment made so much noise that the cooks had to shout to be heard.

The centre of the big industrial kitchen was dominated by long tables, where twenty or so prep cooks were silently busying themselves. Hildur took a closer look and saw the men were chopping something. She found a better position behind the door and focused on observing.

Suddenly, an angry-looking man strode in briskly from the dishwashing bay. His nose was sunken into his face. This had to be the Frying Pan Face Manuel had mentioned. Frying Pan Face stopped at the workstation, waved his hands around aggressively and shouted something. Those toiling at the tables nodded, but no one said anything.

Suddenly, Hildur felt a touch at her shoulder. She jumped and spun around. A tall woman with her hair folded under a hairnet smiled at her in confusion.

'Madam, this deck is not for passengers. Madam, the elevators are at the end of the hall,' she said, pointing down the corridor. She was wearing a long grey apron dusted with white flour.

Hildur pretended to be lost. 'I was looking for a restaurant that was open. I must have misread the brochure.'

'The café is on Deck 10. Madam, take the elevator to the top deck. Press the button that has a one and a zero on it, and it will take you there.'

Hildur brought her hands together at her chest and bowed a couple of times, profusely thanking the woman for her assistance.

Hildur headed past the elevators toward the stairs. She wanted to walk the ship's corridors. The windowless cabins on Deck 3 were less expensive, and some were reserved for crew members. The deck was quiet. The staff were presumably asleep or at work, and most of the passengers were on land.

When she reached Deck 4, Hildur saw an open cabin door halfway down the corridor. Hildur walked slowly, ears tuned to the conversation carrying from within. She stopped a couple of metres before she reached the cabin, ostensibly to tie her laces.

She could make out three voices: those of one woman and two men. The woman was apparently from some Spanish-speaking country. Judging by the accents, the two men were from the Deep South of the United States. But she couldn't make out what the trio was talking about. Before long, the conversation ended and a curvy woman stepped out. She was a little older than Hildur and wore an orange knit dress. Hildur followed her. When they reached the elevators, Hildur pretended to study the information sheet. The other woman pulled a pack of cigarettes from her bag and opened the door leading to the deck. Hildur followed again. Before long, the woman was inhaling with relish, eyes half-shut.

'I'm sorry to bother you, but can I bum a cigarette? I left mine in the cabin and my family took my keycard by accident.'

The woman opened her eyes slightly and gave Hildur a lazy smile. 'You weren't interested in a bus tour of a sheep farm?'

Hildur shook her head. 'These small towns aren't my thing. I've had enough oohing and aahing over wooden barns.'

The woman's curls bounced from side to side as she chuckled. She pulled her cigarettes from her purse. 'It's not exactly Las Vegas,' she said, passing Hildur her lighter too.

It had been years since Hildur had smoked, but she could still puff credibly.

'Do you work here?' Hildur asked.

The woman nodded. 'I'm with the show.'

Hildur looked at her cigarette. It was half gone. She was going to have to pick up the pace. 'My mother paid for my trip so she'd have some company. I've been unemployed for a while and I've been trying to decide what to do with my life.' Hildur took a drag of her cigarette before she continued: 'It looks like a pretty international crew. Is it worth applying to work on board?'

Hildur registered the change in the woman's demeanour. She pulled back slightly from Hildur. The playful smile melted from her face. 'That's one mistake you don't want to make.'

'What do you mean?'

'You're pretty young and you're nice-looking too. This isn't the place for you. Believe me.'

The woman stubbed out her cigarette underfoot and kicked the butt into the sea. Then she gave Hildur a friendly clap on the shoulder and vanished into the bowels of the vessel.

Just when Hildur was about to return inside to continue looking around, someone grabbed her shoulder and pulled her back out to the deck. A hand in a black leather glove was covering her mouth, and her assailant's other hand was wrapped around her torso. She could barely breathe. Hildur didn't resist and tried to predict her assailant's movements so she could free herself, but it was in vain. Her usual techniques weren't of any use. Hildur couldn't even bend her head to see who was holding her, but she knew her assailant was male and clearly larger than she was. Hildur writhed from side to side and bit, but the glove was too thick.

'Who are you spying for?' a low male voice whispered in her ear. 'First at the harbour and now on board.'

Hildur couldn't speak. She settled for shaking her head.

'Don't lie. I know you're a police officer.'

Hildur felt panic welling up inside her. Her field of vision narrowed and blurred. It could have been lack of oxygen. Her body was arched backwards, which made it difficult for her to breathe through her nose.

The man continued whispering softly. His voice was cold, calm and determined, downright frightening. 'Listen to me. I'm only going to say this once. Get out of here. Now. Don't say a word to anyone else. Walk off this boat and never come back. Nod to let me know you understood, and I'll let go.' He tightened his grip as if to communicate he meant business.

Hildur didn't have a choice. She attempted a nod.

The man loosened his grip enough for Hildur to be able to stand on her own two feet. She steadied herself and tried to move her hands. But the man behind her was still holding her arms.

In an even more aggressive tone, he whispered: 'I'll be calling you.'

Chapter 46

8 November

Hey!

Why didn't you answer my last letter? Are you angry?

Are you mad about Railway Street? I had to work the port. I had to make more money than I could earn dealing. The men are at sea for weeks and when they come ashore they have needs. I made more in a few months than I used to earn in a year.

Then one night everything changed. It was lovely from the moment we met. A handsome man wanted to talk to me and promised to take me off the street. He promised me a better life.

Things are looking up, and it feels good.

I have big dreams. I want to change the direction of my life. I hope you understand. Maybe I'm being childish, but I think I can do it. That's why I left without saying anything to anyone. I didn't look back when I left, but maybe I should have talked to you first.

My address is on the back.

R.

Chapter 47

Ísafjörður, June 2022

The steps from the downstairs doors up to the second-storey station felt heavy. Hildur stopped halfway to take a breath. She tried to focus. The sense of helplessness had thrown her off. No one had ever caught her unawares the way the man on the ship just had. Why hadn't she been able to overpower him? Her impotence irritated her, but she refused to regret boarding the ship in an attempt to find evidence on Manuel's behalf. She never regretted anything she'd done with good intentions. Hildur climbed the final stairs and made her way to her office.

Jakob was engrossed in studying the papers in front of him and knitting.

'I have to tell you something. In confidence. You can't tell Beta.'

Jakob stopped knitting. 'You look like you just murdered someone. Is everything OK?'

Hildur told Jakob about her visit to the ship. He looked at her across the desk.

'You must think I'm totally crazy,' she added.

Jakob laughed. 'I'm afraid of you.'

'I had to. I had no choice,' Hildur said.

Jakob swore he had no idea what Hildur had been up to that morning, even if someone threatened to rip his arm off. Besides, her assailant might call later, as he'd promised.

'If I get us some coffee, does Double O Ísafjörður want hers shaken or stirred?' Jakob asked, eliciting a laugh from Hildur.

He headed to the break room and Hildur started up her computer. Jakob's company had put her in a good mood.

Hildur turned on the radio and closed her eyes. She always tuned into the national public radio station. The show began with organ music in a minor key. The radio announcer spoke softly, indicating the time was 11.55 a.m. and the obituaries would be read next. Hildur turned up the volume a little. Aside from the marine weather forecast, the obituaries and announcements of upcoming funerals were her favourite broadcast. Family members sent the information to public radio station 1, where they were read twice a day on weekdays and once a day on weekends and holidays.

'Beloved mother, mother-in-law, grandmother, and great-grandmother, former home economics teacher Hringbrautilta Lilja Heimirsdóttir died at home on 10 June. A memorial service will be held at Húsavík church on 25 June at 1 p.m. She is survived by Birgir, Lóa, Gunnar, and Gunnar's children and grandchildren.'

Today the obituary broadcast was brief: only four were read. While listening to the programme, Hildur realised she would have to write an obituary for Helga and send it in to Radio 1. She'd been the only one close to Helga, and she knew Helga had listened to this same show. In addition to the radio broadcast, the newspaper *Morgunblaðið* published longer obituaries. The multi-page death notice appendixes were the most popular section of the dying print media. Many older people continued to order the print version of the paper just for them. It was natural, she supposed, that as one's own death approached one's interest in the deaths of others grew too.

Hildur emerged from her reverie when she heard voices. Beta and Jakob were chatting in the corridor.

'Chipper mood in here,' Beta said from the doorway.

Hildur grunted and turned off the radio.

Beta took off her summer coat and moved the stack of folders from a chair to the floor. 'Any updates?' she asked, sitting down.

Jakob set the coffee cups on the edge of the desk.

Hildur said she'd looked into the background of the nursing home nurses. 'Jódís has one speeding ticket and the Polish cleaning guy has a few. That's it. None of them are related to Helga, and there's no official indication any of the staff are having money problems.'

She tightened the scrunchie holding her braid and reported on her visit to Jódís's home. 'So it's not evident from official sources, but it seems Jódís might be having financial difficulties,' Hildur said, concluding with what Aron had told her.

'Might that have motivated her to . . .' Beta didn't finish the sentence.

Jódís had been in Helga's room several times a day. That explained the fingerprints.

Hildur was frustrated Helga's bed linen had been immediately put in the wash. The used pillowcase would have been a potential source of saliva traces or fibres from the clothes worn by the perp.

'Maybe the motive wasn't money but shame,' Hildur said.

Jakob picked up the thought: 'If Jódís is stealing from the residents, Helga realised it and was on the verge of exposing her?'

Beta thought it was plausible.

Hildur said she'd checked the CCTV footage to make sure Manuel hadn't been wearing gloves when he was recorded in the passageway. He hadn't. The security cameras also showed that no outsiders had entered or exited the hospital the night Helga died.

'I'll go through Jódís's finances with a fine-tooth comb. That might get us somewhere,' Hildur concluded. She then moved on to Katla's reticence.

Katla was the only resident who'd refused to talk to Hildur. She kept repeating she didn't want to talk to visitors and none of her belongings were missing. Because Katla didn't have any living relatives, there was no way to check whether this was true.

Beta and Jakob listened attentively to Hildur's ponderings. 'Try to talk to her one more time. It's often the thing that's left unsaid that ends up being the most important,' Beta said.

Jakob coughed to draw attention to himself. He turned his computer screen toward Beta and asked Hildur to come closer.

'Although we're not sure whether the nursing home thefts are related to the cabin break-ins, you two ought to see this.'

One of the cabin owners had been in touch with Jakob that morning. Jakob said he'd tried to contact the guy before, with no luck. Apparently, he'd been camping in a location without network coverage. His cabin was in Álftafjörður, about twenty kilometres or so from the centre of Ísafjörður. His neighbour's cabin had been broken into in May, after which this man had installed a surveillance camera outside his own cabin.

'It recorded an unidentified car driving onto the property.'

'Well, well,' Hildur said, enthusiasm in her voice. Beta drew her chair closer.

Jakob clicked play. All the first couple of minutes of video showed were blue sky and some shrubs dancing in the breeze. Then a car entered the image, a white Toyota Yaris. The camera had been installed so close to the ground that only part of the car was visible. The car drove slowly into the yard and apparently parked there.

Hildur brought up the map software and entered the address. 'The private road ends at the cabin, and there are no other buildings on the road,' she said. 'The car couldn't have been just passing by.'

About thirty minutes later, the camera had activated again as the car drove past in the other direction. Once again, the camera angle was such that the police officers couldn't see any of the people in the car or even how many people that might have been.

'But the licence plate is clearly visible,' Jakob said, pausing the video at the relevant spot.

The combination of letters and numbers was registered to an international car rental agency. 'They have an office here in Ísafjörður. I've already asked them for information on who rented it. I'll be getting it today.'

Hildur saw the satisfaction beaming from Jakob's face.

Just then, her phone rang. The number began +49, which meant it was foreign. Hildur couldn't remember which country code was +49.

She answered with her whole name. A minute or so later, the call ended.

Hildur took the lightweight sweater from the back of her chair and pulled it on. 'I have to go and deal with something. I'll be right back.'

Chapter 48

5 February
Hey!
I want to see the look on your face when you read this letter. Maybe you'll smile. Even a little. How are you? Hopefully things are going well. Write to me. I want to hear about you and life back home. I've had some hard days lately, but some OK ones too. I think things will turn out OK. I've been really tired. Some things have happened that have started to affect me. Anytime I have a moment to myself I just lie in bed.

I've been thinking people aren't as nice as they pretend to be at first. In the end, everyone wants something from you. I thought my boyfriend loved me, but he had ulterior motives. I don't want to stand near him during smoke breaks anymore. I've started seeing sides of him I can't love.

Something that happened at the factory has been weighing on me. One night we were woken up at four thirty in the morning. There was nothing unusual about that. The boat pulled into harbour a couple of hours early. Everyone here knows the drill. When the boat comes in, work starts. The passage of our days is determined by trawlers.

The plant is split into two levels. The men are on the first line, because the work is hard. My job is gutting fish. It's smelly work, women's work.

One of the Polish workers has been tired for a long time. And when you're tired, you get cold faster. This morning, he was taking little steps to keep himself warm. He was learning how to use this expensive new machine they want to bring in next spring. It's supposed to cut the processing time by a few seconds for each fish.

Suddenly, there was this loud screech and the line stopped. At first, I thought some plastic or garbage from the sea had caught in the machine. I didn't see what happened, but all of a sudden the Polish guy was screaming . . . Then he stood up straight and I saw his hand was cut off. Blood was spraying from his wrist like water from a garden hose.

The boss ran over to him from his cubicle. People rushed over to help. They shut down the line for the rest of the day until the mess was cleaned up.

We never saw the Polish guy again. I'm afraid.

I'll put my address on the other side again. Mail is only delivered twice a week here. So twice a week I'm anxiously waiting to hear from you, but I'm not holding my breath anymore. I've lost hope.

You mean a lot to me.

R.

Chapter 49

Ísafjörður, June 2022

Hildur walked into the hotel restaurant and realised it was being refurbished. She'd heard about the hotel's planned renovations but hadn't imagined the changes would be on this scale. An extension of a few dozen square metres had been added to the ground floor, windows facing the sea. The décor reminded her of the cute Danish place where she'd stayed during an international police seminar a year earlier.

She ordered a coffee and a croissant and took a seat at a window table with a view of the mountains. There were no other customers. The guests had finished their breakfasts hours before, and even lunch was over by now.

Hildur checked the wave forecast from her phone and decided there was nothing there to see. Summer was an incredibly dull period for surfers in Iceland. Storms were few and weak.

Just then she sensed something at her shoulder. She whirled around so fast she set the table rocking and almost toppled her coffee.

She saw a tall man with short, thick charcoal hair, grey stubble and high eyebrows.

'Max Meyer,' he said, extending a hand. Hildur shook it. 'You must be Mrs Hildur Rúnarsdóttir?'

'Yes. But it's Ms.'

For a split second, Hildur wondered whether it would have been more polite to stand while shaking hands. She never did with Icelanders, because Icelanders only actually had one etiquette rule – take off your shoes before entering a home. She always felt a little unsure of herself with Central Europeans.

Max glanced at the bar and flagged down the server.

Hildur thought a mild correction was due: 'There's no table service here. You have to order at the counter.'

Max laughed and said he'd be right back. Hildur realised he reminded her of Matt Damon. When Max smiled, you could see his upper and lower teeth without it seeming forced.

Hildur had spent a few intense days with Matt Damon on the southern coast of Iceland a decade before, when she'd served as security on a movie set. An acquaintance who worked for the film company had coaxed her to join the production for the duration of the glacier shoot, because Hildur had completed rescue classes and knew how to deal with glacier conditions. Hildur had been responsible for Damon's safety.

'Thank you for making the time. I don't have much myself, so I'll get right to the point,' Max said, seating himself across from Hildur. He spoke English with a German accent. His gaze was stern and penetrating. 'I know you work as a criminal investigator. And what was your other title, something about missing children . . .'

Hildur said she was the only detective in the Westfjords and served as a liaison between child protective services and local law enforcement when it came to missing children, mostly adolescents.

'A lot of juvenile criminality has been prevented in Reykjavík through intense cooperation between child protective services and the police. I coordinate those activities in the rest of the country. It mostly involves trying to convince adolescents to stay in their foster homes and catching up to anyone who runs away as quickly as we can, to protect them from abusers.'

Max listened attentively.

'I'm assuming you didn't just want to talk about my job,' Hildur said.

'As I told you over the phone, I'm in the same field that you are. For the past few years I've been working as a criminal investigator for Interpol France. I'm on undercover assignment. You've been hanging around the harbour and somehow managed to talk your way on board. I don't know what you're up to, but you need to stop snooping around.' Max's words were friendly, but his tone was firm. The request left no room for debate. 'Believe me. It's very important.'

'Why?'

Max didn't reply. He just shook his head.

Hildur felt her chin quiver. No outsider was going to come here and tell her how to do her job. 'You've got some nerve, asking me for a favour without giving me any information other than your name.'

'There's nothing more I can tell you.'

Hildur slid her coffee cup away and lowered her elbows to the table. 'I'm going to do what I want to do and what has to be done.'

The work stress that had accumulated over the past couple of weeks had generated pressure in the cooker, and Hildur let it all out.

'I don't have time for this! I have a bunch of skeletons waiting to be identified, an old woman who died in unclear circumstances, and a half-dead Venezuelan who's so afraid he'd do anything not to return to that cruise ship. And you invite me for a cup of coffee to tell me what I can and can't do on the job. That's not going to fly.'

She drained her cup and stood. She'd had enough.

Max's jaw dropped slightly, and a crack formed in the well-groomed, gentlemanly façade. He gestured for Hildur to sit back down and apologised for his choice of words.

Then he let loose with a barrage of questions: 'What did you say about the Venezuelan? Is that what you're investigating? Do you know his whereabouts?'

'You show me yours, I'll show you mine,' Hildur said, sitting down slowly enough to give the impression she could change her mind at any moment and stomp out the door.

Max rubbed his temples and glanced out the window. The sky was still bright blue. A couple of ravens were strutting across the hotel lawn. Then Max launched into an explanation of his role at Interpol.

Hildur was relatively familiar with the organisation. Interpol facilitated cooperation among law enforcement agencies from two hundred member nations. It was headquartered in Lyon, France. A couple of Icelandic criminal investigator colleagues were currently working there in the financial crimes unit. The other units were anti-terrorism, cybercrime, and organised crime. Every member state, including Iceland, had a national Interpol office. Interpol didn't have a police force of its own; the organisation was primarily concerned with acquiring and communicating information and comparing intelligence.

'I work for the German Federal Criminal Police, the BKA, in their organised crime department. I wanted a little change before I retired and applied to Lyon.'

Max gave a brief summary of his work at the BKA. He'd spent the last five years focusing exclusively on crime related to international cruise-ship tourism.

'It's an extremely difficult area. All sorts of overlapping national legislation, convoluted corporate structures. Every time we're on the verge of catching hold of some strand, it slips through our fingers. Criminal outfits are skilled at exploiting the complex legal status of cruise ships sailing in international waters.'

Hildur listened with interest and without interrupting. No other customers had come in, and the only employee was so far away there was no way she could hear the conversation. Max said he was currently working undercover on cruise ships, acquiring information and reporting essential intelligence onward.

'Tell me about the Venezuelan,' Max said. 'I believe his name is Manuel. A kitchen worker of that name has been missing for days. At first, they thought he jumped overboard. A lot of desperate people do. But then someone began to suspect maybe he'd disembarked. I just went to the hospital and discovered he's no longer there. Where is he?'

Hildur took a moment to think. How on earth could Max get information about a patient without being a family member? And if Max knew Manuel was hiding out, who else did?

Max seemed to read her thoughts. 'I've been hunting international terrorists for half my life. Finding out the information on one patient in a small-town hospital didn't take long.'

Max had done a lot of talking, so Hildur decided to give him something in the name of reciprocity. 'Manuel's staying with a friend and doesn't plan on returning to the boat.'

Max looked horrified. 'If anyone hears he's alive and the police have spoken with him, our entire investigation could be at risk.'

Hildur asked Max to be more concrete. Who was at risk? Hundreds of people worked on the ship. How could one kitchen worker here or there mean anything?

'You can't understand, of course . . . But these are incredibly dangerous, ruthless people. They live by their own code, and the life of one kitchen worker doesn't weigh much. If the criminals have the tiniest suspicion the police are onto them, they'll immediately cut ties to the vessel and continue their activities elsewhere. These guys don't take unnecessary risks.'

Max explained that the organisation's cells operated on a few cruise ships. Narcotics, gem smuggling, worker exploitation, human trafficking. There was so much money involved that any increased risk of getting caught meant immediately getting rid of evidence.

Hildur felt a twinge in the back of her neck. 'So you're saying they have their fingers in just about everything that has to be transported from place to place?'

Max nodded and added that he couldn't provide any more details. He underscored how critical it was Manuel return to his job and come up with an explanation that would satisfy his boss. But the excuse could not involve the police in any way.

'You can't help him. If our investigation dries up, the lives and wellbeing of countless people are in danger.'

Hildur was agonised. Manuel needed help. And now Max was asking her to turn her back on a victim. For the second time, a law enforcement officer was asking her to leave Manuel to his own devices. Should she forget the fate of one individual and prioritise the good of the bigger investigation? Should she sacrifice one person now so more people could have a better chance at being saved? What was the right thing to do?

Hildur eyed Max thoughtfully. His grooved face showed his age. A few deep worry wrinkles ran across his forehead, and he had the eyes of someone who had seen too much.

'How can you keep on doing this?'

Max twirled his spoon around his cup. When talking about himself, he relaxed a little. His words were deliberate and slow, but he seemed sincere. 'I'm not completely sure . . . For years now the team and I have been trying to bring these bastards to justice, and I guess I just don't know how to give up. Besides, I enjoy my work. I guess you have to, to do this work. What about you? Do you have a family?'

Hildur realised she'd lowered one of her hands to her belly. She quickly lifted it to the tabletop and shook her head.

'Me neither. What a pitiful pair,' Max joked, adding that Hildur still had time. He himself was coming up on sixty.

Hildur smiled back. She found something about Max's story intriguing. There weren't a lot of sixty-year-old men out there working undercover. 'Aren't you getting a little old for the job? Couldn't you just sit in the office and watch while your younger colleagues get their hands dirty in the field?'

'I wanted this gig. I wanted to spend the summer on these boats touring Iceland.'

Hildur grunted. Summer was when Iceland put her best foot forward for foreigners. The sea was calm, the sky clear, and you could manage without a down parka for a few days.

'The waterfalls and glaciers must look amazing from the sea,' she agreed.

For a moment, Max stared off into the distance, to a place Hildur couldn't see. She waited. She had the sense he was on the verge of opening up. Hildur found herself surprisingly often listening to strangers tell her things they hadn't necessarily ever shared with anyone.

'This is my last undercover assignment. I accepted it because I wanted to see this place. There was a girl, and she was important to me. Her name was Ruth Weider.'

Hildur didn't generally inquire into other people's affairs, nor did she gossip about her own. Usually she just listened. Even now she just nodded. Maybe it was her quiet presence that coaxed people to unburden their souls.

Max started talking about his first girlfriend. One always fell head over heels the first time, and Max had been no exception. He'd been with this girl for several years, but then a lot of changes had taken place in her life. She'd drifted into bad company.

'She was about ten years younger than me and thought I was boring. She wasn't wrong. Compared to her I was unremarkable, greyer than my hair is now.' Max grunted and sat there reminiscing for a moment. Max had started his career in law enforcement at the age of thirty, and in his free time he'd played floorball and watched soccer on TV. The craziest thing he'd done was listen to Bad Religion. That hadn't quite been enough for his restless lady love.

'She went looking for excitement elsewhere. Ultimately all sorts of substances entered the picture. The debts from her drug habit were massive. When she was finally able to quit, she travelled the continent looking for work and tried to pay off her debts. We promised to stay in touch. She said she'd send me letters and an address where I could write her back. We couldn't afford long-distance calls.'

Hildur still didn't ask any questions, just looked at Max. Not straight in the eye, because that would have been invasive, somewhere in the vicinity of the chin.

'I got three letters from her. After that I stopped hearing from her. She just . . . well, she just disappeared.'

'What do you mean?' Hildur asked, intrigued. 'Disappeared where?'

'In her first two letters, she told me she was in an English port, and in the third she'd moved to Iceland to work at a seafood processing plant. According to the letter, her address was in Flateyri. I saved up for a long-distance call and called the plant, but they said Ruth was gone. Apparently, there was nothing unusual about that. A lot of foreign seasonal workers just picked up and left.'

Hildur was familiar with the phenomenon. It still happened. Young people came to Iceland to work summer jobs at tour companies and horse stables, were paid in cash under the table, and at some point they got bored and moved on. They spent their earnings on travelling around the country, then went back home.

'That was unusual for her,' Max said. Despite her love of adventure, Ruth always kept her word when it came to work. It seemed impossible to Max that she would just vanish without telling anyone. 'Especially me. Even though we weren't together that way anymore, she meant a lot to me. In any case, I tried to find out through official channels, but no one had any information on a Ruth Weider. Apparently, she'd never submitted an official change of address after arriving in Iceland. Everyone kept repeating what you said: that foreigners just disappear.'

Hildur apologised for her words. 'All I meant was, the rapid turnover among seasonal workers is incredibly common. In the past in fishing, and these days mostly in tourism.'

Max nodded. 'It was even hinted to me that she might have killed herself. I don't believe that either. I don't really know if this makes any sense. I just wanted to see the place where she lived before all traces of her vanished. I guess I'm searching for peace for my soul.'

Hildur understood all too well. Her sisters' disappearance a few decades ago had sent a certain restlessness and melancholy churning through her life. Even after her sisters were found, the restlessness had remained. Too many things had happened in recent years that she'd been unable to get a proper grasp on. Some things had been resolved, but not enough. Hildur believed Björk was sitting in prison as an innocent woman. She didn't understand her sister's motive in confessing to a crime she hadn't committed.

The server came by to clear away their empty cups and asked if either was planning on ordering anything else. They both declined. Max had to get back to his tour group so his absence wouldn't spark questions. Hildur had to get back to work too.

Hildur pondered the story Max had shared about his girlfriend. She could check from the database to see who – if anyone – had investigated the case. 'When did she disappear and how old was she at the time?'

Max's jaw quivered a little. Time helped, but it didn't erase the most painful memories.

Max told Hildur about Ruth's long chestnut hair and beauty. He'd never got over her leaving him. Luckily they'd written to each other frequently until the autumn of 1994. After that last letter, he hadn't been able to contact her.

Ruth had been twenty-five years old at the time.

Chapter 50

The low evening sun had stained Ísafjörður orange-red. Two long shadows were advancing toward the public pool. Jakob had packed a big tote with swimming gear for himself and Matias as well as a toothbrush and pyjamas for his son. On summer evenings, the public pool was open until ten. When you came home with your teeth brushed and your pyjamas on, you could hop right into bed. Jakob had asked Guðrún to join them, but she'd preferred to stay home. Jakob knew why. Matias and Guðrún had got into a little squabble. Guðrún had asked Matias to put his dinner plate in the dishwasher. Matias had replied that she wasn't his mum and couldn't tell him what to do. Jakob had told Matias to say he was sorry, but his son had just run to his room and slammed the door. Jakob had seen how badly Matias's words had stung, but luckily Guðrún never yelled back at the boy. Jakob admired her patience.

Jakob liked the cosy local pool. It had been built in the 1940s, and the wooden doors and worn floor tiles reflected the ambiance of past decades. Plus, the tall windows gave onto a mesmerising mountain view.

Jakob and Matias climbed the stairs to the counter, where Jakob paid his entry fee. Children swam free. Tonight it was the men's turn in the sauna. Men and women switched locker rooms every day, because the sole sauna was located in the right-hand locker room.

'Are you going to go off the diving board?'

Matias opened the door to the locker room but didn't respond. Jakob tried not to give too much attention to the boy's acting out.

It was 9 p.m., but Jakob still felt like having a drop of coffee. He was planning on reviewing the material for his next exam when he got home and the caffeine would help him stay awake. There was a coffee Thermos in the corner where pool users could help themselves free of charge. Plastic cup in hand, Jakob made his way to the hot tub to watch Matias, who was practising his diving a little further off. Jumping into the water had turned the boy's frown into a smile. The sight made Jakob feel good.

Two men were sitting in the hot tub. Jakob said hello to both. He recognised one of them as the manager of the local petrol station; the other he'd never seen before. Jakob exchanged a few words with the stranger about the beautiful summer night and the upcoming vacation season. The service station manager listened without contributing. Then he stood, nodded goodbye, and headed for the locker room.

Jakob asked the stranger where he was from. Such questions were completely normal in a hot tub. This was a place where people sat cheek by jowl, discussing politics, sharing the latest news, and complaining about high mortgage interest rates.

'My name is Ómar. I started at the hospital a couple of weeks ago. I'm filling in for the summer.'

Jakob introduced himself and said he worked as a police officer.

'Are you in the field or the office?' Ómar asked.

Jakob replied that he did both. As the situation demanded.

'That's how it is for us doctors too.'

Ómar said he'd been working as an internist in Reykjavík. Here at the small rural hospital he performed C-sections, stitched wounds, and listened to the worries of the lonely. Every day was different.

'On Tuesday and part of Wednesday I was over in the nursing home, checking the residents' eyesight. Those who worked at sea have a lot of hearing problems, but older patients are also worried about their vision. I like having a variety of things to do,' Ómar said, then ventured to ask about Helga. Rumours were running rampant among the staff.

'What do you think? Was the old woman murdered?'

Jakob tilted the plastic cup and poured the lukewarm coffee down his throat. He glanced at Matias, who had just climbed out of the pool and was heading back to the diving board. He and his son waved at each other. Jakob felt himself relax.

'At the moment we're only investigating thefts. I can't take a stance on anything else because things are up in the air.'

Ómar nodded thoughtfully. 'I was over in the nursing home doing my rounds today. One of the residents, Katla Karlsdóttir, mentioned something about the police.'

Jakob frowned. Hildur had mentioned Katla, the woman who'd expressed zero interest in talking to her.

'She said she put her trust in doctors, especially male ones, not the law.' Ómar grunted, then continued: 'She asked if I thought the policewoman who'd come to the nursing home was trustworthy. I said yes. After that, Katla said she wanted to talk to her.'

Jakob thanked Ómar. He would convey the message to Hildur first thing in the morning.

After their swim, Jakob and Matias were sitting together in the sauna. Jakob tossed water on the stones. The steam was soft and wet. The wooden bench creaked beneath them, and the warm wall felt good against Jakob's back.

'Dad?' Matias asked in a quiet voice. He was sitting on the bench, back to his father.

'What is it, son?'

'Can't Hildur move in with us instead? I like her more than Guðrún.'

Jakob had no immediate answer. Of course he'd noticed that Hildur and Matias got along, but he had no idea Matias didn't like Guðrún.

'Um . . .' Jakob tossed water on the rocks to buy some time to think. Blended families weren't so simple. Maybe Matias thought of Guðrún as competition for his father's attention?

'Isn't it nice we have such a great friend in Hildur?'

Matias mumbled something Jakob interpreted as an affirmative response.

'She can visit us as often as she wants, and we've agreed that you can always go over to her place.'

Matias twisted his head around to see his father. 'I know. But I still want her to spend the night sometimes,' Matias said solemnly.

Jakob felt a smile coming on. Luckily, he was able to hide it. His son was being serious. 'Of course she can spend the night some time too. The couch opens up into a bed.'

Matias seemed satisfied with the response. He nodded and said he was going to shower and get dressed.

'I'm going to stay a little longer. I'll be there in just a minute,' Jakob said. After Matias exited, he began ladling water onto the rocks. The hot air settled on his shoulders and warmed his back. He let the steam comfort him.

Chapter 51

Reykjavík, June 2022

The time was coming up on eight. Hildur and Rósa had set out driving that evening for Reykjavík. They would be visiting Björk in the morning.

Things were busy at work, but Hildur refused to give up her visits to her sister.

The winding road made its third turn toward the base of the fjord since their departure and passed the Hvítanes farm junction. They'd been on the road for an hour, and in that time, they'd covered close to seventy kilometres. There wasn't much oncoming traffic, but the sheep grazing on the roadsides slowed their journey.

'You mind going in and getting us coffee and waffles?' Hildur suggested. 'I'll call the prison and make sure we can come outside regular visiting hours tomorrow.'

An Icelandic flag fluttered from the pole outside the café. A few picnic tables and benches stood outside. *It's like something out of a tourist postcard*, Hildur reflected.

'With whipped cream and jam!' she shouted as Rósa walked away.

They'd be able to handle a lot of errands during the trip to Reykjavík. Emma said she had an update on the bodies and bits of textile found in the hole and had scheduled a videoconference with Beta and Jakob that Hildur had got permission to attend. Rósa would have a chance to go to the paint store. The exterior paint she'd been planning on using at Kotsdalur was sold out everywhere in Iceland. She'd eventually found a small hardware store at the fringes of Reykjavík that had a few gallons of the exact colour Rósa was looking for in stock. Plus, the drive to Reykjavík gave the sisters a chance to visit Björk together. That felt important.

Rósa returned a moment later. Hildur pulled out the cup holder and accepted the plates.

With one hand, Hildur steered Brenda back onto the south-bound road, and with the other she steered the waffle dripping whipped cream into her mouth.

Rósa handed her sister a paper towel. 'Tell me about those skeletons.'

Hildur gesticulated that she was swallowing the half-waffle in her mouth, then answered: 'For now it's impossible to say when they were buried.'

'When did our parents move to Kotsdalur?' Rósa asked, taking a bite of her own waffle.

The move had happened a few years before Hildur was born, but she wasn't sure about the year. 'We can find the exact date from the national registry, but it was sometime in the 1970s.'

It was easy talking about things, even painful ones, in the car, because in a way you were talking to yourself. You didn't have to look the other person in the face the whole time. Hildur explained that she'd heard from Helga that their mother had originally inherited the farm from her parents. Tinna had inherited money instead and had used it to buy a home in Ísafjörður. The third sister, Hulda, had moved away from Iceland before her parents' death and refused any inheritance. An only child, Rúnar had inherited his parents' sole asset: a small fishing boat. Rúnar and Rakel had met at a dance at the community centre and began dating. Rakel had found herself pregnant, and they'd basically been forced to marry. That was what had happened, more or less. A typical Icelandic tale.

The sisters continued eating their waffles in silence. The dun mountains rose steeply from the road. The odd trickle of water cascaded down the rockface. The streams formed gulches that carried the troll milk to the sea. The mountains were home to dark-loving giants that had fled the sunlight: trolls. When trolls suckled their children, some of the milk oozed through the mountainsides and into the natural world.

'What do you think: did Mum and Dad know about the bones?' Rósa asked.

Hildur shrugged. Ultimately, she knew very little about her parents' lives. And she wasn't permitted to discuss the investigation.

'I don't really remember much about Mum,' Rósa said. There was no bitterness or sorrow in her voice. She and Hildur had discussed their childhood several times that spring and summer. Rósa didn't like remembering the past, but over the course of those few brief conversations, Hildur had got the impression Rósa knew their mother hadn't been favouring Hildur when she sent her younger daughters to the Faroe Islands. Hildur had been too ill to leave on the scheduled day.

'No one has ever really explained why we had to be sent away,' Rósa continued.

Hildur had pondered the same question during countless sleepless nights and sombre moments on her days off. 'There are some questions we'll never know the answers to. It's just the way it is.'

Helga had told Hildur that Rakel had planned to take all the children to the Faroe Islands and bring Helga along too. The plan had failed, because Helga hadn't been able to leave her husband. Hildur didn't know why the children had to be sent away. If Rakel had wanted to break ties with Rúnar, there probably would have been an easier solution. Her mother's choices seemed incomprehensible. But people had all sorts of things going on that outsiders couldn't see. Hildur didn't believe it was possible to know anyone well enough to fully understand the other's thinking and actions. In the end, we were all here alone.

Bright green grass grew in the valley at the base of Skötufjörður fjord. Snow was still visible on the northern slopes of the mountains rising behind the valley. It never melted, even in the summer. A couple of weeks before, Matias had said the white snow piles looked like vanilla ice cream and the mountains looked like chocolate cake. The idea of a land made out of dessert amused Hildur.

'My guess is Mum tried her best but it wasn't quite enough. Good intentions can lead to catastrophes sometimes. I see it all too often on the job,' Hildur said. She reached over to take her glasses case from the glove compartment and put on her sport sunglasses. 'As soon as I can, I'll tell you about the skeletons at Kotsdalur, but I suggest we don't say anything to Björk yet. She has so much going on as it is.'

Rósa agreed.

The sisters spent the night at an inexpensive chain hotel on the outskirts of Reykjavík. The breakfast was spartan: a plastic-wrapped cheese sandwich and a cup of coffee. After this modest culinary experience, they drove to the prison. Björk was waiting for them in a green plaid flannel shirt and casual cargo pants. She studied the stack of books before her with interest. Hildur had bought some paperbacks from the service station: a couple of Icelandic detective novels and the latest Stephen King in translation.

'How are you doing?' Rósa asked.

Björk stroked her cropped hair and shrugged. 'Fine, I guess. The days are all pretty much the same . . .'

'How are your studies going?' Hildur asked.

Björk laughed. 'You guys sure have a lot of questions.'

Björk planned on completing her specialisation programme in mental health and substance abuse as fast as possible. 'There's nothing to tell. It's just reading and assignments. Let's talk about you instead: how's the renovation going at Kotsdalur? Did you get the septic tank installed?'

Hildur kept an eye on Rósa, who was her usual relaxed self.

'The shit tub is still in the yard. The excavator operator had to postpone for some reason,' Rósa said. 'I'm going to get the last of the exterior paint from Kópavogur today.' She continued with accounts of mundane accidents, like the sheet of roofing metal the wind carried off to the sea.

Hildur had sunk into a reverie. In the meantime, Rósa had given some juicy detail about the excavator operator. Hildur hadn't heard what the story was about, but she saw Björk was smiling. She felt bad that Björk never laughed the same way at her stories.

'Do you remember how I brought you the most recent Yrsa detective novel?'

Björk looked seriously at Hildur. 'Do you want it back?'

That wasn't what Hildur wanted. But something Björk had said had kept occurring to her since. She'd remembered the story the previous evening before setting out for Reykjavík and checked a couple of facts related to it.

'You said you went on a walking tour of Reykjavík that was organised by Yrsa.'

Rósa turned toward Hildur and shot her a quizzical frown.

'She took us to the places mentioned in the first book,' Björk said, eyes fixed on the back wall.

Hildur knew Björk wouldn't be happy about what she was about to say in any event, so there was no point skirting the issue. She cut to the chase.

'Last winter, Yrsa only gave one walking tour. On December tenth.'

The author had confirmed the date with Hildur over the phone.

'And?' Björk said sharply.

'That's the same day the attempt on Hlín's life took place at the pasture.' Hildur paused to let this information sink in for Björk: the dates of Hlín's assault and the walking tour overlapped.

Hildur's acquaintance, the investigative journalist Hlín Jónsdóttir, was one of the victims of a spree of assaults and homicides that had taken place the previous year. Hlín had sniffed out the illicit trade in mares' blood and suffered a horrific assault on the job, coming close to death. The nosy journalist and animal rights activists who opposed the sale of mares' blood had caught the attention of violent criminals. Rósa was mixed up in the illegal business, and initially everyone had thought she'd committed the acts of violence too. The investigating detectives had been sure Rósa had wanted to get rid of the activists and reporter threatening her livelihood.

Then out of the blue, Björk had proclaimed she'd done it. She'd been sentenced. Hildur had been sceptical about Björk's guilt since the beginning, and now she'd caught her sister in a lie.

'There's no way you can be guilty of the crimes you're doing time for,' Hildur said. 'Why can't you just admit it?'

'I want to go back to my cell,' Björk said angrily. She reached for the books and popped to her feet so violently that her chair toppled. The clatter brought the guard over.

'Why are you claiming culpability for something you didn't do?'

Björk's eyes narrowed to slits. Her nose turned up and her top lip rose, revealing her front teeth. 'Maybe I remember wrong! Maybe I didn't take some tour. Maybe I just planned on it and never did it.'

Hildur knew Björk was lying. The author had remembered Björk; she'd made an impression because she'd asked so many detailed questions. And Hildur was on the verge of saying so, but Björk raised a hand and sharply shook her head.

'I appreciate the books, but don't say another word. Why can't you just let me be?'

Then Björk disappeared with the guard. Hildur buried her face in her hands as the sting of failure sank in.

Rósa tugged her by the sleeve and drily noted it was time to go. 'Björk doesn't want to talk about it. She admitted to the crimes, and that's that. Why do you have to stick your nose in something that's none of your business?'

Hildur stood and pushed her chair under the table. She righted the chair Björk had knocked over and pushed it under the table too. 'Do you think she's guilty?' she asked Rósa.

Rósa stepped out in front of Hildur and jabbed her forefinger lightly in the middle of her sister's chest. 'Of course not.'

Now Hildur didn't understand anything.

'But Björk has decided to deal with this in this way. She asked me to trust her. We owe her that.'

'But I don't understand—'

Rósa stomped on the floor to cut Hildur off and said she was acting like a kid who wouldn't accept it wasn't candy day. 'No one has asked you to understand a thing, Björk has made her choice, and we ought to respect it.'

Rósa's face hardened, and her hands clenched into fists. She took a step back from Hildur as if she were struggling to get a grip on herself. Her voice was sharp: 'Which one of us knows Björk better, you or me?'

The turn the day had taken had thrown Hildur off. She didn't know what to say.

'Answer me,' Rósa demanded, backing up another step. The distance between them grew.

Hildur did her best to close the chasm that had opened between them. 'You do,' she said softly.

Rósa nodded her head back slightly. The gesture wasn't aggressive, but the look on her face hadn't softened. Hildur felt herself tense.

She understood less and less about what was going on.

Chapter 52

20 February

Hi, Max!

I'm still working. Every day is the same, stinks like fish, stinks like cigarettes, and I don't hear a peep out of you. Why aren't you answering?

I got in a fight with this one Romanian woman today over the shower. Can you believe it? We're crammed in here like sardines, we work like machines, and we only have one shower that works at our dorm. There was a line outside the bathroom. I knocked on the door, and I guess the Romanian woman thought I was too aggressive. She attacked me like an animal. Luckily there were other people in line and together we were able to calm her down.

Half the workers we live with are locals. Most of the foreigners were hired through employment agencies. Except me.

At first, things were fine, because I could just keep going. I still can! I can chop off cod heads all day long. Grab a fish, put it in the machine – bye bye, head. Grab a fish, hold it up, off with its head. Each fish is in my hands for a few seconds, tops. We make bonuses based on weight. That's an incentive to work our butts off.

I haven't been paid in weeks. They say I'm too difficult and keep trying too hard to change things. Living conditions are cramped. I have very little space and zero privacy. I stand all day at the plant, work hard, and at night I fall into bed drunk. You have to drink if you work here, that's the only way you can take it. The dorm is cold, because the electric heaters don't work properly. The person who runs the dorm doesn't take our complaints seriously.

I'm getting out of here soon. My boyfriend was so attentive and kind when we first met. He helped me get a job and a place to live at the dorm. But now I know I made the wrong choice. He's a monster.

You mean the world to me, now I know it.

R.

Chapter 53

Reykjavík, June 2022

Neither Hildur nor Rósa spoke as they drove out of the prison car park. Hildur had turned on the radio. On public Radio Station 2, a raspy, life-roughened soul voice was singing about women who laughed like the ocean. If you betrayed such a woman, she'd claim your soul and steal off with it. The name of the song was 'Sumar konur': 'women of summer' or just 'some women', depending on the interpretation. Hildur could pick out the delicate tremor of a harmonica in the music.

Hildur looked out of the corner of her eye at Rósa, who had spent much of her life on the outskirts of society, hidden in shadow. Rósa had protected her little sister throughout their childhood. She'd been Björk's safety and stability. The two of them had been raised by their quiet Aunt Hulda, who'd been lost in her own world and remained a distant figure. Rósa hadn't had a chance to live her own youth, because she'd been helping her sister. When hot cooking oil had spilled over Rósa and damaged her face, she'd retreated into her own world as well. Adults had stared at her; children had been frightened by her and whispered the word 'monster'. Rósa had always been a hard worker, and she'd been particularly diligent and efficient at collecting mares' blood. The work had its downsides, but Hildur figured Rósa had enjoyed it at some level. When the illicit nature of the business had been exposed through newspaper articles, Rósa had been involuntarily yanked into the spotlight. The media had written a lot of stories about her. Now, less than six months later, the scandal had died down and Rósa was left in peace. She enjoyed her life in Kotsdalur and her renovation projects.

Hildur's sense of justice meant she had a hard time tolerating Björk sitting in prison, an innocent woman, yet seemingly at peace with her circumstances. Rósa didn't appear to be as troubled by her sister's decision. From now on, Hildur would try to keep her mouth shut about Björk's affairs in Rósa's company, so as not to ruin her relationship with Rósa.

Hildur dropped Rósa off in the hardware store car park and suggested they meet in a few hours at the cafe in the neighbouring garden shop. Rósa growled a one-syllable response Hildur interpreted as agreement.

Hildur drove through the city to the far side of Reykjavík. The three-storey RLE, or national forensic laboratory, was located on Hofsvallagata, the main thoroughfare in the western part of the city known to be a relatively posh residential area. Although part of the University of Iceland, the RLE was housed in separate premises a little off campus. Hildur's student apartment had been in the same neighbourhood, near the Hofsvallagata swimming pool.

When Hildur had called Emma just now and arranged to arrive half an hour earlier than expected, she'd learned Axlar-Hákon happened to be paying a visit to the RLE just then. He usually worked at the central hospital in the old city centre. Emma, Axlar-Hákon, and Hildur had agreed to meet here at the RLE.

The discovery of the skeletons was a link to the past, and Hildur was interested in the past, but her relationship to it was conflicted. If the past was constantly being unearthed, it began to stink. Even so, she couldn't help her curiosity.

Maybe her interest in the pasts of other people, nations, and continents was the reason she'd originally studied history. As her studies progressed, she'd lost interest in the field. Her studies had felt abstract: too many concepts and too much debating matters of secondary importance. And so she'd applied to the police academy. She'd always thought her choice had been motivated by the physicality of the programme, the exercise required, the possibility to help others and do teamwork. But maybe in the end she'd been motivated by curiosity. She wanted to find out what had happened and why.

'How's my favourite detective?'

The cheery greeting roused Hildur from her reverie. Axlar-Hákon had been waiting for her in the lobby. His big frame snatched Hildur up in a bear hug.

'Four complete skeletons. I can't remember any similar discovery during my lifetime,' he said excitedly as they turned from the lobby down a long corridor.

'Why is this place so busy even though it's summer?' Hildur asked, looking around.

Axlar-Hákon spread his arms and said something about European summer studies and an international exchange programme. 'Where there's the EU, there's a programme, a funding application, and a hell of a lot to report.'

The door to the conference room was open and the lights were on. A focused-looking Emma was fussing around with the video projector in the middle of the table so Beta and Jakob could join the meeting. There was a man sitting in the room too, and Hildur walked over and shook hands with him. This taciturn, slightly gruff presence proved to be the new head of the RLE, Magnús Magnússon.

'*Jaejja*. Quite the project you laid on us. Fifteen minutes before summer vacation,' he said to the screen.

'What can I say? It's the wild west,' Beta countered.

Emma brought up an image of a skeleton lying on a metal exam table and got right down to business. Hildur appreciated her brisk approach. Emma began with a quick recap: all the skeletons were well preserved. The soil was cold, so decomposition had taken place slowly. Only a few hand bones were missing. Emma directed her words to the police officers, who, aside from Jakob, weren't professionals in anatomy.

'Over a quarter of our bones are in our hands. Some are very small, so I find it perfectly natural that some have disappeared. Maybe small rodents shifted the tiniest ones. Who can say?' Emma held a pause, then moved onto the next photo. 'But I noticed some things about the skeletons' hand bones that might aid you in the identification of the bodies.'

Emma aimed her laser pointer at the right elbow of the skeleton in the picture. The notes next to the picture indicated the skeleton was that of a woman, about twenty, as yet unidentified.

'This is an antemortem fracture. That means it happened long before the death. The bone shows clear signs of healing. If we ever learn who the deceased is, this information could be used to support identification. The fracture was on the right radius.'

Hildur made herself a note, although quite a few people had broken an arm bone over the course of their lifetime.

'I'm sorry, that's all I can say about this skeleton. But then these others . . .'

Emma switched images again. The next photo was of a skeleton of a man, about fifty, who was missing his left hand from the wrist down.

'This, on the other hand, is a clear perimortem fracture, as I noted at the scene of the excavation. The fracture took place very close to the time of death, in other words it's possible the fracture was involved in the person's passing. Initially the forearm fracture looked clean, but I had a look with a microscope just to be sure.'

Emma clicked ahead to a close-up image. The red laser ran along the rough surface.

'Living bone is wet. When it fractures, the bone ends are uneven.'

'Are you saying the deceased died as a result of losing the hand?' Beta asked.

Axlar-Hákon took the floor. 'We can't know for sure. It may have caused the death. Either that or the deceased had a heart attack or stroke or drowned right after the fracture and the loss of the hand. There are plenty of scenarios.'

Hildur nodded. She was trying to exclude alternatives.

The next questions were posed by Jakob. 'What if it was severed after death? If, say, the excavator bucket hit it? Or when you retrieved the bones from the grave?'

Emma considered it unlikely. If the fracture were recent, the cut would be a lot cleaner.

'I wonder how that hand was cut off,' Hildur reflected out loud.

Emma had clearly anticipated the question, because she had an answer at the ready.

'The fracture is crooked and the bones have fractured at different places. There's nothing I can say for sure, but I think the hand was crushed somehow. Maybe something heavy fell on it, or it was caught somehow and mangled.'

Hildur nodded in interest. Emma really knew what she was talking about.

'As a useful comparison to the previous one . . . This is the second skeleton that belongs to a youngish woman. A few fingers are missing from her left hand, and judging by the evidence, this is also a perimortem fracture, one that took place close to the time of death.'

Hildur squinted to see clearly. In the end, she had to get up and walk over to the screen. She'd have to get glasses soon. She'd been putting it off far too long.

'What makes this fracture interesting is that the cut is very clean. I'd say almost too clean. It appears the blade was extremely sharp. A shredder, a chipper, a big knife, and a lot of force. A fast-moving device with a keen edge. A chainsaw isn't going to produce a cut like that.'

Hildur let her mind wander. Three of the four skeletons were somehow damaged. It couldn't be coincidence. Nor had the skeletons ended up at Kotsdalur by accident. Someone had buried the bodies. But what good would these conclusions do them? Were they investigating homicides? Torture? Or what was going on here?

'Unfortunately, there are no visible traces on the bones that would explain or even hint at a cause of death,' Axlar-Hákon said, moving his jaw back and forth. 'But there are still a couple of minor things we're taking a look at here in the lab,' he added with a deep sigh.

It was typical of Axlar-Hákon to hold off on sharing information to ensure his listeners' focus on what he was about to say. 'Naturally, we've also had a look at everything else that was found in the grave, and I have to say it wasn't much: the silver earrings visible in one of the photos and the bits of fabric found beneath one of the skeletons.'

Hildur felt her senses sharpen. Emma had moved on to the next photo.

'Our investigators looked into the earrings, but there's nothing interesting to say about them. A dime a dozen. There are countless pairs of similar earrings out there in the world,' Emma said.

Hildur was more interested in the clothes than the earrings. She knew clothes didn't decompose very quickly. Either so much time had passed that there wasn't much left of the clothing, or the bodies been buried naked. *But if a bit of fabric had turned up . . .*

Beta was interested in the same thing. 'What material is the textile?'

Axlar-Hákon answered: 'One hundred per cent rubber. Partially decomposed, but some small fragments have been preserved.'

The bits of textile in the photo were badly worn, and there was no way to say what they'd originally come from. Some faded yellow colour was visible here and there.

'And how long—' Beta began.

Axlar-Hákon interrupted: 'It depends on the type of rubber, but generally natural rubber decomposes in about twenty to fifty years. This may give some indication as to the time of burial.'

So in all likelihood, at least one of the skeletons had been buried from 1970 to 2000. Of course, it was also possible that rubber clothes had been tossed in the grave, but it seemed more logical that the garments would have been deposited in the hole with the body that wore them. The investigation had just taken one tiny step forward.

'Let's continue piecing the fragments together,' Beta quipped. With that, she said goodbye to Reykjavík and signed off the videoconference.

Hildur crumpled the empty paper cup into a tiny ball and considered the conclusions drawn about the textile. Thick, natural rubber. It could be a piece of tarp, or maybe a shoe sole or remnants of a rubber glove. Divers used drysuits made of rubber . . . and there was plastic in some work or protective gear . . .

Hildur could feel herself approaching the surface.

Chapter 54

After leaving the forensic laboratory, Hildur headed down Hofsvallagata toward the city's southern waterfront. Hinrik Rökkvason lived a good kilometre away, on the sea.

Something about Hinrik Rökkvason's cantankerous reaction continued to nag at Hildur. All the family members had struck her as surprisingly indifferent with regard to the missing valuables and their elderly relations, but at least the others had spoken in normal tones. Hinrik alone had snapped at her. Now that she was in Reykjavík, Hildur decided to take the opportunity to pay Hinrik a visit. It was late afternoon, so maybe the curmudgeon would be home from work by now.

The handsome white waterfront house rose behind a few old oaks. A tall wooden fence surrounded the yard, but the broad iron gate in it was open. A small stream and a couple of fountains burbled in a Japanese garden encircled by a harmonious assortment of black and grey stones. The grass had been cropped short. The house had an attached, raised deck furnished with outdoor pieces and was perfectly suited to the lush surroundings.

Two Polestar EVs were charging next to the deck. Hildur almost bumped into one as she was searching for the entrance. She found the front door but no doorbell. Nevertheless, the door began to produce sounds: first a tinkling alarm, followed by a question posed in a cold female voice as to the identity of the approaching individual. Hildur brought her mouth to the small black gap in the wooden panel she decided was a microphone and introduced herself. The voice replied: '*Door unlocked. Welcome.*'

The spacious entrance hall was dominated by a polychromatic work of abstract art a good two metres wide. Beneath the painting was an antique-looking vase holding two dry branches.

'Would you mind coming upstairs?'

It wasn't a request; it was a command. Before going any further, Hildur took off her sneakers, which had seen better days. She tiptoed up the glass staircase. She was perspiring from the brisk walk, and her tennis socks left damp splotches on the transparent treads.

Hildur wasn't sure if there was anything Hinrik could have done to look wealthier. Thick, dark hair, a trimmed beard, and a suit that hung so well on his fit, muscular body that the result was casual. The shake of the well-manicured hand was like the voice: friendly but firmly aloof.

'You actually came,' he laughed, gesturing for Hildur to sit with him. 'I was a little cross when you called. My apologies. It was a rough day.'

'No problem,' Hildur said, pulling her notebook and pen from her pocket. 'I'm not in the habit of immediately giving up.'

Hinrik smiled mischievously and looked Hildur in the eye. She explained she was in Reykjavík for a meeting and thought she'd come by for a chat while she was in town.

'The alternative would have been to go to the Reykjavík police station for an interview. I thought this would be a more pleasant option,' Hildur said with an overly friendly smile. She was capable of playing hardball too, if necessary.

Hinrik didn't reply. The smile on his face had narrowed slightly. Eventually he nodded.

Hildur took this as encouragement to get to the point and get out. 'Your father lives in a nursing home in Ísafjörður. His Rolex is missing.'

She repeated what she'd already told Hinrik over the phone: the nursing home had presumably been targeted by thieves. The investigators were compiling a list of missing items and sums of money and needed details so the stolen items could be identified in the event they were recovered.

Hildur had spoken with Rökkvi again before the trip and gleaned more information from the old man. That was another reason she wanted to pay Hinrik a visit.

'Nearly 400,000 krónur in cash is missing too. That's almost a full month's net salary.'

'Not much of a salary,' Hinrik decided to clarify. He rubbed his handsome beard, looking thoughtful. Then he rose to his feet, walked over to the bureau that stood against the room's longest wall, and pulled open the top drawer.

'I gave the watch to my father for his seventieth birthday. Naturally I have the receipt.'

He took a moment to rummage through papers kept in a black plastic folder.

'Here we are, a Daytona-series watch. Green dial. Bracelet and body eighteen-carat gold. You can take a photo of this if you'd like,' Hinrik said, thrusting the receipt at Hildur.

Hildur muttered thanks and accepted the slip of paper.

'I haven't seen that watch on my father's wrist for years. Maybe he accidentally flushed it down the toilet. I offered to look after it for him, but he's so stubborn that there was no way. I let it drop.'

'What about the missing cash? Does that ring any bells? Is your father careful with his money?'

Hinrik laughed as if Hildur had told a hilarious joke. 'He's always been cheap. When we were kids the four of us had to share a banana. We never got new clothes even if he could afford it.'

Hildur held the receipt and considered the alternatives. It sounded unlikely that Rökkvi had squandered the money on purchases.

'Might he have lent the money to someone?' Hildur asked, shifting into a more comfortable position in the high-backed armchair.

Hinrik thought it unlikely. Apparently, the old man never lent money to anyone. 'Unless he earned interest,' he added, correcting himself.

Hildur's gaze focused on the photographs hanging over the broad bureau. Curiosity got the better of her. She stood and walked over next to Hinrik for a closer look. The pictures were of people posing at the harbour, on fishing boats, or at a fish-processing plant. It was immediately clear the pictures were old. They were colour photographs, but they'd faded and the subjects were blurrier than they would be in recent shots.

'The early days of my company,' Hinrik said, pride in his voice.

'I didn't know your company has operations in the Westfjords.'

Hildur had recognised the mountains in one of the pictures. There was no mistaking the ridgelines: three sharp peaks in a row, the tallest of which was Kaldbakur.

There was nothing that odd about it. In the early years of Iceland's history, the wealthiest people had lived in the Westfjords, because that's where the best conditions for fishing had been. There was plenty of coastline, and the long fjords offered shelter from the wind. Residents had ready access to the sea.

Hinrik tapped at a picture in which two men, presumably father and son, were leaning against the door of a warehouse.

'Had. We don't anymore. When my father finally retired and I took over the family business, I moved all operations here to the capital. The old man moved into the nursing home soon after.'

Hinrik studied the photographs on the wall in silence. Then he turned to Hildur and looked her dead in the eye.

'Dad does have one vice, however. He likes to gamble. He might play several times a week. It's a short walk from the nursing home to the corner store. Maybe he's invested his money in gaming.'

This news was a stinging disappointment. Naturally, Hildur would have to verify the truth of the story, but if Rökkvi's money had gone to gambling, it hadn't been stolen. *Well, every stone has to be turned over*, she reflected, returning her attention to the old pictures.

She was fascinated by the snapshots of the past taken in familiar places. She had no trouble identifying the boy standing in front of the trawler as Hinrik: his gaze had been as stern and his eyebrows as thick back then as they were today. Rökkvi she would not have recognised.

'You sold your quotas to fishing concerns in the capital, is that it?' Hildur's tone was prickly.

A small crack formed in Hinrik's manicured appearance. 'Yes. You have to put your money where it generates the best returns. The wages of seventy per cent of the people in this country – including you – are paid with earnings made by the other thirty per cent.'

Hildur didn't take the bait. She knew the vast majority of Icelanders worked in the public sector. She wasn't sure the percentage was quite that high, but what could you do when the island wasn't home to many people and the policy was to keep the entire country inhabited.

'If you get in a car crash in the countryside, I assume you'd need an ambulance too. Or would you rather call a taxi?'

Hinrik grunted to himself. 'At least you're not at a loss for words. I like people who have opinions even if they're different than mine.'

Hildur could sense the sincerity in his voice. Maybe Hinrik wasn't as annoying as she'd originally thought. First impressions could be misleading.

She used her phone to take a picture of the receipt and set it down on the bureau. As Hinrik turned away to return the receipt to the drawer, Hildur discreetly took pictures of the photos on the wall. There were a couple of details she wanted to look into.

As she made to leave, Hildur noticed a colourful and very traditional cross-stitch hanging in the stairwell. It stood out so dramatically from the house's contemporary, minimalistic décor that she couldn't help but comment. 'Nice cross-stitch,' she said, nodding at the handcraft.

It depicted a traditional Icelandic landscape: the roiling sea, a pair of fishing vessels, and snow-capped mountains rising beyond. A phrase recognised by all Icelanders had been embroidered above. It was from the Poetic Edda: *Orðstír deyr aldregi.*

A good reputation never dies.

'Oh, that. There was no room for it at the nursing home, so I brought it here.' Hinrik used his thumb to brush away a speck of dirt he saw on the lapel of his suit coat. 'It's my father's favourite. It was important to him to be a man worthy of his reputation. For him, losing face would have been the worst thing imaginable.'

Chapter 55

As Hildur walked out the gate, her phone rang. Rósa said she needed another hour to do her shopping, and they set a new time to meet. It was no skin off Hildur's nose. She could return the car key Jakob had accidentally forgotten in his pocket. Hildur had meant to mail it to Kristína and Óskar earlier but it kept slipping her mind. She'd take care of the errand now.

The lakeside neighbourhood of single-family homes was quiet. The houses were dark, and there were no cars anywhere. Most Icelanders were at their cabins or on summer vacation abroad. But a familiar-looking car was parked outside Kristína and Óskar's house. Someone was home.

Hildur walked up the flagstone path to the front door and rang the doorbell. Both Kristína and Óskar came to the door. They stood side by side, as if seeking safety in each other. It was a comforting sight. The wrinkles in their faces had deepened, the bags under their eyes spoke of sleepless nights and weeping. Presumably both.

'I came by to return this to you; I was driving past,' Hildur said, pulling the key from her pocket and holding it out to the couple.

Óskar took it. 'Well, um, thank you,' he said. He seemed genuinely surprised Hildur was personally dropping off the key.

Hildur didn't want to intrude or take up the couple's time; nevertheless, she found it necessary to ask how they were doing. A child's death was a difficult subject, but one couldn't bypass it. Family members found it hurtful if conversations skirted the tragedy and focused on other matters. The only thing worse was pretending not to see the dead person's loved one on the street. Or steering a shopping cart into a different aisle at the supermarket to avoid facing the mourner. That was cruel.

'Considering the circumstances, we're doing all right,' Kristína replied.

Hildur nodded.

Kristína thanked her for bringing the key, then continued a little tentatively: 'Um . . . would you like some coffee? We were just about to sit down ourselves.'

Hildur thanked her for the invitation and said she'd love a cup if it wasn't any trouble.

The living room décor was down to earth. Books and decorative items in the wooden bookcase, a plush beige sofa set, and a Moroccan rug on the floor.

'Have you already had the funeral?'

The couple tensed a little at the question, but their faces almost immediately relaxed. The fact that Hildur dared to face death so directly was clearly a relief.

'Yesterday,' Kristína said softly.

Hildur nodded and asked no more questions about the funeral, because Kristína and Óskar didn't continue on the subject.

'Have you been able to sleep and eat?'

Kristína and Óskar looked at each other and nodded.

'I've had to take sedatives,' Óskar said.

Hildur replied that doing so was completely normal. There were several medications that saw people through the worst.

Then suddenly, without warning, Óskar burst into tears and buried his face in his hands. His back twitched, and he doubled over in apparent agony. Kristína wasn't fazed: she must have witnessed this plenty of times. She leaned toward him and stroked his back.

'I never . . . I never should have ever come back home. It's this damn island's fault this happened,' Óskar choked out between his hands.

Hildur watched the moment unfold. She felt as if she were disassociating further and further from the situation, rising out of the boho living room and high into the sky, where the patchwork of coloured roofs looked like a quilt among the summer-green terrain.

Hildur had realised why Óskar looked so familiar.

The framed family photograph on Kristína and Óskar's bookshelf next to the anniversary edition of the Icelandic Sagas had confirmed it. She'd seen it once before. Over two years had passed since then, but Hildur had an excellent memory for pictures. Hildur and Jakob had visited a woman whose attorney husband had just been murdered in a Reykjavík parking garage.

'You're one of Kolfinna and Heiðar's children,' Hildur said.

Óskar sniffled and looked up warily at Hildur. He was too surprised to get a word out. Kristína wrapped her arms around her husband.

'I investigated Heiðar's murder three years ago,' Hildur explained.

She'd actually investigated two other murders linked to Heiðar's as well. The motive for the killings had involved genetics. It had been a tricky case, permeated by sadness. Hildur didn't find it necessary to speak any further on it.

'Your child . . .' Hildur began but couldn't finish the sentence.

She knew the parents already knew. Heiðar had been fingered as one of the murderer's victims due to a genetic illness.

The certain type of hereditary cerebral hemorrhage, a rare condition encountered only in Iceland, wasn't automatically passed down to offspring who carried the mutated gene. But it was sometimes.

'I . . . as far as I know, I'm not sick and neither is my sister,' Óskar managed to say, before bursting into tears again.

Silence fell over the living room. Kristína stroked her husband's back and offered him a handkerchief. She supported her husband with sensitive gestures. Hildur knew grief morphed over time. The stronger party had to do the supporting, and just now that party was Kristína. Time's passage would ensure that the roles would eventually switch.

Óskar dried his face on the handkerchief and straightened up to look at Hildur. But his gaze didn't have the strength to rise all the way to her eyes; it remained resting at the tabletop.

'Mum told me about Dad's illness and warned me, but I didn't listen. We wanted a baby so badly. I believed in good luck. I believed we'd earned it.'

Chapter 56

Ísafjörður, June 2022

The drive home went smoothly. Hildur and Rósa had spent a second night at the chain hotel, set out before breakfast, and grabbed coffee and croissants from the service station. Rósa had drifted back to sleep in the car. Hildur had spent the drive listening to a history of Iceland podcast about relationships between Icelandic women and American soldiers during the Second World War.

'I'll go by my place first to get my surfing gear, then I'll take you home,' Hildur said.

Rósa was stretching her arms and legs in the passenger seat. She'd woken up a moment before the road turned into their home fjord.

The most recent forecast had promised decent conditions at the Kotsdalur shore. There were no big breakers in store, but even smaller waves would do. Hildur thought she might drop by and see Katla again after surfing. Jakob had mentioned that morning on the phone that the elderly woman wanted to meet with Hildur. What had changed her mind?

A good hour later, Hildur was standing hip-deep in the sea in her neoprene suit, gazing at the horizon. The waves were perfect. She dropped onto her stomach on her surfboard and began paddling. She could feel the resistance in her arms and shoulders as she slid forward across the sea's surface. Each stroke carried her board further from shore. Before long, a little wave lifted her up. As she came down, salt water splashed her bare face. The seawater stung her eyes and streamed down her cheeks. She paddled twice as hard.

Hildur leaned onto her arms and rose onto her knees to see better. She looked ahead and decided to wait where she was. The rolling sea reminded her of a sheet drying on the line. There was a roundedness, a familiarity to it, yet it couldn't be predicted with complete accuracy. Hildur turned the board but kept her eyes seaward. She'd done everything as well as she could, and the outcome would come down to chance.

The board rocked with the movement. Then she saw a long, symmetrical wave approach. Hildur got into semi-standing position, still holding the board. When the wave was in precisely the right position, she let go and stood. The board glided shoreward at an angle. For a moment, Hildur felt liberated from everything: work, skeletons, Björk's recalcitrance, Helga's death, Óskar and Kristína's grief, Anton and the pregnancy. The quiet moment lasted less than a minute. Then she was at the shore.

Hildur was smiling. The thing that captivated her most about surfing was the freedom. No matter how well she'd prepared, her own strength and knowledge sustained her to a certain point. After that, the only option was to let go. She had to give herself permission to be free. Hildur felt empowered. Now she was sure what she needed to do.

When she was done surfing, Hildur slipped her board under her arm and walked to the car. The mood-enhancing effect of exercise-stimulated hormones would last the rest of the day. Hildur clicked the board into Brenda's roof rack and stripped off her skin-tight wetsuit. She gathered her braid in her fist and wrung out most of the water . . .

Damn it. She'd run out of garbage bags. Where would she store her wet wetsuit? Then she remembered the tyre-changing kit. She also had a folding snow shovel, rope, and rainproof reflective clothing in the car. She could bundle her surfing gear in her rainwear for the drive home.

Hildur unzipped the big canvas bag and pulled the yellow raincoat out from the bottom. She wrapped her neoprene suit into a tight wad and placed it inside the coat. Somewhere in the distance, a sheep bleated. She fingered patterns into the now-wet surface of her raincoat. She realised something important had just occurred to her. She quickly slammed the door to the cargo space, hustled into the driver's seat, and started up the car. There was one detail she had to check as soon as possible.

Chapter 57

The air conditioning hummed faintly. Soft speech could be heard somewhere at the far end of the corridor. Hildur lightly rapped on Katla's door with her knuckles.

Katla had an inquisitive gaze. Her knee-length, polka-dotted linen dress covered her plump arms. The top two buttons had been left undone. But it was the big, almost perfectly heart-shaped mole on her left cheek that first drew one's attention.

'There you are,' Katla said, turning around with her rollator to make room for Hildur. Katla leaned on the rollator as she walked, and her progress looked laborious. Her footsteps were slow and low, the soles of her feet dragged against the floor.

Hildur waited for the old woman to seat herself first. Then she took the free chair at Katla's side. 'You wanted to talk?'

Katla fiddled with the lace trim stitched to her linen dress.

'When you were here visiting, I heard you talking about the bones you found,' Katla said.

Hildur thought for a moment. She might have discussed the Kotsdalur excavation with Jakob a few days ago. Apparently, Katla had excellent hearing. Hildur knew it was only a matter of time before some journalist – for instance, some acquaintance of the excavator operator – began asking questions. But at least for now the media hadn't sniffed out the story.

Katla made herself more comfortable in her chair.

'I can hear again now that I got this gadget,' Katla said, indicating her hearing aid. 'You're one of the girls from Kotsdalur, aren't you? I'm from the same area. I remember you. You have two younger sisters too, don't you?'

Hildur nodded. 'Did you know my parents?'

Katla shook her head. 'Not very well. I bought those salves from your mother, like half the women in the area. I knew your father by appearance. I worked at the fish-processing plant. Your father worked for the same boss. Your father's name was Rúdólf?'

'Rúnar,' Hildur said.

'That's right!' Katla said, slapping her plump palms together. She looked visibly delighted to be remembering old times. Her whole body jiggled as she laughed. There was no trace of the gruffness that had marked their earlier exchanges.

'Did you know Helga well? You visited her often, I noticed,' Katla said.

Hildur admitted this and asked why she'd never met Katla during her visits. 'At first, you didn't want to talk to me. I'm interested in why not.'

Katla lowered her gaze to her palms and fingered the lace hem of her dress again. She told about distant relatives who had placed her in a nursing home less than a year ago, against her wishes. In their view, she couldn't manage on her own at home anymore, even though that's what she wanted most in the world: to live at home and look after herself.

'I'm not much of a people person. I prefer my own company.'

'Why?' Hildur tried to steer the conversation in the direction she wanted.

'Because you can't rely on anyone here but yourself. And I'm afraid.'

The answer had come directly and without hesitation. Hildur was suddenly alert.

'There's no reason to be afraid.'

Katla grunted in a way that filled Hildur with shame. Who was she to go promising emotional states on someone else's behalf?

'I heard you whispering about those bones with that handsome colleague of yours. And I heard what you and Helga said when you visited her. I know what happened. That nice male doctor said you were a trustworthy police officer.'

Hildur didn't comment; she didn't want to interrupt the old woman. She simply nodded to indicate she was listening.

Katla lowered her voice. Hildur could barely make out what she was whispering.

'He's like a beautiful spider who weaves his transparent webs from one side of the fjord to the other. Then when you want to get away, you can't.'

Katla's face had grown gloomier, and she glanced around as if checking to make sure no one was listening. What on earth were these spiders Katla was talking about?

'Who do you mean?' Hildur asked.

Katla shook her head decisively. 'He's incredibly intelligent. That's all I can say.'

Hildur tried to coax Katla into talking, but it was no use. And so she turned the conversation elsewhere for a moment.

'The old photographs in the lobby are from this area. There are some of the Hagfiskur fish-processing plant too. I recognised you in the picture,' Hildur said, running her finger across her left cheek. Katla's heart-shaped mole had been easy to identify.

'Yes, indeed,' Katla exclaimed. She said she began working at the plant in the early 80s and worked there until 1998, when the plant was closed and its operations moved south. 'They gave me a silver spoon for my service.'

Katla took a small sip of water from a mug on the coffee table and adjusted her glasses.

'That devilish law should never have been made,' she snapped, underscoring her outrage by slapping the arm of her chair a couple of times. The determined eyes flashed behind the thick-rimmed glasses as she whispered: 'A national asset was turned into the property of the few. The villages emptied. A lot of people around here were left without work too. Before that, things were fine.'

'Does this have something to do with the bones that were found?' Hildur said. She tried to lead the conversation without rushing, so as not to put Katla off.

'There were accidents at the plant,' Katla said, eyeing Hildur with a knowing look.

'Aren't there always at factories?' Hildur asked.

Katla swatted the air in frustration. 'Let me finish.'

Hildur realised her tactic of pretending to be sceptical had worked. Katla wanted to talk.

If the accident wasn't serious, the employee was sent home or to the dormitory with an aspirin and a package of band-aids to recover. If the accident was serious, an ambulance was called.

'Unless' – Katla said, tapping her forefinger against the mug in her hand – 'you were a foreigner.'

A shiver ran through Hildur. 'Why?'

Katla snorted and kept her eyes on the floor, as if considering how to put it. She let out a deep sigh and looked up at Hildur: 'No ambulance was ever called for them. They just . . . they just never came back to work after being injured.'

'Didn't anyone notice?' Hildur asked.

Katla shook her head. 'No one missed the foreigners. After recovering, some just left and went back to their homelands, so no one paid much attention if someone just didn't show up on the line anymore. But a company is worth more if it doesn't kill its employees, right? The statistics looked better if the foreigners' accidents weren't recorded anywhere.'

Hildur conceded this was the case.

'I had sharp ears back then. I know everything. But I kept my mouth shut because I needed the job,' Katla said. For a moment, a sly, one-sided smile formed on her face. It quickly melted. 'But I didn't have any evidence. I thought maybe my coworkers were just flapping their gums to stay warm.'

Katla grazed her left ear. 'But now that I heard about those bones, I thought to myself, darn it, maybe the old rumours are true after all!' She held a brief pause. The heart-shaped mole quivered as the corner of her mouth tightened. She nodded at her nightstand. 'Check the top drawer. There's a big brown envelope at the bottom. I want you to take it.'

The drawer squeaked as Hildur pulled it open. The envelope was unsealed. Inside were a few smooth handwritten sheets of paper. They looked like letters. Hildur quickly scanned them. She understood nothing about them but the greetings and the sign-offs. The address on the back was familiar.

'I not only did my job in the plant, I also handled the mail and cleaned the offices. For some reason these letters were never sent. I found them in the wastebasket and kept them. I speak German, so I immediately understood the contents.'

Hildur gave Katla a quizzical look. 'You've kept these letters all these years?'

Katla nodded and smiled, visibly pleased with herself. 'The love in them was palpable. And they proved he was bad, just as I'd always suspected.'

Katla said that by the time she found the letters, the woman who sent them was no longer around. 'The full name and address were on the back. I went to the dormitory to ask about the woman who wrote the letters, but I was told Ruth Weider had moved out a couple of weeks earlier.'

Hildur had to close her eyes. Too many questions were elbowing their way forward at the same time. Hadn't Katla asked anyone about the contents of the letters? Hadn't she tried to find the person who'd written them? Weren't they in envelopes? Weren't there addresses on the envelopes?

Katla took off her glasses and began cleaning them with the hem of her dress.

'It was easiest to get by when you just minded your own business. No one at the dormitory knew where that girl had gone. Back home, I suppose. Or at least that's what the Fisherman told anyone who asked. I heard him.'

The old woman put her glasses back on and looked probingly at Hildur. 'And they weren't in envelopes.'

Katla said that when the plant employees sent mail abroad, they brought the letter to the office, with the address written on a separate sheet of paper. The office staff handled the mail, and the postage costs were deducted from the employee's pay.

'The Fisherman read through everyone's mail. He probably didn't want these letters in particular to be sent. I'm assuming that's why they kept ending up in the wastebasket every time. Either the Fisherman was jealous about the letters or he wanted to protect his reputation. I found the letters fascinating, so I always fished them out of the garbage for myself to read. But I didn't have the nerve to defy the Fisherman and send them on.'

Hildur digested what she was hearing. She only had one question left: 'Do you remember what kinds of clothes you wore while you were working at the factory? Could you tell me about them?'

Chapter 58

13 March

Dear Max,

I still haven't heard from you. That makes me sad. Things have got really bad here.

I've been following the price of fish on the markets. The rumour going around is our boss is richer than I could have ever imagined. We don't see any of it. The roof of our dorm is still leaking. Our workdays keep getting longer, and I haven't got my pay on time for ages. Apparently, I'm not obedient enough. I shouldn't be demanding things all the time. He says it makes him feel bad. He hasn't told me he loves me in ages. He's the boss here, no questions asked. If I don't do what he says, he says I'll end up in jail. I entered the country illegally on a fishing boat so I don't have a valid contract. I can't get a social security number. I can't get anything. He's blackmailing me. I exist for him alone. That's what he tells me every night. He says he owns me because he saved me from working the streets.

I've made my decision. I'm getting out of here by the end of the month. I'll come back to you if you'll still have me and I have the money to leave. I have to get out of here. Could you help me, even if it's just this one last time?

I've been thinking about all sorts of things. A secure, stable relationship is better than constant adventure. Thinking about you gives me the strength to keep going through this terrible situation. I've come to realise I love you.

R.

Chapter 59

Ísafjörður, June 2022

Jakob heard Hildur clatter into the office. He remarked on the water dripping from the tips of her hair to the keyboard.

'It's raining out there,' Hildur mumbled, taking a rubber band from the pen holder. She tied back her hair and logged into her computer, then the national police database, LÖKE.

'The embassies handled the dental records quickly. We know the identities of two of the deceased now,' Jakob said in satisfaction. This information momentarily captured Hildur's attention.

Jakob had been surprised by the embassies' efficiency. Sometimes it could take months to get a response to international requests. He rolled his chair over next to Hildur's and spread two documents across her desk.

'Wait, there's one thing I really have to check first,' Hildur said, turning back to her computer with a look of concentration.

Jakob couldn't sit still, and he popped up to release his excess energy. He was dying to share the news he'd just received with Hildur. A moment before, he'd let out a wild cheer that the teeth of one of the female skeletons was a match for information received from Madrid. He'd also learned that Catherine Martin Ruiz had done a lot of riding as a child. Her radius had fractured at the age of fourteen. Catherine would finally be buried in her family's shared plot.

Jakob heard Hildur cursing to herself.

'Listen to this,' she said.

But Jakob cut her off. He'd spoken up first, so he got to go first. When he reported what he'd learned about Catherine, Hildur's expression changed. To Jakob it seemed as if she'd got lost somewhere in her own world.

'She'd been living in Iceland for about a year when she vanished. She came to work at the Hagfiskur fish-processing plant. Her parents and brother stayed in Madrid. Catherine's mother reported her missing when she didn't hear from her daughter one Sunday, when Catherine always called. Catherine's coworkers were sure she'd gone back to Spain. They said she'd said something about leaving earlier.'

Hildur looked at the documents Jakob had laid out. 'You mentioned two victims.'

Jakob reached over to his desk for his notebook, where he'd just made himself some notes. His entire body was tingling with the thrill of success. 'It was the Jan you asked about.' He read from his notes: 'Jan Nowak, a Polish citizen, disappeared in Iceland at the age of fifty. He found work at a seafood-processing plant in the Westfjords in the late 80s through an employment agency.'

Jakob had reached Jan's son and spoken with him on the phone. The son had remembered his mother saying his father had been injured on the job. His hand had caught in the filleting machine and been chopped off.

'The coworkers said Jan was immediately taken to the doctor after the accident. He'd been placed on extended sick leave, then decided to return home.'

'Except he never did?' Hildur ventured.

Jakob nodded. Jan's wife hadn't believed the story about Jan's return to Poland, because no one had been able to confirm it. She'd been left with no option but to report him missing.

But no investigation was ever launched, because so many people at the factory said the same thing: Jan had been injured and then just took off.

'That old newspaper article . . .' Hildur muttered. 'Helga was right.'

'Could it be a coincidence that these two missing people had the same employer?' Jakob asked.

Hildur reminded him that almost the entire town had worked at the plant. 'But it's not a coincidence. Check this out.'

Hildur clicked on the document she'd looked up in LÖKE. Jakob stood behind her and bent over to see the image on the screen. Her wet hair smelled of salt.

'The forensic investigators found a few scraps of textile in the grave and had them analysed,' she said. Sturdy rubber was still used for workwear in extremely cold, wet conditions, such as fishing boats but also fish-processing plants. 'Wool beneath, rubber on top,' she summarised.

Jakob took a closer look at the photograph. It was the same one they'd looked at during yesterday's videoconference. The bits of fabric were very worn, but faded black stripes could be seen beneath the yellow surface. Hildur pointed at the stripes and said she'd seen a similar pattern, thin black lines against a yellow background, in two different photographs.

'Do you remember the Rolex that went missing from the nursing home?' she asked, explaining that she'd visited Hinrik.

Jakob grunted; he wasn't surprised. If someone refused to talk to Hildur over the phone, she found it perfectly natural to drive five hundred kilometres and ring their doorbell.

'I saw this same pattern in an old picture at the nursing home. It showed workers from the fish plant and . . .'

Hildur pulled out her phone, browsed through her photos, and when she found what she was looking for turned her phone so Jakob could see. He studied the old colour photograph taken at the harbour and instantly grasped its significance.

'I also saw it in photos in Hinrik's living room. The bits of rubber are from Hagfiskur employee uniforms.'

Jakob plopped back down in his chair. Something about what Hildur had just told him was upsetting him.

'I just remembered something related to this,' he groaned, reached for his phone, and brought up the local hospital's website.

When Jakob had met Ómar at the pool, the message from Katla had consumed Jakob's full attention, and he hadn't remembered what else the summer temp had said.

'Ómar told me he'd been conducting vision exams,' he said, raising his phone to his ear. 'There's one thing I have to check right this second.'

He asked the receptionist at the hospital to put him through to Ómar.

'You told me you went over to the nursing home to conduct eyesight exams. You also mentioned the days you performed them, remember?' Jakob began. 'Were you examining any of the residents while I was taking fingerprints?' He told Ómar the exact date and time he'd been taking fingerprints, information he found in his notes.

Ómar didn't need much time to think.

'Well, I was a little mystified by the patient's eagerness,' he said, recounting how one of the residents had insisted on coming in for an exam without an appointment.

Jakob shivered.

'The patient had just got new glasses during a trip to Reykjavík but still wanted their vision tested. To make sure the new glasses were the right strength. I didn't have the heart to refuse.'

'And you performed the exam?' Jakob confirmed.

Ómar replied that he hadn't had anything more pressing to do at the moment.

'What was the patient's name?' Jakob asked, although he already knew the answer.

Chapter 60

'Would you care for coffee or tea?' Hildur asked the old man sitting in the conference room.

'She has great legs, but does she know how to make a cup of coffee?' Rökkvi Baldursson said with a wink at Jakob, who was sitting across from him. A laptop and a small camera stood on the table between them.

Hildur had assumed Rökkvi would try to establish a connection with Jakob. That's why she and Jakob had decided Jakob would play the good cop and handle the talking while she hung back.

Jakob and Hildur didn't have any evidence of Rökkvi's involvement in anything. They were missing one necessary piece of the puzzle. They'd come up with a plan and hoped it would work. They had a strong suspicion, but they needed more proof. If they were too hasty and revealed their hand too soon, it would give the suspect time to come up with explanations.

Hildur headed to the break room to fetch the coffee and accompaniments. She knew Rökkvi's eyes would be on her as she left the room, so she swung her hips intentionally.

Beta was in Reykjavík for a seminar. Hildur had called her and explained the turn the investigation had taken. The chat with Katla had confirmed the suspicions that had been growing in Hildur's mind and provided the missing link. Beta had approved Hildur and Jakob's proposal.

'Help yourself,' Hildur said upon returning to the conference room. She placed three coffee cups, the sugar dish, a carton of milk, and a pack of cookies on the table.

'Why don't we men begin,' Jakob said, turning on the video camera. He recited the pre-interview formalities and jotted down Rökkvi's contact information.

Rökkvi was visibly relaxed as he sat there at the table. Now and again he stroked his thick, well-groomed silver-grey hair. He was wearing a dress shirt under a lightweight purple sweater. His dress trousers fitted well. As a matter of fact, he looked much younger than his age.

'So we're investigating the death of Helga Ingimarsdóttir, and you're being questioned as a witness,' Jakob began.

Rökkvi's face showed no reaction. He poured a little milk into his coffee and stirred it in.

'I thought you were investigating those thefts?' he then asked, raising an eyebrow. He stared into his coffee cup as if he'd dropped something important in it. 'Sad that she died, although of course she was quite old. How can I help?'

Jakob ignored Rökkvi's questions. 'Did you know Helga well?'

Rökkvi raised his cup to his lips and drank. His movements were slow and deliberate. 'If I'm being questioned as a witness, then I have to know the crime involved.'

Hildur knew Rökkvi wasn't stupid. He knew how to ask the right questions. She and Jakob had to state the crime they were investigating.

'We suspect Helga was the victim of a homicide,' Jakob said sharply, then repeated his previous question.

'I knew who she was, but we didn't know each other. We exchanged a few words now and again, but that's it.' Rökkvi took another sip of coffee and looked Hildur in the eye. 'Delicious.'

'So the fact of the matter is . . .' Jakob held a dramatic pause, glancing at the documents in front of him and then Rökkvi, '. . . Helga was suffocated.'

Rökkvi spun the coffee cup around, apparently studying its floral pattern. 'How awful. Does this have something to do with the thefts?'

'It's possible. We believe we've found some of the items that were stolen.'

Hildur noticed Jakob's words send a tremor through Rökkvi's face. Then his facial muscles relaxed slightly.

Hildur had known from day one that Jakob would make an excellent police officer. When they'd looked into the backgrounds of the nursing home and hospital employees, Jakob had paid particular attention to any trips abroad the employees had made recently. Jódís's travels to Scotland over the past couple of years had caught Jakob's attention, because she didn't have any relatives there. Jakob's research had confirmed Hildur's observations: Jódís's finances were catastrophic. Apparently, opportunity had made a thief of her.

There was only one pawn shop in Iceland, but Glasgow had several, and Scotland was served by budget airlines. Jakob had called through the Glaswegian pawn shops and found most of the nursing home residents' missing items, including Rökkvi's Rolex. They'd be launching a criminal investigation into Jódís's activities too, but it wasn't time for that yet.

Hildur slid a photo of a Rolex sent by a Glasgow pawn shop across the table. The name and location of the pawn shop were visible in the photo. 'This ought to look familiar. Do you recognise this watch?'

The look of confusion on Rökkvi's face seemed genuine. He stared at the photo for a moment, then smiled broadly. 'In Scotland? So I didn't lose it; it was . . . it was stolen?'

Jakob conceded this was the case. The watch would be returned to Rökkvi at the first opportunity.

'Who took it?' Rökkvi asked. He was having a hard time hiding his curiosity.

Jakob said the investigation was still underway, but they'd get to the bottom of it. Rökkvi would be informed in time.

Hildur took the floor. She explained the police considered it highly likely that Helga had woken up when the thief entered and tried to shout for help. 'It's possible the thief was frightened of being caught and killed her by smothering her with a pillow.'

Rökkvi had stopped joking and was now listening carefully to Hildur's words.

'Your room is off the same corridor as Helga's, just two doors down. Did you see or hear anything out of the ordinary the night Helga died?'

Rökkvi frowned and fingered one of his earlobes. He appeared to be thinking. 'I don't remember. I sleep pretty soundly, thanks to melatonin and my ear plugs.'

Jakob made a note of Rökkvi's response, then announced the interview was over and Rökkvi was free to leave after signing the transcript.

Hildur watched Rökkvi's movements. Nothing about his body language suggested signs of nervousness or hesitation. He read the transcript and signed it.

'Damn it, you guys are pretty good. I was sure I'd misplaced that watch, but you found it. Thanks a million,' Rökkvi said.

After he exited the conference room, Hildur shot Jakob a look and smiled. They'd done it. Hildur put on a pair of disposable gloves, took the coffee cup Rökkvi had held in his hands, and dropped it in a sealable plastic bag:

'Now we'll catch that bastard.'

Chapter 61

After talking with Rökkvi, Hildur drove to Guðrun's yarn shop. Jakob was on a videoconference with the investigative team in Reykjavík about the cabin break-ins and hadn't answered Guðrun's call.

Matias had ditched soccer practice in the middle of the warm-up. He'd kicked over the plastic cones and bolted, eventually ending up at Guðrún's workplace.

Guðrún was standing behind the register, fiddling with skeins of yarn and looking like she didn't know what to do. She nodded toward the back left corner.

Matias was sitting on a cardboard box bearing a yarn mill's branding, tapping at his phone in concentration. He was still wearing his soccer gear; the local team's uniforms were blue with white sponsor logos. His calf-high socks accentuated how skinny his legs were.

Hildur called Matias's name, and he looked up from his phone. His expression was curious.

'You want to go for a drive?'

'Did you come in a police car?'

Hildur told Matias to go on out and wait. 'The car's unlocked. You can sit in the passenger seat if you promise not to touch anything.'

Matias nodded.

'I'll be out in a minute.'

Matias jumped down from the box and raced out the door, which was still ajar. Hildur watched him go. She had the car keys, so there wasn't any risk to speak of.

Guðrún leaned back against the shelf behind her and shook her head.

'What's with that kid? I can't get through to him. He came here from soccer practice but won't talk to me at all.'

Hildur stayed near the door. She had a direct line of sight through the display window to the vehicle. 'He doesn't know who he is.'

Guðrún looked questioningly at Hildur. 'Am I doing something wrong? I try so hard to be nice to him, but . . . but it feels like every time I open my mouth I say the wrong thing,' she said and sniffled.

Hildur found Matias's behaviour completely normal. A new place, new people, a new language. What would you expect but defiance? 'Give him time. It's the only thing that helps.'

'How long?'

Hildur shifted her weight to her other foot. She glanced back out at the car. Matias was sitting rigidly in the front.

'There aren't any rules. At least a year.'

The transition from new to familiar was hard to explain, but a year made for a good rule of thumb. Once the holidays, graduation parties, and Easter were experienced the first time, the next occasions went more easily.

Hildur knew Jakob's meeting would be over in half an hour at the latest. She suggested to Guðrún that she close up early and go home and relax. Jakob would be there soon.

Hildur pulled the door shut behind her and strode across the street to her car. She climbed in at the wheel and inserted the key into the ignition.

Matias immediately began asking about the switches and buttons on the dash. He wanted to know what would happen if he pressed this or that. Hildur explained about the ventilation, the emergency lights, how to open the bonnet, and how police radios worked.

'The world's shortest tunnel isn't too far away. When you honk the horn in it, you hear this strange music. Should we drive there?'

Matias nodded, clearly excited about the idea: 'If I can honk the horn.'

He had to tilt his head back to see Hildur's face from under the visor of his ball cap.

'If you buckle your seatbelt first,' Hildur answered and started up the car.

As Matias turned toward the door and fumbled with the seatbelt, Hildur saw the hollow below his hairline. Light fuzz grew there; it was like a tiny bird's nest. The neck was a little child's; the ball cap a big boy's. Matias's fingers weren't plump anymore, but his cheeks still were. The impression was one of a foal that had just risen to its feet but was already running its heart out. The sight somehow made time's passing concrete. She felt a lump form in her throat.

She swallowed it down and buckled her seatbelt too.

Chapter 62

The next morning, Hildur and Jakob were back in the conference room with Rökkvi again. Rökkvi had just been finishing his breakfast when the two investigators had appeared and asked him to come with them. Hildur had sensed Rökkvi's irritation as well as his skilful concealment of his emotions.

As they exited the nursing home and walked to the police car, Hildur had spotted Katla at the window, watching them. Hildur was sure she'd caught a small smile flash across the old woman's furrowed face.

Rökkvi had deposited his felt hat on the table and folded his coat over the back of an unoccupied chair. This time he was not offered coffee.

'You got the watch back already?' he asked.

Jakob didn't answer the question. He just recited the usual pre-questioning litany.

Hildur observed Rökkvi's face when Jakob told him he was suspected of having killed Helga. Not so much as a tremor.

'Listen, Rökkvi. Would you tell us what you did before you retired?' Jakob began.

The police knew all about Rökkvi's work history, but they wanted him to explain it in his own words. Rökkvi had once owned a big trawler, and he'd established a fish-processing plant in a nearby village. Hildur and Jakob had dug through old documents and made calls to people who'd been around at the time. By piecing information together, they'd been able to paint a relatively comprehensive picture of Rökkvi Baldursson's contributions to the Icelandic economy.

'Dances in the evening, gutting fish in the morning,' Rökkvi said, then whistled a couple of bars of some tune Hildur didn't recognise. 'What I'm saying is, I was a fisherman. Or I still am. You can never get rid of the smell of fish.'

Hildur glanced at Rökkvi's hands. They didn't look like the hands of a working man. Nor did those of his son, Hinrik Rökkvason, who lived in a waterfront home. *The work at sea and the factory was done by other people altogether*, she thought to herself.

Jakob shepherded the conversation onward: 'You once owned a big enterprise in the area.'

Before the interview, Jakob and Hildur had known they probably couldn't get Rökkvi to confess to his role in old crimes. Even so, they wanted to hear how he reacted.

Rökkvi sat up straighter and swiped the surface of the table with his forefinger, as if searching it for dust. 'The biggest in Iceland. My son picked up where I left off.'

Hagfiskur had been a significant company and major employer in the Westfjords. Rökkvi had been granted a large fishing quota in the late 1980s. As soon as the law permitted, Rökkvi had begun buying up boats along with their quotas from smaller-scale fishermen. He waited a few years and accumulated a massive fortune when the quotas were decoupled from locations and boats fishing in specific waters and converted into transferrable assets. Hildur had made a note of one particular name she spotted among the old documents.

'My father sold you his boat in the early '90s,' Hildur said, poker-faced.

Rökkvi grunted. 'I was wondering why your name was so familiar . . . But yes, that's right. I bought *Herdís* from him. Your mother tried to stop him, but your father stuck to his guns.'

Now it was Hildur's turn to grunt. 'My mother was probably right.'

Rökkvi shrugged and said it depended on whose point of view you looked at it from. One person's loss was another person's gain.

'I silently thanked your father many times. From my perspective, he made a good deal. I got a good boat, fish, and a loyal worker.'

Hildur stared at Rökkvi without saying a word. Jakob didn't speak either. They had agreed to use silence at this point of the interview to pressure Rökkvi into saying something. Most people didn't tolerate silence very well and tried to fill it with talk. And that was exactly when they usually said something they normally wouldn't have.

'Your father got his share. I paid him well,' Rökkvi added.

Prior to the interview, Hildur and Jakob had known the statute of limitations would have expired on any workplace safety crimes, as well as assaults, abandonment, and desecration of the dead.

But now it was Jakob's turn to twist the screws.

'Four bodies were found buried behind Rúnar's house. They've been identified as those of foreigners who worked for you in the early 1990s. Age, ethnicity, gender, and dental records match people who worked at your plant. What do you have to say about this?'

Jakob wasn't exactly telling the truth. They hadn't succeeded in verifying the identity of all the bodies, but they had confirmed enough details to pretend they knew more than they did.

Rökkvi sat up straighter again and nudged his chair toward the table. 'I don't know anything about that. Rúnar was a little strange. He might have had some dark secret of his own.' He leaned back in his chair and smirked. 'I'm sure you can't prove anything, so I assume we can stop this nonsense?'

'How well did you know Ruth Weider?' Hildur shot back.

Hearing the name caught Rökkvi off guard. He appeared to carefully weigh his response. After a minute or so, he calmly answered: 'Yes, I knew her well. She worked in England as a harbour-front whore. I got to know her when we brought in a cod catch. I hired her to work at my factory. She was a hard worker, gutted fish all day and screwed all night. She was wild and unpredictable. Maybe she got pregnant and went home. There's nothing more I can tell you about her.'

Hildur was pleased by Rökkvi's now-hostile attitude. An angry person was easier to derail. The biggest mistakes were always made in a state of heightened emotions.

Hildur said small bits of fabric had been found in the grave at Kotsdalur and been analysed at the forensics laboratory. 'We compared them to photographs displayed in your son's living room and here in the nursing home's corridors. They show workers wearing coats that are exactly the same colour as the textile samples and bear your company's logo. The textile fragments in the grave are from Hagfiskur workers' coats. The kind used at your facility in the 1980s and 1990s.'

Rökkvi shook his head. A mocking smile spread across his face. 'Some old coats? Is that the best you can do? You can't call me to account for ancient history,' Rökkvi snapped, and looked at Jakob as if he were an imbecile. 'So if you don't have any more questions—'

'As a matter of fact, we do,' Hildur said. She asked if Rökkvi used a pillow when he slept.

Rökkvi rubbed his face and remarked on the idiocy of the question.

'We decide what questions to ask,' Hildur snapped. 'Your job is to answer.'

Rökkvi sighed. 'Yes, I use a pillow.'

Judging by the look on Rökkvi's face, he was getting a sense of the direction the conversation was heading. Because it was too late to back out, he fell silent.

'You and Helga were neighbours at the nursing home. The distance between your rooms is no more than a few metres. There are no CCTV cameras in the corridors. The doors aren't locked.'

Rökkvi stared straight ahead. Jakob glanced down at the documents again and continued with how easy it was to move between the two rooms.

'Call me a taxi. I'm going back to the nursing home. I don't have to sit here listening to silly insinuations.'

Jakob pressed both palms to the tabletop, signalling for Rökkvi to cool it.

'Calm down and let me finish.' Jakob took a piece of paper from the folder of printouts in front of him. 'This is a photograph of one of the fingerprints found on Helga's bedframe. The print is clear. The killer wrapped his left hand around the aluminium support while he held the pillow in place with his right hand.'

Jakob shifted his finger over to the image on the right: 'We took this fingerprint from the coffee cup you held in your hands yesterday. The prints are a match.'

They'd received confirmation from the forensics laboratory that morning. They'd been fortunate to get the fastest fingerprint analysis possible.

Hildur waited a moment for Jakob's words to sink in. Rökkvi's back had slouched slightly.

'I went into Helga's room to pay her a visit earlier in the week,' Rökkvi said. 'Maybe that's where the prints are from.'

'No, you didn't,' Hildur said drily. 'Helga would have told me.' She lowered her fingers to her laptop and typed as she spoke. 'I visited Helga the evening before she died. At first, the things she told me struck me as odd and not grounded in reality. She talked about ghosts that visited her, and she mentioned foreigners who had gone missing.'

Hildur remembered the door to Helga's room had been open at the time. If Katla had heard the conversations, it was perfectly likely Rökkvi had too.

'You were afraid Helga would keep talking and you'd lose your reputation . . . and that your son would lose his. You were afraid everyone would learn about the missing foreign workers. You took your pillow with you into Helga's room, pressed it to her face, and kept pressing until she stopped breathing.'

Hildur paused. She saw Rökkvi shrink before her eyes. His back was fully hunched.

'You just made one big mistake. You left your pillow next to Helga,' Hildur said.

Rökkvi's complexion had gone a shade whiter. Suddenly, he looked incredibly old. But his eyes flashed with willpower and determination.

'Ultimately this is about money too. A Canadian investor is presently assessing the value of the company your son runs.

You didn't want your old deeds to come out. You wanted to safeguard your own reputation, your son's reputation and wealth.'

Hildur saw Rökkvi's sharp Adam's apple bobbing up and down faster. It was strangling his throat like a tightening noose.

'When I visited your son . . .' Hildur added, this time more slowly, 'I saw the cross-stitch.'

Rökkvi's favourite saying had been hanging in the living room of his son's massive house.

A good reputation never dies.

'Respect is important to you, Rökkvi. You murdered Helga because you didn't want to lose your reputation. In the end, that's the only thing that remains when we pass on.' Hildur held a dramatic pause before continuing: 'I think once Helga was dead, you left the pillow there because you couldn't bear to look at her. Tough guy or not, murdering another human being with one's bare hands is unnerving. When it comes down to it, you're weak. A weak man who craves respect.'

Chapter 63

The thick caramel coating crunched between Hildur's teeth. She'd picked up ice creams for herself and Jakob from the store. Their cooperation had been seamless.

Rökkvi had imagined he'd get everything he wanted. He'd considered himself untouchable. And so he'd misjudged and murdered Helga. The poor woman had died because Rökkvi had wanted to protect his reputation to the end. A small catastrophe used to try and prevent a big catastrophe often resulted in an even bigger one. *How shortsighted and stupid*, Hildur thought to herself, turning the ice cream bar. She always gnawed off the crust before moving on to the insides.

The fingerprints on the bedframe wouldn't have been sufficient to charge Rökkvi, but he didn't know that. They'd set a trap the old man had fallen for. He'd confessed; he hadn't been able to stand the suggestion that he was weak.

'It was my only mistake. Otherwise it was the perfect murder,' Rökkvi had stated. And with those words he'd locked himself in a prison cell for the rest of his life.

Two patrol officers had set out after the interview to escort Rökkvi to Reykjavík to await his detention hearing. Beta, who answered for the investigation, had already spoken with the prosecutor. As soon as Hildur completed the preliminary investigation documents, they'd be delivered to the prosecutor, who would then decide whether to press charges.

The case seemed clear cut. In addition to circumstantial evidence, they had a motive and a confession. Rökkvi was an octogenarian and didn't have many years left. But a suspect's age didn't play a role in preliminary investigations or decisions to press charges and presumably not in sentencing either. Rökkvi wasn't ill. On the contrary, he was in excellent shape for a man his age.

'I'm frustrated we can't bring him to justice for those workers,' Jakob said, munching on his chocolate ice cream cone.

Hildur shared Jakob's pain. Although it seemed relatively certain the victims had died at the fish-processing plant, Rökkvi could no longer be called to account for their deaths. A murder conviction could get him a life sentence, which meant there was no statute of limitations. But for the prosecutor, trying to determine whether Rökkvi had murdered any of the people found in the grave would be a waste of resources.

Hildur hadn't revealed how painful Rökkvi's cruelty toward her family had felt. Rökkvi claimed Rúnar was the one who'd buried the bodies in his own backyard.

'He worked for me,' Rökkvi had said, giving Hildur a pointed look. That was all he'd said about Rúnar, but there had been no need to say more. Hildur had understood. Rúnar's financial stress and dependence on the wealthiest man in the village had presumably pushed him into darkness. For the first time, Hildur saw the motives lurking behind her father's behaviour. She didn't approve, but she understood. Her father had been forced to live not only with financial destitution he'd brought on himself but also the resulting shame. Hildur could only guess at what else the subordinate relationship between her father and Rökkvi had entailed.

After finishing his ice cream, Jakob held up the sweater he was working on to get a better look at his handiwork. 'Should we have pressured Rökkvi even more?' he fretted. 'If Rökkvi was capable of murder now, maybe he also committed it as a younger man.'

'Rökkvi will die in prison in any event,' Hildur said, comforting herself with the words. She settled in to write the preliminary investigation report. She wanted to be sure the groundwork was completely solid. There was no room for error. When she finished the document, she would travel to Reykjavík personally to get Rökkvi's signature.

A couple of hours later, the sound of her phone ringing roused Hildur from her writing. A German number.

'Hi, it's Max. I got your message. Are you free to meet now?' He said he'd be leaving soon for Reykjavík to make it to his next cruise on time.

Hildur's thoughts turned to Manuel, who was still hiding out at Andri's summer cabin. 'Come to the station. Grey building, second storey. I can offer you a cup of coffee.'

Hildur reread what she'd written one final time, then made her way to the break room. As she measured out the coffee into the machine, she heard tentative footfalls and two voices in the corridor. She recognised the language as Finnish. Hildur peered out into the corridor and saw an elderly couple standing at the door to the office she shared with Jakob. The woman's silver-grey hair was cut in a neat bob. The broad-shouldered man was wearing a long, lightweight coat and carrying a leather satchel. Their backs were turned to Hildur. She couldn't make out individual words, but she could hear Jakob speaking in an unusually loud voice.

Hildur stepped out and approached the couple. Apparently, they heard her, because they turned around.

'Excuse me, is everything all right here?' Hildur asked in English. She'd never seen the man or woman before, but his jawline and her eyes told her everything she needed to know.

'Are you Jakob's parents?' she asked and introduced herself.

She glanced at Jakob, who was standing behind his desk, fists clenched and jaw tight.

'Yes, they're my parents and they're just leaving,' Jakob replied firmly in English.

The man and woman exchanged a helpless glance and then gave Hildur an apologetic smile. 'We don't want to cause any drama. It's probably best if we leave,' the woman said. Her husband nodded haplessly at her side.

The woman took one last look at Jakob and said something to him in Finnish. Then she and her husband left. Hildur watched the hunched couple recede.

'What was that about?'

Jakob collapsed to sitting in his chair and rubbed his face. 'I don't understand them at all. How dare they come here! They . . . Why can't they just leave me in peace?'

Now Hildur understood. 'Those messages . . .'

Jakob nodded. 'They're difficult people. I haven't replied to their messages for a long time. I never would have guessed they'd go to the trouble of tracking me down here.'

Hildur sat down at her desk and glanced at her watch. Max would be here any minute.

'What did they want?'

Jakob laughed incredulously and shook his head. 'They told me they were sorry about everything and asked me to help them one last time.'

Hildur waited for Jakob to continue his story, but just then they heard footsteps again. Max Meyer was striding purposefully down the corridor.

A moment later, Max was sitting in the conference room. Despite Max's reluctance, Hildur had invited Jakob to the meeting, because she'd be sharing everything she knew with him anyway. Max had given in because he had no choice.

Now he sat there staring at Jakob, who was finishing the collar of a sweater. 'I've never seen a man knitting before.'

'Well, pay close attention and you might learn something,' Jakob replied, with a smile so bright it revealed his upper and lower teeth.

Max said he'd been on land for a couple of days doing some investigating. He didn't go into any greater detail.

Hildur asked Max to give them a rundown of the shady things that took place on cruise ships. Max placed his hands behind his neck and stretched his arms. He seemed to be weighing up the situation.

Hildur didn't want to drag things out, so she opened the conversation with her trump card. 'I have information on Ruth Weider.'

Jakob started. There was a clink as one of his needles dropped to the floor. The look on Max's face revealed that he'd been caught off guard too. He lowered his hands to the table and leaned forward.

'What did you say?' he asked sternly.

Hildur kept her face neutral. She held a binder in her hands, and she knew its contents would be of interest to Max. 'You go first. Has anything else come up in the investigation that we should know? I want to know what's happening in my hometown.'

Max sighed. 'I've kept my word. I haven't done any more looking into Manuel's situation. We didn't look into who rented the rental car. What more do you want?'

Hildur glanced at Jakob. He'd already told her the investigation into the break-ins was wrapping up. The two of them had analysed the details of the case. They'd linked the break-ins that had taken place at cabins in the Westfjords to those that had taken place elsewhere in the country and found a pattern. Max looked on indifferently as Hildur and Jakob spread a map across the table marked with the times and locations of all the incidents.

'The cabins have been vandalised but not robbed. The perps appear and disappear without taking anything.' Jakob stressed the last three words by tapping the tabletop with his forefinger. Then he handed Max a printout from the rental agency, including the information on the car caught on the surveillance camera and the identity of the hirer.

Max read the printout and raised an eyebrow. 'You're kidding . . . That's a name I recognise. Could I have the footage from the camera? It might be of use in our investigation.'

Jakob promised to give him the video. But he and Hildur wanted information too. The police were responsible for maintaining public safety in Ísafjörður and needed to be aware of everything that was happening in their jurisdiction.

Max told them the cruise ships were supplied at the departure port. Thousands of kilograms of clean laundry, food, beverages, and other goods were loaded onto each ship for a week-long cruise.

'Passengers have to go through a security screening upon boarding and their baggage is X-rayed. Goods brought on board some other way, like clean bed linen and food supplies, aren't X-rayed. The passengers are allowed ashore at the intermediary stops. Anything at all could be taken off the ship during those stops. The shipping companies don't X-ray upon disembarking.'

Hildur knew what Max was about to say next and said it first: 'Distribution of illicit goods.'

'Yes. It's been made ridiculously easy. Drugs, cash, stolen valuables, small works of art, anything at all that doesn't take up much space. They're brought on board with supplies, and criminal gang members posing as ordinary passengers distribute them to day-tour destinations.'

Hildur was on the verge of speaking when Jakob interrupted her: 'Those cabin break-ins. There was never any intention of stealing anything. They wanted to use them as caches.' He related the observations he'd made at Skálavík, where a small hole had been dug under the porch.

'A typical diversion,' Max said, adding that the scheme was used outside Iceland as well. 'Since nothing is taken from the targeted cabins, the police, the insurance companies, and the owners have no motive to look any further. Later, criminal gang members retrieve the stash and distribute it onward. If some neighbour catches them, they just say they're from the insurance company or the police and investigating the break-in that had taken place a few days before.'

'Pretty ingenious,' Hildur mused, this method being completely obvious yet hidden at the same time.

Max said the distribution was honed down to the finest detail. It was the outcome of years of trial and error. 'That surveillance camera footage would be a big help for us.'

Jakob pulled out a black USB stick and handed it to Max. Max thanked him, slipped it into the inner pocket of his jacket, and zipped up the pocket.

'So who exactly are these perps? Should the National Police be informed?'

Max raised his hands. 'By no means. Not yet. Only when they can't screw anything up anymore.' He paused and softened his tone: 'All I mean is, everyone in this country knows each other. Information would leak from cousin to cousin, and that's a risk we cannot take. Connections between police command and politicians are too close here.'

Max had clearly done his homework.

Jakob and Hildur listened to Max's account of a criminal gang founded by Germans and long-time Turkish immigrants in Germany. The gang didn't have any ideological aims. They were just focused on making money.

'The organisation operates like a multinational conglomerate. Markets are precisely divided, and different crimes are committed in different areas. In Germany, they make money off an unofficial workforce and construction-industry tax evasion. Here in Iceland, the activities are primarily dealing narcotics, the through-transit of illegal diamonds, and the black-market trade in mares' blood.'

Hildur's heart skipped a couple of beats. She felt as if she had lead sinking down into her legs. 'What did you say about the trade in blood?'

'The blood of pregnant mares is used to produce hormones for the food—'

Hildur cut Max off. 'I know all about that. We had an investigation into violent crimes last year that involved the industry.'

Max nodded. 'I know about your sisters. I have my sources.'

Hildur didn't respond.

'It's just a small part of the organisation's activities, but according to our estimates, the trade in illegally sold mares' blood brings in a few million euros a year here,' Max continued.

It had become clearer and clearer to Hildur what a tempting country Iceland was from the perspective of international crime. It was remote and people trusted each other. It was easy to collect blood in the sparsely inhabited countryside without attracting attention, then sell it on to international buyers.

'It was lucky the investigation into the business side of the mares' blood trade dried up. Its ballooning into an official investigation and the subsequent publicity could have put the entirety of this bigger investigation at risk.'

Hildur and Jakob were perfectly aware of what Max was talking about. Last year's spree of assaults and homicides had centred on confrontations between mares' blood collectors and animal rights activists. But there had been no media coverage of the illicit business involved in the collection of the blood.

'Do you know who's running the Icelandic arm of the organisation?' Hildur asked casually, setting the binder on the table in front of her.

Max eyed the binder in Hildur's hands.

'We won't intrude on the investigation, and whatever you tell us stays here,' Hildur promised.

Max chose his words carefully. He explained about the structure of the organisation, which was similar everywhere. The leaders didn't avoid publicity. Just the opposite: they were ordinary people who drew no attention to themselves and blended into the masses. 'But we never had this conversation, and you guys aren't going to start digging into anything.'

Hildur and Jakob promised. They didn't even have anything to dig into.

'We think it likely the ringleaders on the Icelandic end are Árni Emilsson and María Magnúsdóttir. They own a farm and tourist industry enterprises.'

Hildur made a mental note of the names, then slid the orange binder across the table to Max. Max tried to open it quickly, but Hildur placed her hand on it and looked him in the eye.

'Would there have been any unique features of Ruth's skeleton that she could be identified by? Were you aware of any major fractures or, for instance, deformities?'

Max thought for a moment, then answered in a confident voice: 'Her left forefinger was much shorter than her right. She cut off the tip while she was shoeing a horse. I remember, because I'm the one who took her to the hospital.'

'How do you remember it was the left hand?'

'She was incredibly frustrated because she was left-handed.'

'Had Ruth ever been to the dentist?'

The answer came quickly: 'Not that I know of, at least as an adult. She was afraid of the dentist.'

Hildur nodded and slid her hand off the binder. Max opened it and began to read.

Hildur had put together a file consisting of the photographs of the remains of the second, as-yet-unidentified young woman, a summary of Emma's report that she herself had translated, and the stack of old letters Katla had given her.

'A woman about the age of twenty. It could be Ruth or not,' Hildur said. 'We can't know for sure, because the left hand is missing, so there's no way to check the fingers on that hand. Some sharp object had severed the hand just prior to death. But those letters prove she was here around the time she went missing.'

Hildur explained how Katla had set aside the old letters she'd found in the wastebasket in the fish factory office and held on to them until today.

'Katla's mother was German, so Katla speaks German fluently. She could read the letters, and she set them aside. The letters weren't in envelopes, so she wasn't able to send them on.'

Hildur saw signs of powerful emotion on Max's face. By the time he reached the end of the file, his eyes were welling up with tears. 'You found her.'

Hildur asked Max to maintain his scepticism in spite of his excitement. Ruth had been in the Westfjords, but the body found in the grave wasn't necessarily hers. It would have been possible to take a DNA sample of the bones, but they had nothing to compare it to, as Ruth had no living relatives.

Max shut the binder and handed it back to Hildur.

Hildur shook her head and told Max to keep it. 'That's everything we have. You had a right to know, even though we can't be completely sure.'

'I don't suppose we can ever be completely sure about anything,' he said, wiry fingers stroking the binder.

They sat in silence for a moment, eyes on the binder.

'Sometimes all we can do is accept things as they are,' Hildur said.

Ruth's fate stung Hildur. She'd gone and tried her luck in search of a better life. She'd been brave and set out. Grasped at opportunities. Those opportunities had just proven to be cruelly unfortunate.

Hildur told Max the bones were in the possession of the forensic pathologist. Because there was no way to positively identify the body, it might be impossible to turn it over to him. If he wanted to try to bury Ruth, it would behoove him to reach out to the pathologist. Axlar-Hákon's contact information was in the pocket of the binder.

'I wish I hadn't been such a dunce,' Max said softly. 'I wish I would have been able to keep her close.'

The words were directed at himself, and Hildur didn't know what to say anyway. She just listened. That was enough.

As if by joint decision, they rose to their feet. The meeting was over. Before Max exited the conference room, Hildur said: 'You'll find the bag in the bathroom on Deck 8. I stashed it behind the wall. You know what to do, right?'

Chapter 64

Hildur had one final errand to handle before her trip to Reykjavík, so she headed out for a run.

First, she ran past the old cemetery in front of the church, where no one had been buried for ages. The former wooden church, over a hundred years old, had been destroyed in a fire, and the new church had been completed in the early 1990s. The oldest graves had had to be moved out from under the new building. Everyone who died in Ísafjörður these days was buried in the cemetery at the base of the fjord.

Hildur liked cemeteries. It was an aspect of the same fascination she had for printed obituaries and death notices read on the radio. Ministers, janitors, old and young. After death, each and every one of them left behind one and the same thing: an empty shell that disintegrated and turned to dust. Family members and the community ensured the memories remained. That's why Hildur found it interesting to read people's birth and death dates, names and other tidbits of information on the gravestones. A farmer from Nes, born in high summer 1922, died on Christmas Eve 1979. The gravestone showed that his wife, a stay-at-home mother, had lived twenty years longer than her husband. The beginning of life was foreign to Hildur, the end of life much more familiar. She felt safe in the company of the lost and the deceased.

After her stop at the cemetery, Hildur returned to the pedestrian-slash-bike path. As she ran, she considered the farmer's wife. Had she been unhappy for twenty long years following her husband's death? Or had an independent life, one lived on her own terms, only begun after he died?

Each one of us had our private hidden life. Hildur's thoughts glanced on Jakob. She didn't know whether he'd agreed to see his parents again. They'd showed up unexpectedly and asked for help, and those who asked for help deserved to get it. But Hildur hadn't started giving Jakob advice, because she didn't know what she would have done under the circumstances herself. Hildur also had secrets she'd never told anyone, and she knew if she lived to an old age, she would continue to face many things she would keep wholly to herself.

Kilometre followed kilometre, and the birds twittered in the riverbank bushes.

'Hey, Ribs!'

Manuel was sitting on the porch at Andri's cottage. He greeted Hildur with a wave.

'Ribs?' Hildur asked.

'Well, you're kind of . . .' Manuel said, lifting his arms away from his sides to make himself look more muscular.

Hildur laughed. Oh, those Venezuelans and their nicknames. A couple of golden plovers were strutting through the yard, heads bobbing. They looked around for a moment, then took to the wing. These were the longest days of the year.

'You said you had something you wanted to talk to me about,' Manuel said, holding his gaze toward the evening sun.

Hildur took a folded envelope from the pocket of her running jacket. 'I can't tell you anything else, but I can swear you shouldn't go back to that boat. We can't protect you there.'

A doubtful gleam sparked in Manuel's eyes. 'What other option do I have, do you suppose? You said I could trust the police.' Manuel's voice grew louder as he spoke. 'You promised telling you what happened would help!'

Hildur had promised Max not to endanger the BKA and Interpol investigation into organised crime.

'There's a bigger picture here. Investigating these things takes time.'

Hildur felt a weight inside. This was so incredibly difficult. It was unfair to sacrifice one person to a major investigation. But ultimately she'd thought of a solution.

'Manuel, when the cruise ship pulls into harbour, you're not going to board.'

Manuel moaned. 'I have to! They'll notice if I don't go back to work. They'll assume I snitched, and then my parents in Venezuela will end up in trouble. You don't understand: these people have tentacles everywhere. I can't get away from them.'

Hildur asked Manuel to listen. 'Everyone on board thinks you're dead. I've arranged it that way.'

She explained her plan, which she could share now that Max was in on it. Back when she'd been looking for Manuel, she'd taken his bloody clothes from the hospital. She'd crammed them in a bag and hidden them in the bathroom on the cruise ship.

'Before long, everyone on the ship will think you jumped.'

Max had promised to stage Manuel's clothes and shoes on the ship's foredeck. It had been his favour to Hildur in return for the information she'd given him about Ruth.

'You're going to have to apply for asylum in Iceland.'

Hildur said she'd spoken with an acquaintance who worked at the immigration authority and had given her some off-the-record advice. 'I think you and Andri should consider getting married and tell the authorities about your plans when applying for asylum.'

It wasn't easy for Venezuelans to get asylum in Iceland, because the immigration authority viewed the country as safe. Nevertheless, sexual minorities had been subjected to persecution lately.

Manuel listened to Hildur and said he knew all about it. He'd had plenty of experience with hardened attitudes and state-sponsored discrimination in his everyday life. It had been one reason why he'd applied for work abroad.

Hildur advised Manuel to report to immigration after a couple of days and claim asylum. That would presumably give enough time for someone to find his clothes. She passed Manuel the envelope, which contained instructions for applying for asylum that she'd printed out from the website.

'When you get married, you can consider changing your name. A new surname will give you some anonymity,' Hildur said. 'And delete all your social media accounts.'

Manuel turned the envelope over in his hands, looking lost.

'I hope everything goes well,' Hildur said, and bid Manuel goodbye.

'Thank you.'

That was all Manuel said, but it was enough.

Consequentialism was a matter of raw mathematics. According to that philosophy, it would be ethical to sacrifice one life if doing so ended up saving a hundred. But you couldn't determine the virtue of an action by the achieved benefit alone. The ends didn't always justify the means. Hildur felt a profound gratitude that she'd succeeded in saving this particular one.

Chapter 65

Hólmavík, June 2022

A slow count to three while rising onto the balls of the feet, a slight pause, and a slow count to three as the soles of the feet dropped back to the floor. After repeating the movement three times, the blood began to circulate in Hildur's calves. On long drives it was wise to make use of every stop, even short ones.

Hildur had hit the road at six that morning. Now the clock showed eight thirty. She'd pulled into a pit stop for coffee a moment before. There was a small grill attached to the sole grocery store in the village of Hólmavík. Ice cream, yesterday's pastries, and coffee from the Thermos were on offer too.

The bald man in an apron nodded at the coffee maker: 'The truck drivers just emptied it. It'll be a minute.' Then he turned back to scrubbing the sandwich grill.

'You have any cream?' Hildur asked hopefully, once the coffee was done percolating.

'We have milk.'

Hildur flashed her credit card at the payment terminal, took her coffee, and exited. A couple of cars zoomed past. The sea roiled behind the shop; behind the car park stood the local savings bank, now empty, and a couple of buildings that had seen better days. Beyond them loomed the great wilderness of lava fields threaded by a single road that connected the Westfjords to the rest of Iceland.

Hildur's phone began vibrating in her pocket. She climbed into Brenda and turned the key in the ignition. She connected the phone to the audio system via Bluetooth. The speakers needed a slap to work, even though she'd just bought a new set for the front seats. *Why does everything fall apart these days*? Hildur wondered, giving the speakers another smack.

A confused female voice could be made out through the crackle, speaking English. 'Is this Hildur Rúnarsdóttir?'

Hildur answered in the affirmative and turned up the volume. At the intersection, she flipped the indicator to the left, toward Reykjavík. She still had a three-hour drive ahead of her.

'This is Lisa Weber. Do you remember me?'

Hildur frowned. She wasn't sure. The name sounded familiar. The woman's accent also sparked recognition, but she couldn't immediately place it. *Lisa Weber. Lisa* . . . Yes, she'd definitely heard the name before somewhere.

'We met last winter. You came to the horse farm with that tall Finnish policeman. My coworker Luka had died, and you . . .'

Now Hildur remembered: the young German woman who worked at the Sel horse farm in northern Iceland. A fish-ravaged body had been found in a salmon pen in the Ísafjörður fjord. The deceased had been identified as Lisa's Slovenian coworker Luka. At first, the police had suspected the death involved drug debts, but it had proved to be something much more complicated: Luka had been an animal rights activist and tried to put a stop to the illegal trade in mares' blood in Iceland. But the real crooks behind the blood business had caught wind of the activists and silenced them. Some had been frightened into silence through assaults, but Luka had died.

'You guys had those mares . . .' Hildur said.

Lisa was delighted that Hildur remembered her. She explained that she'd spent a few months in Germany; she'd returned to her homeland to recover from Luka's death and the emotional and psychological weight of the investigation.

'But I found a new job in Iceland and I just got back. I train horses at a place outside Reykjavík. I wanted to call you because . . .' Lisa's voice was drowned out by the crackle of the speaker.

Damn it! Hildur swore to herself and pulled over. The road was straight. She could see for kilometres up ahead and behind, and there were no other cars in sight. She disconnected her phone from the car's speakers and raised it to her ear.

'I'm sorry, I'm driving and my Bluetooth isn't working. What did you just say?' Hildur said. She was getting a strange feeling about this call.

'I read some old news in English after I got back to Iceland. There were quite a few stories about those horrible crimes . . .'

Hildur knew the newspaper Lisa was talking about. Iceland's free English-language paper contained restaurant and tour recommendations for tourists. In addition to articles on culture and tourism, it published stories of interest to foreigners, and the abuse of Icelandic horses was a topic that spoke to tourists visiting the country.

'Last winter when the investigation was still underway, I was in Reykjavík and I went to see some colleagues of yours. I don't remember their names. A Bella and . . . a . . .' Lisa hesitated.

'Beta and Tumi,' Hildur suggested. Beta and Tumi had handled the investigation into the assaults against Luka and the other victims while Hildur was in Finland helping Jakob.

Hildur let her gaze circle the dark grey lava field. Patches of green moss clung to the rock here and there, looking irresistibly soft. For a moment Hildur considered stepping out of the car and lying down in the lava, head resting on a bed of moss.

'I heard mares' blood is being collected again,' Lisa said. Now there was certainty in her voice.

Hildur was aware of the trade in mares' blood. 'There's nothing illegal about it. If you observe the veterinarian's instructions and the blood is collected properly, it's a completely legal activity.'

Hildur heard Lisa sigh deeply. 'I know. But they have a new girl doing it for them,' Lisa said.

'What do you mean? Who's "they"?'

Lisa held a brief pause. 'It was a lot later when I realised my former employers knew what was going on the whole time.'

'You've lost me,' Hildur said. She had no idea what Lisa was trying to say.

'Árni and María knew what was going on the whole time.'

Hildur felt her blood freeze. What exactly was Lisa saying? *Árni ja María* . . . Hildur rewound to her most recent conversation with Max. Max had mentioned an Árni and María too.

They do everything. Everything that turns a profit . . .

'Lisa, now it's important that you remember correctly. So have you seen them, your former bosses, recently?'

Lisa said she'd seen the couple the day before. They'd been talking to a woman Lisa didn't recognise at the stables in

Reykjavík. The woman had handed over two heavy-looking canisters to them.

'I was cleaning the stalls. They didn't see me, but I heard some of what they were saying. They made the girl swear to do a better job sticking to the schedule, because they had a big buyer in China . . . I'm sorry. That's all I heard.'

Hildur pressed the phone to her ear. She and Jakob had personally visited Árni and María's farm the previous winter when investigating Luka's death. Not to mention years ago, she'd had some dealings with the couple through the missing children's unit, while helping some kids who'd run away. Árni and María owned a foster family business. And now . . . and now, six months later, the names of the couple that lived in the countryside had popped up in an Interpol investigation.

It was clear from Lisa's voice that she felt bad. She'd mentioned Árni and María to Beta and Tumi the previous winter, but the names hadn't been recorded anywhere, because other information had led the police to Rósa, and Rósa had been arrested for having carried out the assaults on the animal rights activists.

'Lisa, I'm really glad you called.' Hildur couldn't tell Lisa about the other suspicions regarding Árni and María, but she knew the information she'd just been given was incredibly valuable.

Lisa was worried about the welfare of the animals. 'You'll make sure the horses aren't abused anymore, won't you?'

Hildur promised. 'Spot checks are being carried out at mare farms regularly these days. The activity is being monitored more actively,' she said, then ended the call.

Hildur heard a massive stone roll from her gut back to the lava field. She didn't know what to do yet, but there had to be some way of freeing her sister, and now there was no doubt as to Björk's innocence. Björk had an alibi, and the police had new suspects. But before she did anything, there was one thing she had to take care of. The thing she was driving to Reykjavík for.

Chapter 66

Reykjavík, June 2022

> Hey, lady . . . How are things? <3 Greetings from your favourite reindeer herder. It's calf-marking day . . .

Hildur was sitting on a park bench, phone in hand. On the next bench over, two homeless guys were drinking red wine from a bottle. They seemed to be enjoying the sun. Hildur wasn't. Even so, she'd had to rest for a moment. She'd felt weak after her visit to the hospital. Her vision had been blurry and her footsteps loose. She'd sit here for a moment, finish the half of a kebab sandwich she had in her purse, then hit the road and head home.

The text had come with a photograph. A handsome man looking straight into the camera. His smile was so broad that the left eye narrowed to a squint. He had a reindeer under his arm. Hildur recognised the animal as Maire. Maire was one of Anton's oldest reindeer. She was easy to recognise, because her head was completely white and her ears were dark.

Hildur stared at the message for a moment, then tapped out a polite reply. Anton was marking the ears of the calves that had been born that spring. In the autumn there'd be the round-up, and then it would be time for winter grazing. Calving in the spring. And so on. Hildur returned her phone to her purse and pulled out the sandwich.

Spicy sauce and a double helping of meat. The best kebabs in Iceland still came from the place next to the Parliament Building.

Hildur already knew how things would go. Deep down, she'd known from the start. Anton wouldn't move from Lapland, and she understood him perfectly well.

She just never should have agreed to meet him a second time. The hotel dates in Finland were supposed to have been a bit of fun, and they had been. But then fate had wrung out a different kind of rain from the clouds. Their trip together to a tropical island had been a big mistake. She should have never grown attached to Anton – or been impregnated by him.

Anton wouldn't leave his reindeer, and Hildur wouldn't leave her Westfjords. Hildur was reminded of her old friends Selma and Greipur. Neither one had accepted the second-best option. Hildur crammed the last of the kebab in her mouth and crumpled the wrapper into a ball.

Anton was a nice guy, but he wasn't her guy. Their lives were too different. She was happy she understood that now. Hildur's life was good the way it was. She didn't need someone else every day of the week. At least not Anton.

Things feel hard now, but this will pass, she thought to herself and stood.

Hildur twirled the car keys in her hand. She'd got the keychain as a present from her Aunt Tinna. For Hildur's eighteenth birthday, Tinna had made her a cross-stitch embroidered with her name and its source in ancient Nordic mythology. On her most recent birthday, Tinna had ordered a gargantuan keychain based on the cross-stitch so Hildur wouldn't lose her keys so easily. In a month's time, Tinna would return to Ísafjörður from her summer vacation. Hildur realised she missed her aunt. She looked at the keychain with a smile.

Hildur. Battle. A spirt of war and death tasked with deciding whose turn it is to win a battle and whose to die.

Hildur started walking to her car. Her step was light, and her thoughts felt clear. Her strength seemed to have returned. She'd made a choice that had been the only right option for her. She was alone again.

The emptiness felt good. Sometimes the greatest love was admitting what you didn't want.

Epilogue

The removal of two badly mangled bodies from a car in late winter 1995 took hours. The police had immediately seen that neither passenger had been wearing their seatbelt. The man in the passenger seat had been trapped between the crushed nose of the vehicle and the seat. The lower half of his body had been pulped into a nasty-looking jelly in the collision, but his face had been recognisable.

The woman's body had suffered more serious injury. The accident investigators had concluded that a wave-sharpened lava formation had pierced the car right where she'd been sitting. The sharp rock had peeled off her face. Her head was badly battered from the other side too. At first, the police officers had been perplexed by her lack of clothes, as when she was discovered she'd only been wearing a long skirt. But the disfigured bodies, the frigid wind, and the difficult rescue conditions had ultimately consumed their full attention.

The car was identified by the licence plate number, Rúnar by his face, and Rakel by her long hair. The funeral was a closed casket affair, as there was nothing left of Rakel's face to show. Rúnar and a faceless woman who was missing half her left forefinger were lowered into the ground after the memorial service. The pastor tossed a shovelful of dirt into the grave; Tinna and Hildur sang a poem about a bird.

The driver's door had been torn open during the accident. The force of the crash had been powerful enough to open the door and let the sea's current take hold of the driver's earthly remains. Lapping slowly, the currents had carried her body further out to sea.

Hildur wasn't aware of any of this when she boarded a small fishing boat in Ísafjörður harbour twenty-seven years later, a white urn under her arm. The boat pulled out of the harbour and puttered into open water. Hildur had written a death notice to be read on the radio, then an obituary for the newspaper. Now she was going to perform one last service for Helga. Helga had wanted her ashes to be scattered in the fjord.

Hildur stood the way she'd learned over the course of her lifetime: both feet planted firmly on the deck and eyes on the horizon. The air smelled of the sea; the breeze tossed her long hair.

The boat slowed. The captain killed the engine, nodded at Hildur from the cabin, and opened his newspaper. Scattering ashes in the sea wasn't allowed, but there was always the option of looking away for a moment.

A pale grey swan was swimming near the boat, and its wing slapped softly as it launched into flight. Hildur had never heard such a beautiful sound. She removed the lid from the urn and tipped it. From out of nowhere, a small gust of wind blew through the calm summer evening. It snatched up the grey dust and twirled it through the air. Then it died as quickly as it had appeared, and the ash rained slowly into the sea. The grey dust lingered on the surface, then sank and was gone.

From the radio in the captain's cabin came the voice of the singer Bubbi Morthens:

If I drown, I drown tonight
If they find me
Come seek me out
Let this be my reminder

Acknowledgements

The Secrets from the Deep is dedicated to my grandmother Sirkka. She died the week I began writing this book, exactly a year after my mother's death. I dedicated the previous book in the *Hildur* series, *The Shadow of the Northern Lights*, to my mother, who died the week I began writing it. What can we deduce from this? Nothing. Life is incomprehensible in all its tones and hues.

Writing stories is my way of making some sense of a chaotic world. Most of the places mentioned in *The Secrets from the Deep* exist. Major changes were enacted in fishing legislation in Iceland in the late 1980s and the early 1990s, and decision-making related to fishing quotas remains a hot topic in domestic politics. The cruise ship business also sparks opinions for and against in present-day Iceland. Although the societal themes touched on in *The Secrets from the Deep* are real, all events and characters in the story are fictional. The village of Flateyri exists but has never been home to a fishing company named Hagfiskur or any company resembling it. Cruise ships stop in Iceland's harbours, but the cruise ships and other vessels mentioned in this work are inventions. Any potential similarities between the novel and real life are complete coincidence.

A warm thanks to all the helpful people who supported me through the process of writing this book and responded to my queries on all manner of subjects, from the security checks on cruise ships to fishing boats and the human anatomy. A special thanks to Ingibjörg Elín Magnúsdóttir and Aldís Hilmarsdóttir for patiently answering my questions about police work in Iceland.

A big thanks to author, translator, pastor, and former woodworking teacher at the Ísafjörður school, Tapio Koivukari, for his knowledge about fishing. If any errors have made their way into the book, they are naturally mine and mine alone.

A warm thanks to my publisher, WSOY, especially Timo Julkunen, Reetta Miettinen, Veli-Pekka Mattilainen, Laura Lyytinen, Mika Hänninen, Pirita Hietalahti, Mari Nieminen, Heidi Möksy and Kaarina Lehto, Silja Koivisto, Satu Sallantaus, Iina Moukola, and Harri Mäki.

I'd like to give a special thanks to Anna-Riikka Carlson, publisher of Finnish fiction at WSOY, who originally saw something in the *Hildur* series and gave it a chance! A thank you to my rock-solid, solid-gold editor Hanna Pudas – you are always and simply the best! Senior brand manager Satu Sirkiä, thank you for the extraordinary work you have put into the *Hildur* series. You have been an irreplaceable support in every way.

A thanks to literary agent Toomas Aasmäe at Bonnier Rights Finland for helping bring the *Hildur* series to an international readership. Thanks as well to Ebba Erolin, Arja Siitonen, and Nicole Myyryläinen at Bonnier Rights. Thank you, Lippo Luukkonen, for the legal assistance.

Most of all, thanks to my family – Björgvin, Saga, and Sæla, and my sisters Suvi and Sini – for travelling this life alongside me.

Satu Rämö

Ísafjörður, August 2024